SHAD

Diane Guest lives
husband and childr
of *Lullaby*, *Forbidden Garden*,
and *The Nightwalker*.

DIANE GUEST

Shadow Hill

A BERNARD GEIS ASSOCIATES BOOK

HarperCollins*Publishers*

HarperCollins*Publishers*
77–85 Fulham Palace Road,
Hammersmith, London W6 8JB

A Paperback Original 1995

1 3 5 7 9 8 6 4 2

Copyright © Diane Guest 1995

The Author asserts the moral right to
be identified as the author of this work

A catalogue record for this book is available
from the British Library

ISBN 0 00 637782 3

Set in Palatino at The Spartan Press Ltd,
Lymington, Hants

Printed in Great Britain by
HarperCollins Manufacturing Glasgow

Prologue

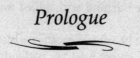

Darkness.

Are my eyes open or are they closed?

But how could she know? Eveline was paralysed, unable even to lift a hand to her face to feel if there were tears.

Darkness. No light.

Nor was there sound. Not even the beating of her own heart.

What's happening to me?

She tried to open her mouth to cry out.

Silence.

You are asleep. Wake up.

But she wasn't asleep. Eveline was wide awake. Trapped, frozen in some mysterious arctic wasteland where nothing moves. Slowly the truth of it all sifted into her mind. *This is no dream. This is no arctic wasteland. This is the first step down the road to everlasting hell.*

Then faintly Eveline heard something. Someone approaching.

There was the sudden lifting of a sheet that had covered her, kept her from seeing, and in the flickering candlelight she found herself looking up at a circle of faces. People staring down at her – her mother, her best friend. Grief-stricken. Weeping. Dr Aubin, shaking his head. And then, coming into view from behind them, someone else.

Adrien.

Black fear like burning acid spilled into her brain. *Oh God, not Adrien.*

And then she heard her mother whisper, 'Dr Aubin, is my child, my sweet Eveline, really dead?'

The doctor nodded. 'I'm sorry, Camille.'

An agonized sob. 'But how? What happened?'

A gesture of helplessness. 'We won't know until after the autopsy is performed.'

Her mother moaned.

No! No! I'm not dead! I'm alive! Eveline wanted to shriek it. But she couldn't.

Dr Aubin reached down and gently closed her eyes.

Again, darkness. Again, the sheet was pulled up over her face.

Gradually the sounds of mourning faded away and she was alone once more.

The only thing active in the room was her own brain. All that was left to her was her ability to think – and she knew with certainty that she was doomed.

How had she allowed this to happen? How had she been so blind? She never should have told Adrien she was leaving Shadow Hill. She never should have refused his advances. She should have allowed him what he wanted. And afterwards, she should have crept away in the dead of night, fled to some distant land where he would never find her. She should have gone while she was still able.

But she hadn't believed in his power. She had thought it was all pretence. Smoke and mirrors. Threats without substance designed to terrify simple people into submission.

Now it was too late.

Too late. Unless . . .

2

Unless somehow Dr Aubin discovered that she was still alive.

Please, Dr Aubin! Please!

Dr Aubin exhaled. He was relieved be heading away from Shadow Hill. A magnificent plantation to be sure – but so remote. And so . . . so intimidating. Like its owner, Adrien Ravel. Until this morning Dr Aubin had known the man only by reputation – a shadowy figure, powerful and wealthy. A man as mysterious as the source of his fortune. There was one thing Dr Aubin knew for certain: in Saint James parish there were a lot of folk who were truly afraid of Adrien Ravel, though exactly why, the doctor didn't know. Nor did he care to know, but if ever he was asked to go to Shadow Hill again he would refuse. He had responded this one time because when Camille had called, begging him to help her daughter, Eveline, he had felt obligated. After all, Camille had been his patient for most of her life.

So he had come to Shadow Hill, but he had arrived too late. Poor Camille, he thought. Such a good woman. And poor dead Eveline. Though just how she had died he didn't know.

He came to the end of the long shaded drive, stopped for a moment to wipe his brow, then turned onto the sparsely travelled road that led through the marshlands and back towards Brancheville, the small town west of New Orleans where he had his practice. This morning he had felt just fine but now he was increasingly light-headed, kind of queasy. Probably nerves, he thought. He had never become inured to seeing people die, especially in such a sudden manner. That's why he was so anxious to get to his office, make some phone calls. First of all he had to get in touch with Ben Luzanne over in New Orleans. The Medical Examiner was sure to agree that there should be a coroner's inquest. He'd have to send someone out to Shadow Hill right away to collect the body.

◦Poor girl. Only seventeen years old. Strange case, he thought. Impossible to diagnose. When he had arrived at Shadow Hill she was already comatose, breathing with great difficulty, and within the hour she was dead. There had been some evidence of pulmonary oedema and cyanosis. But nothing he could determine as causal.

According to Adrien Ravel, her employer, she had been ill earlier in the day, vomiting and such. But it had been chalked up simply to a touch of the flu. It wasn't until after lunch when she hadn't appeared for clean-up duties that the housekeeper had gone to look for her.

That's when Camille had been notified and, near hysteria, she had called Dr Aubin.

The doctor came to a V in the road and stopped, cursing himself under his breath for not having paid stricter attention to the route on his way to Shadow Hill.

'Damn,' he muttered angrily, then drove off again, hoping he had made the right decision. Hoping he wasn't heading deeper into bayou country. Oh well, he thought, if I don't cross the Choctaw Bridge pretty soon, I'll turn around.

The sun had dropped below the moss-draped trees and, sweating profusely now, Dr Aubin rolled the car window down, hoping to get a breath of cool air, hoping it would help him shake off this growing malaise. Maybe he had better not go to his office. Maybe he had better go straight home.

4

Of course he should. He had no choice. The queasiness he had felt earlier was rapidly turning to griping pain low in his abdomen, and now he was aware of a tingling sensation in his right hand that spread up his arm, across his shoulder and down his left side.

Just ahead he saw the bridge, a rickety wooden affair without rails that looked like a raft floating on a sea of marshgrass. A poor excuse for a bridge, he thought. But at least he knew where he was. He knew he was heading in the right direction. The dull throb in the back of his head was clouding his vision, making it more and more difficult to see. He slowed the car to a crawl.

'God damn,' he moaned, 'I *am* sick.'

The next moment his throat closed. Gasping for breath, he threw his head back, jerking his legs forward, his right foot jamming against the gas pedal on the floor.

The car flew off the bridge, skimmed lightly across the surface of the water, then sank like a stone.

Dr Aubin didn't care. He was already dead.

Eveline's brain was a pulsing mass of pain and horror. And no one knew. She could not tremble or scream or flail out with her fists, or weep. She knew why. She knew what was in store for her, and it was worse than death. Death would have been welcome.

She prayed to die. But her prayer went unanswered.

She felt hands lifting her, gathering her body up, carrying her somewhere. Finally setting her down on a soft cushion covered with satin.

Her mind exploded but no one heard it.

Jesus God! Help me!

And then came a muffled thud and she realized that the coffin lid had closed down over her.

In a state of numb horror she thought about what was coming. Adrien had described it in detail but she hadn't believed.

Now she did.

She was to be entombed. Buried alive. And again she would pray for death. But death would never come. Death was not what Adrien had in mind for her. He would bury her, but he would never allow her to suffocate. That would be too kind. At the last minute he would come for her. He would lift the lid of the coffin and bring her forth. He would call upon his Voudou spirits and they would take her soul from her body. She would pass from this perpetual horror into a state of living death.

She would become a zombie with only one function: To serve Adrien. To obey him in all things.

Her master.

Adrien.

Chapter One

New York City, 21 December.

Snow.

David Wickliffe pulled his collar up around his ears but he didn't quicken his pace. He loved it when it snowed, especially in mid-December. In time for a white Christmas. It was one of the things he missed, living in New York City. It seldom snowed here, at least not really heavy snow. Not like back home in the mountains of Utah. There in winter it seemed to do little else.

He smiled to himself, remembering fondly the long walks through frozen woods, the squeaking sound of the snow underfoot when it was so cold your throat ached, the exhilaration of skiing the steep mountain trails. David was still passionate about the sport and he was glad to be going home if only for a week. He, Galen, and their daughter, Katy, were flying west on the twenty-second to Provo to see his mother, spend the holidays, ski.

He cut across Washington Square and with a last look back at the whispering snow, he ducked into his office building. He would have spent more time outdoors but it was almost four o'clock and he was eager to talk to his assistant before she left for the day, to find out if she had heard anything from Baird Laboratories. He knew that if the Directors were going to commit any of their funds to his project it would have to happen before the end of the year. And if they decided not to, well, he would have to begin all over again. The interminable, convoluted, godawful process of looking for research money.

David headed up the stairs. At fifty-eight, he was beginning to feel his age, and he grew angry that life was rushing past so quickly. He had been here at New York University for almost twenty years. Teaching, writing volumes explaining the effects of diet deficiencies on the human body, describing the mechanisms of the immune system, outlining the steps in the development of chemotherapy. But all of his writing, all of his teaching had been explanatory, describing what already was, what had been discovered by someone else. True, he had worked on a number of research teams, but never one that was his very own. His real ambition was to be *the* discoverer. A man who would take all the bits and pieces of his own knowledge, put it together in a different configuration, and have something new and astonishing come out of it. The way Fred Banting had discovered insulin, or Waksman streptomycin.

He often wondered how such men must have felt. How *he* would feel if he were to find what he was looking for: a drug that would induce chemical hibernation in humans. Such incredible potential. For one thing, if metabolism could be lowered almost to the point of nonexistence, there would be a surgical revolution, possibly changing the application of anaesthetics for ever.

In his search for such a formula David spent every free moment in the laboratory. He had watched closely the efforts of a group in Canada who were working on a similar project for NASA, trying to find a way to put humans into deep sleep during long-term space travel. Thus far they hadn't come up with much. Another group of scientists in Maryland were experimenting on squirrels, trying to discover why the loss of blood to their brains during hibernation didn't result in stroke – another mystery that David would have to solve if he were to be successful.

His own preliminary work had been vastly encouraging. David had already formulated a chemical which, when applied in proper dosage, had induced hibernation in some species of smaller animals without any ill effects. Now it was time to move on. The next step was to create the same state of suspended animation in more advanced specimens, and for that he needed more money. He had already received modest grants from a variety of sources but they were no longer enough. He needed substantial funding – big money – from someone willing and able to give it. Like Baird Laboratories.

When he entered his office Sylvie Valois was at her desk. 'Am I glad to see you,' she said, leaning back in her chair. She smiled. It was one of the most striking things about her, that smile. It transformed her, turning her almond eyes up at the corners, startling the viewer with a glimpse of flashing white against the milk chocolate of her skin. Sylvie Valois was an attractive thirty-eight-year-old, but there was nothing spectacular about her looks until she smiled. Then she was dazzling.

She stood up and thrust an envelope at David. Return address, Baird Laboratories. A thick manila envelope. Not the usual skinny kind that signals rejection.

Heart pounding, David held it for a minute in a shaking hand. 'Jesus,' he said softly.

'I didn't think that Baird would ever consider anyone east of California,' Sylvie said, incredulous.

'Me neither.' David ripped open the envelope and pulled out a sheaf of papers. Glancing down he saw only one word: Approval. 'Jesus,' he said again. 'We did it, Sylvie! We got funded.'

She rushed around the desk and hugged him fiercely, then pulled back, a frown replacing the smile. 'How much?'

'I don't know. I have to read it.' He scanned the letter. Then numb, he handed it to her. 'Third paragraph.'

'Wow! Two hundred thousand a year for two years. That's more than you ever hoped for.'

'It is.' He was trying to catch his breath.

She read the rest of the letter aloud.

'Although there is a great deal of interest here at Baird in the development of a drug for use in modern surgery, our prime objective in funding your research is to obtain a commercial product that will safely and effectively induce hibernation in human beings for the purpose of weight reduction. We were most impressed with your statistical tables which proved conclusively that the loss of body weight during hibernation is significant in every instance, without any resultant biological damage. We believe this would have immeasurable worth as a commercial product. The enclosed evaluation of your proposal was prepared by our own research team for your use as a guide.'

Sylvie dropped the papers on his desk and grabbed David by the arm. 'I can't stand any more! Let's go celebrate!' She grabbed her coat. 'Let's call Galen. Tell her to meet us at Samell's.'

Still numb, David picked up the phone. If anyone would realize how much this meant to him it would be his wife, Galen. It meant a great deal to Galen, too. Not because she had a serious interest in biochemistry, but because, while she had pursued her own career with flawless success, he hadn't. Thus far he had spent his life reaching for, but never quite attaining, that elusive goal: to be a discoverer. He was still reaching.

Galen, on the other hand, had never faced a hurdle she couldn't clear. She was a paediatric cardiologist, one of the most respected in the city. Her career was a perfect blend of her two prime passions: children and medicine, and to those ends she had devoted her life.

Not that David didn't count, but he wasn't her top priority. Both of them had accepted that fact from the very beginning. When they had married twelve years ago it had been understood; Galen was a doctor first, a wife second.

And then Katherine had appeared. Their precious daughter. And in that first breath of life Katy had accomplished what David had never been able to. She became the light of her mother's life, her first priority. The one person, if the need ever arose, that Galen would give up her career for.

David understood. He accepted it – and he rarely thought about it, except sometimes in the dark of night when he would suddenly wake to find Galen gone, off on an emergency call, and for a fleeting moment he would wish that she had refused to leave his side, because she loved him more than anything else in her life.

But he knew that it was an absurd wish and it would fade as quickly as it had come, thank God, and he would turn his thoughts to other things. Like the latest experiments in cryogenics. Then gradually he would fall asleep to dream new dreams, forget old ones.

'Answer, damn it,' he said into the phone. And now one of those dreams was about to come true.

'Dr Wickliffe's service.'

'Is she there?'

'I'm sorry. She's in consultation. Is there a message?'

'No. No message.' He hung up. 'No luck,' he said to Sylvie. 'She's not there. So I guess it's just you and me, babe. Let's go celebrate.'

The snow was still falling and the air was bitter cold.

'This weather intimidates me,' Sylvie muttered as they hurried along the street. 'It must be my Deep South genes.'

'Speaking of the Deep South, are you still planning to go back home to New Orleans for the holidays?'

'I am. Although it's a sad time for one of my cousins. I just got news that her daughter died.' She shivered. 'Poor Camille. When I spoke to her she was almost incoherent with grief.'

They crossed the street to Samell's, sat at the bar and ordered drinks. A gin on the rocks for David, a Campari and soda with a wedge of lemon for Sylvie.

'Well,' she said, lifting her glass, 'here's to artificial hibernation.'

He smiled. 'Here's to a whole new world filled with happy skinny human beings.'

They clicked glasses.

'Here's to a monstrous commercial success worth millions of dollars,' she said.

'Here's to a Nobel Prize for Chemistry.'

Hearing himself say it, the reality of it all suddenly

hit him. Until now, the thing he had been waiting to discover had been hidden in a nebulous world with no parameters, no absolute direction, nothing concrete. Now it was real, a prize within his grasp, and he had been granted a considerable amount of money – enough perhaps to attain it.

He took a long slow sip, felt the gin warm the back of his throat. 'Liftoff,' he said to Sylvie. 'I think we're on our way.'

'I *know* we are,' she said. 'On January fourth I'll be back in the lab, ready to go for the gold.' She paused. 'By the way, are you and Galen still going to take care of Mingo while I'm gone?' Mingo was Sylvie's cat.

'You bet. Katy has the guest room all prepared. And while we're away Helen will be happy for the company.' Helen was the Wickliffes' housekeeper.

'I don't know how Helen feels about cats,' Sylvie said, running her finger around the rim of her glass, 'but I do know that Katy loves Mingo almost as much as Edie does.'

David frowned. 'How *is* Edie, by the way?' Edie was Sylvie's fifteen-year-old daughter, still alive thanks to Galen. Seven years ago she had been struck down by rheumatic fever. Galen had been called in on the case, using her considerable skills to help Edie survive the dreaded childhood disease. It had been a long gruelling battle, and in the process Galen and Sylvie had become warm friends. It was because of their friendship that David had given Sylvie her job at the University, and for that he would be eternally grateful to his wife. Sylvie was the best – a brilliant technician, as inspired as she was dedicated. A very special person to all the Wickliffes.

'Edie seems to be holding her own,' Sylvie said

13

cautiously. 'But with this rheumatic business you never know. Who was it said rheumatic fever is the disease that licks the joints but bites the heart?'

'I don't know,' David said grimly, 'but it's true. I don't envy you, Sylvie.'

There was a moment's silence. 'I have to take Edie to see Galen tomorrow afternoon. Usual checkup. And as always, I pray that there will be no bad news. I don't know if I could endure what Camille has just suffered. The loss of a child has to be devastating.'

'Were you close to your cousin?'

'Once upon a time. I haven't seen her in years. Her family moved to a small town west of New Orleans back in the sixties, and it might as well have been to another planet for all I ever saw of her after that. But we've kept in touch – letters, an occasional phone call. In any case, I'm definitely going to visit her on this trip. When I spoke to her she sounded desperate to have me come to Brancheville, though I don't know what good I can do. Eveline was all Camille had. The loss has to be immeasurable.' She took a deep breath. 'But enough of this depressing chatter. We're supposed to be celebrating.' She lifted her glass again. 'Here's to Professor David Wickliffe.'

'Here's to Sylvie Valois, his brilliant assistant, his treasured friend.'

They finished their drinks and were about to leave when something hanging on the wall at the far end of the bar caught Sylvie's eye. It was a primitive drawing of a serpent with its tail in the water and its head resting on the top of a high mountain.

'Huh,' Sylvie said, leaning over to get a better look. 'I've never seen that here before.' She pointed. 'Typically Haitian. I wonder where Sam got it.'

David turned.

'That's one of the things I was telling you about,' she said. 'Remember? That's Damballah Oueddo. The most ancient of all Voudou spirits.'

David moved to the end of the bar so he could see the drawing more clearly. What little Sylvie had told him about the Voudou religion and its mysterious rites had intrigued him.

'Now that you've reminded me,' he said, coming back to pull on his overcoat, 'are you still going to see if you can find out anything about that zombie powder stuff?'

A month or so ago, in the process of evaluating one of their experiments, Sylvie had compared the paralysis they were seeing in one of their guinea pigs to what she called 'zombification'. 'From what I've been told,' she had said, 'zombies are not like vampires or werewolves. They are living human beings, brought from a state of suspended animation into a state of mindless slavery.'

At first David hadn't believed any of it, but Sylvie had pressed. 'I'm serious, David,' she had said. 'The Voudou priests do it by applying different kinds of chemical agents. One drug puts the poor devil into a deep sleep, and another brings him back to spend the rest of his days a robot, without a will, to be used for whatever unearthly purpose the priest intends.'

David had been intrigued, not because he was convinced that such transformations were possible, but because, like most people, he felt an eerie fascination when the words 'zombie' or 'Voudou' were mentioned. 'How'd you ever hear about such things?' he had asked Sylvie.

'From my mother. She never knew anyone who

could turn a person into a zombie, but she knew it was done. And she knew that the sorcerers who performed such hideous deeds – they're called *bocors* in Haiti – were part of the dark side of Voudou. True followers of the religion wanted no part of their evil-doing. I suppose in much the same way that Christians deplore Satanism. In any case,' she had continued, 'I do know that *bocors* exist in Haiti even today. They say that some of them possess all the lethal knowledge that belonged to the ancient death cults of West Africa.'

'Did your mother believe in Voudou?'

'Absolutely. In fact her dearest friend was a *mamaloi*, a Voudou high priestess. My mother and Ti Reine came out of Haiti together with their families in the fifties and both settled in New Orleans. Ti Reine lives there to this day.'

'Do you think she knows anything about these secret concoctions that they claim suspend life?'

'I'm sure she does.' Sylvie had said it with certainty. 'I'm just not sure she'd ever talk about it.'

Now as they stood on the sidewalk outside the bar waiting for a cab, David repeated his question. 'Do you still think it's worth your time to try to find out something about this zombie potion?'

'Why not?' she shrugged. 'It can't do any harm.'

David nodded. 'No, it can't.' *Can it?* He paused, feeling a sudden peculiar twinge of uneasiness. He shrugged it off. 'Good luck,' he smiled.

A taxi pulled up. 'Are you going to share the cab with me?' she asked.

'Nope. I'm going to walk. See you later.'

Sylvie climbed in and he shut the door. He stood watching as the cab inched its way down the snow-covered street. Then he turned and headed uptown, not caring that his feet were getting wet. He felt wonderfully alive. Happy. Successful. About to undertake the most incredible challenge of his life. And to top it off, it was snowing.

David never noticed the shadowy figure standing motionless in the doorway next to Samell's. Why should he? New York was a city full of faceless people standing in doorways.

The black man made no move. Nothing that would attract attention. From his vantage point in the doorway he watched and listened. Not that he needed to hear. He already knew where she was going, how to find her.

He shivered. His blood was thin, unused to this cold, but that didn't matter. In three days' time she would be flying south to New Orleans. And he would go with her.

He had been sent to New York City by Monsieur Ravel to locate a woman named Sylvie Valois and to watch her. That was all. To find her and to watch her. Sylvie Valois, a name to which he could now attach a face. It never occurred to him to wonder why Monsieur Ravel had an interest in her. That too was unimportant. The fact was that he had done his job, would continue to do it until Monsieur Ravel told him to stop.

When he was sure he wouldn't be noticed he stepped out onto the street and began to walk uptown. He knew where she lived. He would find her again.

Chapter Two

Snow.

'Look, Peter,' Galen said, reaching across the hospital bed, taking the small hand of the eight-year-old boy who was lying on his side, not moving. 'It's snowing. Just in time for Santa Claus.'

Slowly the child turned his head to look out the window. 'Will I really be home for Christmas, Dr Wickliffe?'

She smiled. 'You will.'

'Promise?'

She let go of his hand. 'Cross my heart. And you know how good I am with hearts. And I'm telling you now that everything about yours looks perfect, inside and out.'

He put his hand on his chest. 'No pus?'

'Nope. It's healing just fine. Two more days and you're out of here.'

Galen felt a familiar twinge of sadness. She would miss Peter. He had been here for three weeks now, recovering from surgery to correct a congenital constriction of his aorta. He had had a rough time but, like almost every child she had ever treated, he was a fighter. Brave. Uncomplaining. Willing to give it his all – one of the reasons why, as a young medical student, she had turned her attention to the treatment of children. They were the least deserving of their fate, but when stricken they were the most accepting of it.

With a last look at Peter's chart, Galen left the room and headed down the corridor. She had only one more patient to check and then she would go home to her own sweet child: Katherine Devon Wickliffe. Katy. The provider of eleven years of endless delight. Katy, with her serious-silly approach to life, her limitless flights of fancy, determined to be either an Olympic ski champion or an archaeologist, at the same time doggedly clinging to all the magical dreams of childhood, never considering for a moment that the time would come when she would have to give them all up.

And then there's me, Galen thought wryly. At age forty-three I still haven't abandoned the magic. I still believe that the impossible can happen.

She glanced out the window. I hope it keeps snowing for ever and ever so that Katy and I can go out to the park and build an army of snowpeople.

And then she remembered that her daughter wasn't at home. She was at Edie's, baking Christmas cookies.

Edie, Sylvie's daughter. Another precious jewel in Galen's box of treasures. A child Galen had watched endure the agonies of rheumatic fever, and had grown to love during the never-ending vigil that had come afterwards. Galen had been her doctor for seven years. She had seen the child struggle, survive, grow into a gentle doe-eyed beauty.

Dangerous business to be so pretty at fifteen, Galen thought as she hurried down the hall. Dangerous business to be that pretty at any age.

Not that Galen had ever experienced such problems herself. She was not pretty and she knew it. Feature for feature she was flawed. Overly wide mouth, nondescript hazel eyes, short curly hair that frizzed at the mere mention of water.

But there was something instantly likeable about Galen. She had not been blessed with good looks but she was the possessor of other, more endearing qualities. A keen sense of humour and a sharp intellect, softened by genuine kindness. Adults trusted her. Children loved her.

She pushed the down button on the elevator. A quick stop on the fourth floor to see how Marcy Luciano was doing in recovery, and then home for a hot shower and, because she wasn't on call tonight, a well-deserved martini. She wondered if David would be home. Probably not. He spent as many long hours at the University as she did at the hospital and it was rare when they had uninterrupted time to spend at home together.

Oh well, she thought, stepping out of the elevator, not long and we'll all be off on our trip, and if we don't ski until we drop maybe we'll have some time left just to talk, catch up. She often wondered how many marriages were like theirs – two people running parallel, rarely touching.

Not that she didn't love David, she did, but not as much as he loved her. She knew that David would do anything for her. Anything. But would she do the same for him?

No. She wouldn't. Not if it meant sacrificing her career. There was only one person in Galen's life that she would do that for: Katy. And David knew it. He never asked, never made any demands. But sometimes she saw it in his face. A kind of sad acceptance. And she was filled with a wrenching sadness herself, that David had never had the kind of wife who would be happy just to be at his side. If anyone deserved it, he did.

Not that there had ever been any illusions about their relationship. David had been in his mid-forties when they met and he had known from the beginning what her priorities were. When he accepted her as his wife he had done it with an open heart, with no unrealistic expectations.

Sometimes, though, Galen couldn't help wondering. Not just about David's loss but about her own. She was forty-three years old and yet in a rare moment she would see something that would make her pulse quicken, something simple, like the sight of a young couple, absorbed in each other, walking hand in hand at dusk along a city street. Suddenly the young girl that still lived somewhere in her soul would wonder what it would be like to be mindlessly, passionately in love.

She smiled to herself. Every time she thought she was past the fantasy stage, a foolish thought like that would pop into her head and she would be properly put back in her place. Still a romantic at heart. 'Dr Wickliffe,' she said under her breath, 'when are you ever going to get real?'

She pushed open the door to the recovery room and went in.

Katy stood in front of Edie's mirror, holding a pair of her friend's earrings on either side of her head, looking at herself with a critical eye. She couldn't try them on because her ears weren't pierced yet. Mom said not until she was twelve. Only four months to wait and then Katy would be one step closer to her goal: full-grown womanhood. No more stupid braces on her teeth, no more flat chest, no more frizzy hair. No more fear of dogs, no more hiding her face in the middle of a horror movie, no more waking at night, crying for her mother.

Not to mention the fact that when she became an acknowledged adult she would be able to go full steam ahead in pursuit of her goals, either to be an Egyptologist or an Olympic skier. Katy loved to ski even though she didn't get to do it often. On a few weekends during the winter months her parents would take her to Stowe. And every December she went to her grandmother's house in Utah where she could ski every single day.

Katy wasn't a great skier. Not yet. But she was willing to work at it. And she had high hopes. Next to being pretty she wanted most of all to be good at some kind of sport. There wasn't much she could do about her looks – her yukky curly hair, her straight legs, her funny nose. But with lots of practice she might succeed at skiing, become a slalom champion, or maybe downhill.

If not, she would become an Egyptologist.

She put the pair of earrings back in the jewel box. 'What are you doing, Edie?' She glanced over her shoulder.

Edie was standing in her closet on tiptoe. She reached up and took her big straw bag down from the top shelf. Her *makout* she called it, where she kept all her most treasured religious paraphernalia.

Katy watched, breathless. It wasn't often that Edie let her see what was in the bag. Edie was very protective of Katy, as though she were her mother.

But Katy didn't need another mother. She needed a friend who would treat her like an equal. Katy might be only eleven years old but in mental years she was at least fourteen, maybe older. There were things she knew about that most eleven-year-olds had never even heard of. Like who the Philistines were, and what did it mean to have a vasectomy, and how the Appalachian Mountains were formed. True, Katy's knowledge hadn't come from experience. It had come from books. When she could persuade her father to let her loose in the University library, one of her favourite ways to spend a Saturday afternoon was browsing there. But just because she got most of her information from books didn't mean she was a baby, even though Edie thought she was.

Today Edie was treating her more like a friend, and that made Katy very happy. Edie was allowing her to stay while she looked through her possessions to decide which she would take with her on her trip. Twice a year, once at Christmas time and once in the summer, Edie and her mother went to New Orleans. While they were there they stayed at the old Beauchamp house in the French Quarter where Edie's grandmother had worked as a housekeeper for years and years. Edie's mother had been born and raised there, and even though Mr and Mrs Beauchamp were dead, their son, Jonas, always welcomed Sylvie back with open arms.

'Between Christmas and New Year's Day it is the season of *maji*,' Edie was saying, 'and if Mama lets me, I'm going to be able to take part in one of the Voudou ceremonies with Ti Reine.' She set the straw bag down on the floor. 'I can't wait to show her some of the things I've found.'

At the mention of Ti Reine, Katy drew in a sharp breath. The name alone scared her to death. Ti Reine.

The Queen. Katy had never seen the woman nor a picture of her, but in her mind she knew precisely what Ti Reine looked like. She was tall, very tall – a giantess in fact – with black flashing eyes and black hair pulled away from her face, covered with an elaborate headdress like the ancient Egyptians wore. Whether she had any teeth or not Katy didn't know because in her mind Ti Reine never smiled. Never. Because she was a *mamaloi*, a High Priestess of the Voudou religion.

Katy didn't know very much about Voudou except what Edie was willing to tell her, but she had every intention of doing extensive research on the subject the first chance she got. She had already asked her own parents about it but they didn't know much either. Her father said it was a little understood religion that had come to the New World in the seventeen hundreds, during the years of the slave trade. Why was she asking?

Katy had shrugged. Just curious, she had said. She knew that Edie wouldn't like it if she told her parents that Edie was a Voudouist. With Edie it was a well-kept secret. Her own mother didn't believe in the religion. Not that she thought it had no value. For those who needed it, she knew it was a sacred faith, but Sylvie was not one of them and she didn't want Edie to be one either. It had been Edie's grandmother who had served the spirits of ancient Africa, and she had tried to teach Sylvie, but Sylvie had been too critical, too sceptical, too modern.

Edie was different. Edie was what her grandmother had called *ti fey*. A child of the house. And while her grandmother lived, she and Ti Reine had schooled Edie in the practices of Voudou. But now her grandmother was dead and Ti Reine was Edie's only teacher.

'I've read everything I can find in the library,' Edie had told Katy, 'but there is very little written. Very few people seem to understand the religion, so I have to depend on Ti Reine.'

'Want me to do some research?' Katy had asked.

'I don't think so, Katydid,' Edie had said smiling, patting Katy on the arm. 'But thank you anyway.'

Katy hadn't been surprised. As usual Edie thought she was just a nice little kid who wouldn't be able to understand. Ti Reine, on the other hand, understood everything. She could work all kinds of magic. She could call upon the *loa*, the Voudou spirits, to do her bidding. She could get rid of enemies just by sprinkling salt and pepper into the four corners of a room. And she could heal sickness without ever taking the person to a hospital.

'Is she a doctor?' Katy had asked.

'No. She is a healer. A *mamaloi*. It's what I hope to be someday.'

Katy hadn't understood exactly what that meant but it made her nervous. 'Does . . . does your mother know you want to be one?'

'No,' Edie had said in a hushed tone, 'and I don't want you ever to tell her.'

'How come?'

'Because she won't like it.'

And in spite of herself, Katy had been scared. She had always been awed by Edie. The way she looked, so beautiful, so grown-up. The way she wore her hair sometimes, braided with coloured beads her grandmother had given her. Her smooth dark skin was always perfect, with never a trace of a blemish, and her eyes turned up at the corners to make her look just like the bronze sculpture of the Egyptian moon goddess

Isis that Katy had once seen in the Metropolitan Museum. But the nicest thing about Edie was the way she treated Katy. Sometimes like a little kid, sometimes like a friend, but *always* like someone she cared about.

Katy had tried her best not to act stupid and spoil everything, but this revelation of Edie's plans to become a *mamaloi* had made her shiver. As far as she was concerned it was the same as saying you were going to become a witch.

Now she sat on the floor beside Edie and watched, wide-eyed, as Edie reached into her straw bag. She took out a small white candle with strange markings carved around the centre. She set it down carefully but she didn't light it.

'I don't want to burn it until Ti Reine sees it and tells me if I inscribed it with the right symbols,' she said seriously.

Then she took out a most curious thing. It looked like some sort of squash with a long stem. 'This is my *ason*,' Edie said, shaking it. 'It is the symbol of the *mamaloi*, filled with sacred stones.'

'Where'd you get it?'

'I bought it.'

'Where?'

No answer.

Edie put it back in the bag. 'I haven't decided yet whether I should take it to New Orleans,' she said. 'It may not be the right time.' She looked over at Katy. 'I'm not sure I should show you any more.'

'Oh, please,' Katy begged. The eleven-year-old in her was nervous but the almost-grown-up couldn't resist.

Edie looked hard at Katy. 'You'll never tell?'

'Never.'

She paused, considering for a minute, then decided in Katy's favour. She took out a small square box tied with red string. Carefully she untied the knot and lifted the lid.

Katy stared. She had no idea what to expect but already she wished she hadn't asked to see.

Edie reached in and took out a small brown jar. 'This is a *govi*.' Her voice sounded far away, like she was dreaming. 'It contains the spirit of an ancient ancestor,' she whispered. 'I am going to take it to Ti Reine so she can release it into the trees.'

Katy's mouth fell open. What was Edie saying? That inside this jar was the soul of a dead person? Like a ghost or a demon or something? It couldn't be true. But if it was . . .

With a weird look on her face Edie held the jar out in front of her. 'Be patient, little spirit,' she crooned. 'Soon I will set you free.'

Hearing those words Katy was no longer just nervous. She was scared. 'Edie!' she gasped.

And then the front door slammed shut. 'Girls? I'm home.' Sylvie's voice.

Within seconds Edie had put the jar back in the box, the box back in her straw bag, and the bag back on the shelf in her closet. She turned around just as her mother appeared in the doorway. 'Hey, you two. What's up?' Sylvie didn't wait for an answer. With a click-click of her heels she continued down the hall to the kitchen.

'Come on, my little Katydid,' Edie said gently. 'There's nothing to be frightened of. My spirit won't harm *you*.' She took Katy by the hand and pulled her to her feet. 'Let's show my mother all the fantastic cookies we baked.'

27

Chapter Three

Baton Rouge, Louisiana, 20 December.

A vibration. Then a low rumbling sound, and within minutes a southbound express train roared through the station. But Joseph Marron did not want to head south. He wanted to go north or east or west. Anywhere but south. Anywhere but back to Brancheville.

Along the edge of the platform four other people stood waiting but Joseph hung back behind the schedule board out of sight, desperate not to be noticed. In case one of the passengers wasn't really a person at all. In case one of them had been sent by Adrien Ravel to find Joseph. To kill him – or worse. Not that Adrien Ravel needed anyone to do that for him. He was a sorcerer. If he wanted to, he could kill from a distance, without ever coming near.

But did he really want to kill Joseph? Or would he be content knowing that he had succeeded in driving him away? Joseph didn't know. All he could do now was run, and hope that he could hide.

He eyed his fellow passengers. All white but one, a woman. Joseph wasn't afraid of the whites. He knew that if Adrien had sent someone to find him it would be a black. Like Adrien himself. Like Joseph.

He felt the sweat break out on his forehead, trickle down the sides of his face. It was hot as hell for this time of year but it wasn't the heat that was making him sweat. It was the fear.

He looked at the lone black woman who stood with her back to him, impatient, shifting her big leather tote bag from one hand to the other. Though he couldn't see her clearly, she looked harmless enough.

But then, what was harmless? He knew what could happen to people when the drums sounded across the bayou, when the candles were lit, when the low fearsome chanting began.

An icy terror seized him and he shrank back against the wall. Where was the goddamn train? And in the next second, out of the dust it came, so fast that for a moment Joseph thought it wasn't going to stop.

He stumbled aboard and took a seat at the far end of the last car, so he could see without being seen. He put his battered brown valise on the seat beside him, resting his hand on top. Just under its closed zipper, inside his faded denim jacket was a snub-nosed thirty-eight special that Marcel had given him, showed him how to use. If, that is, he had time.

Joseph had never killed anyone. But he would now – if he had to, to save his own life. Not that he was certain a bullet would stop whatever was coming to get him.

Joseph took a deep breath. He had always believed that you either lived or died. Until Adrien Ravel came to Brancheville, that is. And then Joseph found out that there was a third possibility. You could become a 'thing', neither dead nor alive. A thing that existed somewhere in between. A zombie. Joseph had never seen such a thing before, never even believed that one could exist. And then he saw *her* – Blue's woman – and he believed. Remembering, Joseph shuddered.

29

The train moved out of the station, and as it picked up speed Joseph began to relax a little. Baton Rouge was a big city and he had made his way here without being followed. He was sure of that. Besides, the other people in the car had settled down without so much as a glance in his direction.

He leaned his head against the back of the seat and closed his eyes. Only for a minute, he thought. To rest them. They burned, and in the pit of his stomach he could feel a big queasy lump, although he couldn't imagine what it was. He hadn't been able to eat a scrap of food for two days. Not since he had seen *her*. Since then Joseph had been crazy with fear, and because he couldn't think what else to do he had gone to Marcel, told him what he had seen. Marcel had given him the gun, advised him to get the hell out of Brancheville while he still could. And Joseph had run, because he trusted Marcel to tell him the truth.

Marcel was his best friend. Had been, as far back as Joseph could remember. They grew up together on the bayou, spending long lazy days out on the water in Joseph's father's old pirogue, fishing for redfish, swatting mosquitoes, sucking on oranges. A good life while Joseph was a boy. In fact, even after he was grown, life in Brancheville wasn't bad. He had a job down at the end of Fitch Street, tending bar for old Mr Reynaud. It was a tin-roofed bar called La Dauphine, on stilts with its own landing to tie up boats. A busy place after dark. Joseph was happy there, and to make life even more pleasant, he had his own home. When his father died a year ago he left his house and his parcel of land to Joseph and his brother, Blue. It was a small house a short distance from town, not much to brag about, but it was a quiet place, right on the creek just below the

Choctaw Bridge. A private place with no neighbours to bother you, no poachers to raid your traps. Life had been good. No worries, no headaches, no fears.

Until Adrien Ravel came to town.

Adrien Ravel. The mysterious black man who bought the old Dumas plantation way up on Breaux Creek. The place had always intrigued local folks even back then, because it was built on a *cheniere*, a peculiar patch of high ground that rose right up out of the swamp. Like it was fighting for air. Joseph guessed that was why Ravel named the place Shadow Hill. Folks said he had come all the way from Haiti, bringing with him trunks and trunks of money, lots of Haitian servants, and dozens of beautiful Haitian women.

At first, folks in Brancheville were curious about the stranger. Curious but nothing more. Until weird things began to happen – things that had to do with more than just the living. Things that had to do with the dead.

Joseph Marron was not a church-going man. He didn't believe in much, except that you lived while you could as best you could, and you died when your time was up – a simple persuasion for a simple man. Religion, he thought, was fine for some folks, not so good for others. But then he began to hear things that made him wonder. Secret things about powerful spirits that had come to the bayou country with Adrien Ravel, and about the people out at Shadow Hill who served them. About rituals and magic ceremonies that could drive believers into a frenzy, and spells that gave power to those who demanded it, those who deserved it.

There was a whispered name for it: Voudou.

Joseph snapped his eyes open. The train had pulled into a station and some people were getting off, some getting on, but no one came into his car. Joseph stood up and went to the restroom, barely making it inside the door when the vomit came rolling up into his mouth, spilling over into the toilet. What had caused this awful sickness he couldn't imagine. He had eaten nothing for two whole days. Shee-it, he thought. I really *am* sick.

He kneeled on the floor and retched until there was nothing left to retch, nothing coming up but a yellow-ish green bile. He stayed there, gasping, until a knock came at the door. He felt too queasy to get up but he knew he had to. He lifted himself to his feet, stumbled out into the aisle and collapsed back in his seat. He closed his eyes. How could he be so sick? Was it only his nerves? He had to admit that it was a real possibility, since what he had seen had scared him half to death.

But what if it wasn't his nerves? Could it be that what he had heard about the Voudou spirits was true? That they could punish anyone, any time, any place? Joseph didn't know. But it didn't matter. He had only one hope now: to run for his life.

His mind raced back to the beginning. After Adrien Ravel took up residence out at Shadow Hill, life in Brancheville had gone on as usual. Joseph and Blue continued to live together in their father's house, rarely seeing each other, what with Joseph working nights at La Dauphine and Blue working days sweeping up over at the St Charles Hospital.

And then one day, for no reason at all, Blue upped and quitted his job and went to work out at Shadow Hill. From then on everything changed. Especially Blue. He became as mysteriously unapproachable as the man he worked for. Joseph never knew exactly what his job was. How could he, when no one knew what Adrien Ravel did either? Blue took to wearing dark clothes and dark glasses and began to walk with a threatening swagger. He began to push Joseph around, give him orders. Blue didn't seem to like Joseph any more, and in response, little by little, Joseph began to dislike his brother in equal measure.

Then two nights ago the worst happened.

Joseph was working at La Dauphine. Nothing much was going on until he overheard whispered talk that Blue had a woman, who for some mysterious reason Blue didn't want anyone to see. So he was bringing her out to the house only when Joseph was gone.

Joseph couldn't believe what he was hearing. It had to be a joke, he thought. First of all, Blue had never been successful with the local ladies. They considered him a big slob, nothing like Joseph, who had always been a winner when it came to a quick score. Blue was not good-looking nor was he one for smart conversation. In fact, to Joseph's knowledge the only women Blue had ever taken up with were the ones over in the cat houses in New Orleans.

But if Blue really did have a woman of his own now, why was he hiding her away? Joseph was sure he knew the answer: because Blue didn't want Joseph to see her, didn't want to give his brother a chance to steal her away. And that was when Joseph decided to leave work early, sneak out to their house on the creek, and see for himself.

The moon was full that night, bright enough to see the house even from a distance. Joseph left his truck parked along the road and walked down through the swamp. Sure enough, Blue's pickup was in the yard.

33

Joseph crept through the marsh grass and up onto the porch. If there was a woman inside Joseph was going to catch them in the act. It would serve Blue right for sneaking around, trying to hide his prize from his own brother.

Joseph opened the door a crack and peeked in.

No one in the front room.

Without a sound Joseph went across the floor to the bedroom door and threw it open. A broad grin appeared on his face. Sure enough, there they were, Blue and the woman together on the bed, stark naked, Blue on top, doing his thing.

'Oooeee!' Joseph howled. 'Look at you, big brother! Ain't you somethin'?'

Blue stopped moving. He didn't look around. He didn't get up. He just stopped moving. Still covering the woman with his bulk, he lay there stiff, like he'd had a stroke or something.

'Come on, Blue, what you got there?' Still grinning, Joseph walked to the edge of the bed and bent over, determined to see Blue's trophy.

And what he saw filled him with sheer, mind-gagging horror. She was pinned under Blue so he never glimpsed her naked body. But he saw her face. A face with the wide glassy eyes of a dead person. A face that Joseph recognized. A face that had once belonged to a girl named Eveline Carne, a Brancheville girl who everyone knew had *died*.

Joseph didn't mean to scream but he did. A high blood-curdling scream that never ended until he was almost into Brancheville.

He never went back to his house.

Now, remembering the horror, he snapped open his eyes and for a single terrifying moment he thought he

34

had gone blind. Everything was pitch dark, but in the next instant the train rumbled out of the tunnel and he could see again. His eyes still burned as if someone were sticking red hot needles in them, but at least he could see. He wondered what time it was. He had no watch. But then what difference did it make? He'd get to St Louis when he got there. *If* he got there.

Again he took count of the passengers – still only three of them, none seeming even vaguely interested in him. But he was not convinced that he was safe yet. If someone was coming after him, whoever it was would walk in shadow, most probably never seen. And Joseph would die never knowing his executioner.

He broke out in a sweat, felt it soak his shirt, gluing him to the back of the seat. He had a powerful urge to jump off the train and run all the way back to the Choctaw Bridge where he could throw himself into the sweet warm water and stay until he felt good again. And then maybe he'd get his fishing pole, or maybe he'd go down to the boat launch and look for crayfish.

But he couldn't do that. Not now. Not ever again.

He shifted in his seat. His feet felt tingly. He had been sitting so long that they must have gone to sleep. He wondered if he should walk back to the restroom, then decided not to. He didn't have to go, and although he still felt sick he knew he wasn't going to vomit again. There was nothing left in his gut but gnawing fear.

The train rumbled on and Joseph slept. He dreamed about Blue. Blue, telling him in a flat deadly voice that Joseph was doomed. That he had seen something he never should have seen, a girl brought back from the dead. *A zombie.* And for that, Joseph must pay with his own life.

'But what if I take an oath never to tell?' Joseph wept.

'Adrien Ravel doesn't want your oath,' Blue thundered. 'He wants your life.'

Joseph woke from the nightmare with a start. He hadn't needed Blue to tell him such a thing. He knew it was true. Marcel had told him to run. And he had. But would he ever be safe? Could he ever hide from Adrien Ravel, a man who could bring people back from the dead? A man who spoke with the spirits?

The conductor came through the car and took his ticket. 'You okay, mister?'

Dumb with fear, Joseph could only nod.

The conductor stared at him sceptically for a minute, then shrugged and turned to make his way back down the aisle. The black woman, toting her big leather bag, brushed past the conductor, heading towards Joseph's end of the car. When she reached him, their eyes met, locked in a terrible gaze for a seemingly endless moment before she moved on.

Joseph reached up and wiped the sweat off his ashy face with his shirt sleeve. He was sweating like a hog but maybe it was because he was breathing so hard.

He tried to catch his breath, tried to swallow, but could do neither. The woman was gone, and suddenly he knew he needed help. He wasn't just sick. It was something far worse. Something deadly.

He tried to lift himself from the seat but he couldn't. His whole body had gone numb. His eyes were starting from his head, burning as if someone had thrown a bottle of acid in his face, but he couldn't close them. Joseph knew that he was doomed, that somehow Ravel and his Voudou spirits had worked their deadly magic against him without his ever knowing how. He wanted to scream a warning: *Don't mess with Adrien Ravel!*

But he couldn't. He managed to make a small gobbling sound low in his throat. But no one heard him.

No one noticed him at all for almost an hour.

By then, Joseph Marron was stone-dead.

Chapter Four

New Orleans, 29 December.

Sylvie's eyes opened wide and for a moment she felt a rush of panic. *Who the hell are you? Why are you following me?* She closed her eyes tight, then opened them to stare once again from the second-floor window in the Beauchamps' house down to the street below. But the man had vanished. The only person in sight was an old woman walking her spaniel in the morning sun. She paused while the dog sniffed around Jonas' front gate. Then she moved on.

Am I going nuts? Only a moment ago Sylvie had seen him clearly – the same shadowy figure she had noticed three times before. At least she *thought* she had.

The first encounter was about a week ago, outside her apartment building, just before she hailed a cab to go to Galen's office with Edie. He was standing at the corner, waiting to cross the avenue and Sylvie would never have noticed him had it not been for the fact that his shoulders and bare head were covered with snow. Even his eyebrows were white. It was as if he had been standing there for hours waiting for the traffic light to change. But when it did, he never moved.

The second time she saw him was at Macy's, standing just to one side of the escalator. And again she never would have noticed him except that at first glance she thought he was a mannequin. He was that still. But when she looked at him she was surprised to see that he was watching. *Her?*

The thought had been unsettling but she had brushed it aside and had hurried on. She had a lot to do before she left for New Orleans and not anywhere near enough time to do it. No time to wonder about what ifs. Or things like: who the hell are you?

And then again in the airport. She had stopped to buy a pack of Lifesavers and when she turned around there he was, standing at the edge of the waiting area, in full view. And this time she knew he was watching her.

She had stifled an urge to walk over to him, slap him hard, demand: what do you want? What the hell do you think you're doing?

But Edie was waiting, about to board their plane so she put him out of her mind. There was no way she was in any danger. Was there?

And now here, safe in Jonas' house, the house where she had grown up, she wasn't in any danger either. Besides he wasn't there any more. Perhaps he never had been. Maybe she *had* imagined. Maybe she hadn't seen him at all.

Sylvie turned away from the bedroom window and went downstairs to find Edie. Ever since they had arrived in New Orleans Edie had seemed preoccupied, and this morning Sylvie knew she had put it off long enough. Today she was definitely going to have to take her daughter to see Ti Reine. There was something in Edie's manner that always disturbed Sylvie when she saw it, and she was seeing it now – a pensive, withdrawn quietness. Sylvie knew it meant that inside, Edie was thinking about Ti Reine, thinking about Voudou. Sylvie had tried to ignore it. For the past six days she had put off their visit to the old woman, offering all kinds of excuses, making other plans. But now she knew she could put it off no longer. This morning she was going to have to take Edie to see Ti Reine.

On her way to the kitchen, Sylvie glanced into the front room. Edie was sitting quietly by the window, looking out at the passing cars, waiting. But Sylvie wasn't ready to go – not yet. She needed to gather herself together.

Jonas had already left for his office, but Sylvie went into the sunroom anyway to pour herself a cup of coffee. She was dreading this visit because she knew that she was going to have to talk sternly to Ti Reine, tell her that she was not to encourage Edie in any way to become a Voudouist. Right now Edie was a very impressionable, very vulnerable young girl, standing in absolute awe of Ti Reine, hoping that someday she might be chosen to follow in her footsteps. Not so unusual for a fifteen-year-old to dream, Sylvie thought, but as far as she was concerned that was all it should be. A dream. Never a reality. Sylvie did not want her daughter ever to embrace Voudou as a part of her life. She knew that it was a religion focused on healing, but it was also a religion born out of desperation, to a culture that knew little else. For most Haitians there had never been any hope except to turn to their priests and their ancestral spirits for help. For mending. For guidance. Edie didn't need that. Edie was not part of that world. The last thing Sylvie wanted was for her daughter to follow a religion rooted in dark despair.

This was what she was going to try to explain to Ti Reine, and hope that the old woman would understand and not take it as an offence or a betrayal.

Sylvie took a sip of coffee. She had promised David she would ask about zombies, but that was the least of her concerns right now. It would have to wait. With Sylvie, first things always came first.

She set her cup down on the table. There was no point in delaying any longer. Ti Reine was expecting them.

Edie was still in the chair by the window, her lovely young face composed, the picture of patience.

'Let's go, Edie,' Sylvie said with unexpected sharpness. Annoyed with herself she held out her hand. 'Come on, sweetie, Ti Reine is waiting.'

There was little conversation in the cab, and Sylvie could see that now Edie was no longer calm. A thoughtless Sylvie had taken care of that.

'Mama, are you angry with me?' Edie asked.

'Of course not.' Sylvie smiled and put her arm around her daughter. 'It's just that I'm upset about Camille, my cousin. You remember I told you about her? How she has lost her only child?' She felt Edie relax.

'Poor Cousin Camille,' Edie said. 'Are we going to visit her?'

'Yes. As soon as I can arrange it. Perhaps this afternoon.'

The cab pulled up in front of a small grocery store and they got out. Edie didn't wait for Sylvie. She ran down the alley and up the back stairs.

Sylvie watched as Edie disappeared. I've been coming here all my life, she thought suddenly, and I never noticed before how shabby it is. She followed Edie up the stairs to Ti Reine's apartment. The door was ajar and she went inside. She could hear voices from the kitchen but she stood in the parlour for a moment and looked around. Nothing had changed. It was a dark room with shades drawn, furnished with only absolute essentials: two straight-back chairs, a worn sofa, a few assorted tables, and at the far end a chest of drawers, clear evidence that Ti Reine had little interest in the material world.

'*Ma petite.*'

Sylvie turned to see the old woman standing in the kitchen doorway.

Ti Reine looked exactly as she always had. A small woman, thin as a rail, and old, though no one knew precisely how old she really was. Somewhere in her eighties, Sylvie guessed. But in spite of her years there was an ageless quality about her. To those who knew her she seemed indestructible and infinitely powerful. Perhaps it was because she always carried herself with a regal air, radiating confidence, shoulders back, head held high. Like her name. Like a queen.

Sylvie felt a rush of affection. 'Ti Reine,' she said, and went to her.

They did not embrace. They never had. Instead, as was her habit, the old woman put her hands on either side of Sylvie's face and looked hard into her eyes. 'You are troubled,' she said softly.

Sylvie turned away. 'Where is Edie?'

Her daughter appeared in the doorway. 'Ti Reine would like me to go downstairs and pick up her groceries. May I?'

Sylvie nodded, grateful for the chance to be alone with the old woman, but not surprised at the opportunity. Somehow Ti Reine always knew when Sylvie needed time to talk.

What she had to say didn't take long but it was painful, so painful. She loved Ti Reine, she had limitless respect for the woman, but she feared her, too. Ti Reine lived in a world guided and controlled by the *loa*, the Voudou spirits. Some benevolent, others brutal and vindictive.

While Sylvie spoke, Ti Reine listened, her eyes hooded, impassive.

'I love you, Ti Reine,' Sylvie said earnestly. 'And I have the deepest admiration for you. Your strength is limitless. But I must ask you not to encourage Edie in any way.'

There was a long pause, and then Ti Reine put her hand to her head and leaned forward.

Sylvie shuddered. She knew what was coming. As a child she had seen it happen in Voudou ceremonies. It was the prelude to a spirit possession. Ti Reine's body would be taken over by one of the *loa* where, for good or evil, the spirit would speak through her mouth. The few times Sylvie had witnessed such a thing she had been terrified.

And she was terrified now. She stared at the old woman who sat rigid in her chair, eyes glazed over.

And then to Sylvie's great relief the moment passed. Ti Reine had stayed in control. 'I will do as you ask, Sylvie,' she said quietly, and for the first time she sounded truly old.

Sylvie reached out to take her hand but Ti Reine drew back, shaking her head, then got to her feet. 'You will take Edie with you when she returns,' she said. 'Do not bring her to me again. She is no longer a child of this house.' Without another word she left the room.

After lunch Sylvie rented a car, and she and Edie began a trip west to Brancheville. The trip served a double purpose. It meant that Sylvie would get to see her cousin Camille, and that Edie would have something to think about besides Ti Reine. That morning when Edie had returned to the old woman's house with the groceries, Sylvie had lied to her, told her that Ti Reine wasn't feeling well and they would have to reschedule their visit for another day.

Edie had been visibly upset, had begged to stay, but Sylvie had insisted that it was impossible. Now, as they headed out of the city and made their way along the north bank of the Mississippi River, Edie's mood began to lighten a little, perhaps because of the magnificent landscape unfolding on both sides of the road: mile after mile of live oak trees dripping with Spanish moss, flat fields and rolling hills with glimpses of the mighty river in between.

'Can we take a boat trip on the river?' Edie asked.

'Absolutely,' Sylvie answered. She had four more days to keep Edie occupied and happy. And away from Ti Reine. A full day's riverboat ride would do just fine.

They crossed the river at Vacherie and headed south. Sylvie had no idea where in Brancheville her cousin lived, but the town was small, the gas station attendant helpful, and she found the house without any difficulty.

It was a pretty house, painted white, with a wide porch and pots of ferns hanging on either side of the front door. Rose bushes lined the walk, underplanted with all kinds of flowers.

Sylvie took a deep breath. 'I hope she's home.' Then, 'I hope she recognizes me.'

They were almost to the steps when the front door opened and a woman stepped out onto the porch. A short, solid woman whose black skin was as smooth and unlined as it had been when Sylvie last saw her. Twenty-five years hadn't changed Camille one bit.

She looked from Sylvie to Edie, unblinking, without a flicker of recognition, and in her eyes Sylvie could see a deep sadness. And more than that: something that looked like fear.

'Can . . . can I help you?' Camille asked.

'Camille? It's me. Sylvie.'

The woman stood still for a moment, then threw her arms wide and rushed forward. 'Sylvie! My dear, my dear, my dear! Thank goodness you've come!' Tears streaming down her face she hugged Sylvie with a fierceness that was almost painful. Then she stepped back and turned to Edie. 'And who is this?'

'This is Edie,' Sylvie said softly. 'My daughter.'

'Oh cousin, she's beautiful.' The tears came back in a fresh flood. 'Almost . . . almost as beautiful as my Eveline was.'

Sylvie took her hand. 'Poor Camille. You sounded so desperate when I spoke to you that I had to come. To tell you how sorry I am. To see if there's anything I can do.'

'There is, there is,' Camille stammered, almost breathless, gripping hard. 'I don't know why I did it but I . . . I threatened him. I told him about you, that you have friends in high places who will help me.' She was clearly frightened now and the words tumbled out. 'Will you come with me? He's sending a car to get me. To take me to Shadow Hill to get Eveline's things. Right now. Please, please, I don't want to go alone. I am so afraid.'

'Of course we'll go with you.' Sylvie hadn't a clue what was going on but she put her arms around her cousin. 'Won't we, Edie?'

Camille rested her head on Sylvie's shoulder. 'I knew the Lord would answer my prayers and He has. He sent you.'

Sylvie had no chance to ask Camille any questions. In the next moment a black Mercedes pulled down the road and stopped behind Sylvie's car.

Camille straightened up. With Sylvie on one side and Edie on the other, she made her way down the walk.

The car door swung open.

Off they went.

Sylvie learned very little on the way. Camille would only say that they were going to a place called Shadow Hill, where Eveline had lived, worked, died, and now was buried. She was going to pick up her daughter's possessions.

'This must have been unbearable for you, Camille,' Sylvie said softly. 'How did it happen? Was there an accident?'

In response Camille threw a fearful glance at the driver, then shook her head and fell silent.

They drove on, along narrow back roads that led deeper and deeper into the bayou country, roads that Sylvie would never have dared to travel by herself. Magnolia trees and live oaks crowded the way, and beyond them she could see the brooding murky waters of the bayou.

And suddenly, in the midst of nowhere, the car stopped. The driver got out, walked a few feet off the road and unlocked a high wrought-iron gate, almost hidden by vegetation.

The next minute they were on a gravel drive, hardly more than a path really, cutting its way through a thick all-enveloping tangle of green. Suffocating, Sylvie thought. And then she heard them. Dogs. Snarling menacing dogs, not yet seen, but seeming to close in from all sides.

She felt Edie's hand grab hers and she squeezed it.

'Don't worry,' Camille breathed. 'We're almost there.'

In the next instant the trees parted, the drive widened, and the sounds of the dogs faded away.

Sylvie couldn't believe what she was seeing. Even at a distance, through an archway of ancient oaks under-planted with masses of flowering camellias, the house was clearly visible. Set at the top of a gentle rise, with terraced lawns sweeping away in all directions, it was breathtaking. A magnificent antebellum mansion, painted cool white with dark maroon shutters, fronted with two-storeyed colonnaded verandahs edged with intricate wrought-iron grillwork.

'Shadow Hill,' Camille whispered, and Sylvie felt her shudder.

The driver stopped the car, got out and opened the passenger door.

'Please, Sylvie,' Camille whispered, 'come in with me.'

Sylvie nodded, feeling oddly unnerved. She turned to Edie. 'You wait here,' she said. 'We'll only be a minute.'

'No way,' Edie whispered, grabbing her mother's hand. 'I'm not staying here alone. Besides I can't wait to see the inside.'

In spite of her uneasiness, neither could Sylvie. What kind of people lived here? Why did her cousin seem so afraid? And even more unsettling, why did she herself suddenly feel so threatened?

Had Sylvie turned at that moment she might have had an answer. She might have seen a familiar figure standing at the edge of the driveway. The same man who had followed her all the way from New York. And she would have realized that it was no coincidence, that he had been watching her. She wouldn't have known why, but she would have known that she was in real danger. She might have left Shadow Hill and never come back.

But she didn't turn. She never saw him. Instead she walked with an unsteady Camille and a breathless Edie up the wide step onto the verandah.

The front door was opened almost immediately by a white-smocked servant who led them across a huge entry hall to a room at the rear. But not so quickly that Sylvie wasn't able to get a look around. As much as the exterior had overwhelmed her with its splendour, the inside was bizarre. All the walls were painted with murals depicting ancient battles, and the furniture was more appropriate to a French palace than a Louisiana plantation house. Each chair was etched in gold, elaborately carved with swans and griffins. The tables were marble-topped with curved legs. At the far end of the hall, impossible to miss, stood a huge marble bust of Napoleon Bonaparte.

The servant ushered them into a large room with high vaulted ceilings and a marble floor. Heavy crimson drapes hung at the windows and in the centre of the carpet stood a huge mahogany desk supported by legs shaped like gargoyles.

'I'll tell Monsieur Ravel that you have arrived,' said the servant. He left.

'Who is Monsieur Ravel?' Sylvie whispered.

Camille shivered. 'He owns Shadow Hill.'

'And your daughter worked for him?'

Camille put her finger to her lips. 'I'll tell you later,' she said in a hushed tone. 'Once we're safely away from this place.'

Sylvie nodded.

Within minutes the servant returned. 'Monsieur Ravel will be with you in a moment. Please sit.'

Camille began to sway on her feet and Sylvie reached out to steady her, helping her to one of the gilded chairs. Camille sat down with Edie sitting close beside her.

Sylvie remained standing. A large painting over the mantel had caught her eye and she moved closer to get a better look.

It was a primitive work, utterly out of place in the ornate surroundings. Gruesome, Sylvie thought, although what it represented she wasn't sure. In the background was a skeletal figure draped in black, wearing a wide-brimmed black hat. He was riding, oddly enough, what seemed to be a goat. In the foreground, seven other bony figures, all similarly draped in black, walked one behind the other. And where their eyes were supposed to be were only round blobs of white paint.

Sylvie felt an unexpected chill touch the back of her neck.

'*Corpses Walking in the Sunlight*,' she heard someone say.

Startled, Sylvie turned to see a man standing in the doorway.

'That's the title of the composition,' he said, coming toward her. He was a strikingly handsome man, lean and muscular, dressed in a khaki shirt, riding breeches and polished leather boots. He moved with

49

the grace of a panther, and spoke with a soft accent that Sylvie recognized at once as Haitian. 'It's something I picked up years ago in Port-au-Prince. I like it, don't you?' He smiled, revealing a perfect row of strong white teeth, but his dark eyes were not smiling. They were cold, expressionless, like pieces of obsidian. 'I am Adrien Ravel,' he said.

Rattled for an instant, Sylvie quickly regained her composure. She held out her hand. 'I am Sylvie Valois, Camille Carne's cousin.'

His grip was cool, firm. 'I know. In her time of grief Mrs Carne mentioned you as someone who might help her. Welcome to Shadow Hill.' He turned to a wide-eyed Camille. 'My dear Mrs Carne, how are you?' Without waiting for a response he turned to Edie. For a long minute he stared at her with an almost hypnotic intensity, as if he had just discovered a priceless work of art. 'You, *mademoiselle*, are exquisite,' he said. 'And you are . . . ?'

Sylvie moved quickly to Edie's side. 'She is my daughter.'

Adrien Ravel nodded, looking from one to the other. 'Two extraordinarily lovely ladies,' he said softly, then turned back to Camille. 'I have had one of the servants pack your daughter's possessions. You may go through them here and decide if there is anything worth keeping. Or you may take all of them with you. As you like.'

Camille stood up. 'I'll take them,' she said in a tight voice.

Camille didn't utter another word until they were delivered back to her house in Brancheville. There, in the safety of her own home, she poured out her heart to Sylvie, frantic words rushing out so rapidly that it was difficult to understand them. Things about sorcery and witchcraft and madness. But there was one thing that Sylvie understood clearly: someone, Camille said, had murdered her Eveline. And that someone, she knew, was the devil himself. Adrien Ravel.

Chapter Five

New York City, New Year's Day.

All the snow had melted and the city looked uniformly grey, but even so, David was happy to be back. They had spent a wonderful week in Utah. He had found his mother in good health, ski conditions had been perfect with almost three feet of new powder, and he had managed a lot of uninterrupted time with Galen. Long evenings spent by the fire after his mother and Katy had gone to bed, sorting out their plans. Discussing the news from Baird Laboratories. What he would do when he got back to New York. How far he had come in his research and where he was headed. Galen's trip to San Francisco for a medical seminar in March. Katy's request that she be allowed to have her hair straightened. Sylvie's dissertation on virus proteins.

'Someday we'll have to bring Sylvie and Edie out here to your mother's, put them on skis,' Galen had said.

'No way.' David had found that idea hilariously funny. 'If there is anything Sylvie hates it's the cold. Cold weather of any kind. She reminds me of Sam Magee. Remember that poem? "He was often cold but that land of gold seemed to hold him like a spell, though he'd often say in his homely way he'd sooner live in hell."'

They had both laughed then, agreeing. Sylvie did indeed hate the cold almost as much as David loved it. 'When is she due back at the lab?' Galen had asked.

'On January fourth.'

Galen had grown pensive. 'Tell me honestly, David, if you could choose, would you rather stay here in Utah, live the rest of your life here? Never go back to New York?'

And he had answered her honestly, a little surprised himself at the certainty of his feeling. 'Right now there is nothing I'd rather do than go back to New York. Nothing is as important to me as this project. Nothing.' He had emphasized the word. Then he had smiled and kissed her cheek. 'Nothing except you, of course.'

She, too, had smiled at that. 'You, my darling, are a liar. But I love you all the same.'

Now they were home. The traffic coming out of the airport was light and their taxi made it into the city without any delay, turning onto Fourteenth Street, then down Fifth Avenue, dropping them off right in front of their building.

'Hurry up, Dad,' Katy said as he fumbled for the key. 'I can't wait to see Mingo.'

David opened the door and set their bags down in the foyer as Helen came through the living room, a smile of relief on her face. 'Welcome home, Wickliffes,' she said. 'Was your trip everything you had hoped it would be?'

'Everything,' Galen said, hugging her. 'No crises while we were gone?'

'No. The cat piddled on the hall carpet but that's all.' She took Katy's coat and hung it up.

'Where is he?' Katy asked, heading down the hall.

'Asleep in the front window, as usual. Except for that first accident he's been a very well-behaved cat.'

'What's for dinner?' David asked, sorting through the mail on the hall table.

'Shrimp piccante,' Helen said.

'You are so good.' Galen picked up her suitcase. 'How'd you know I was just thinking about that? As soon as I unpack I'll be down for a taste.'

David took the other bags and followed her up the stairs.

'Oh, by the way, Professor,' Helen said. 'Sylvie called from New Orleans yesterday. Wanted you to call her there as soon as you had a chance. She said it was nothing to worry about, but she did sound anxious. The number is on the desk in the library.'

'Huh,' David said, following Galen into the bedroom. 'I wonder what's up.'

Galen glanced at her watch. 'It's almost six. Why don't you call her right now. Then I'll call my service.'

'Good idea.' He left the room and went back down to the library. Helen had left a pile of notes on the desk, Sylvie's message on the top.

He punched in the number.

Only two rings and a soft voice answered. 'Beauchamp residence.'

'This is David Wickliffe, returning Sylvie Valois' call.'

'One moment, sir.'

There was a click, then a long pause, so long that David thought he had been disconnected. Just as he was about to hang up he heard another click, then Sylvie's voice, sounding out of breath. 'David. You just caught me on the way out. But I'm glad you did. By the way, Happy New Year.'

'Happy New Year to you too. What's up?'

'Something extraordinary has happened and I'm not quite sure how to handle it. Remember when I told you about my cousin's daughter? That she had died?'

'Yes.'

'Well, three days ago I drove over to Brancheville to see Camille. And the short of it is, she believes that her daughter was murdered.'

'You're kidding.'

'No. And do you know what else? Talk about weird coincidence, the rumour in Brancheville is that Eveline is not dead at all. That she is a *zombie*.'

David couldn't believe what he was hearing. 'A *what*?'

'A zombie. Strange, isn't it?'

'Preposterous is more like it. Does your cousin believe it?'

'No, she doesn't. Camille is a hard-line Baptist. But she does believe that Eveline was murdered by her employer, a Haitian named Adrien Ravel.'

'Has your cousin contacted the authorities?'

'No. She's too afraid. And that's where I come in. I've been trying to get some information myself but it's been impossible because all of the state and local offices are closed until the fourth of January. This morning I talked it over with Jonas. Criminal law is not his field but he knows what questions to ask. Tomorrow morning, even though the state offices are closed, he's going to check with a friend who works in the Medical Examiner's office downtown, ask if he would be willing to spend a few hours accessing the computer files, see what Eveline's autopsy showed. Find out if there was any reason to suspect foul play.'

'And if there is?'

She sighed. 'I may be here longer than I expected. I just wanted you to know.'

There was a pause while Sylvie talked to someone in the background. 'Sorry, David,' she said, coming back on the line. 'My car is here.'

'And where are you off to?'

'I'm having dinner this evening with a very interesting gentleman. His name is Jeremy Calder, a surgeon at the Tulane Medical Center.'

'Ah ha,' David said. 'Someone special, perhaps?'

She laughed. 'No, no. Nothing like that. When I told Jonas about Adrien Ravel, he suggested I call this fellow for information. Jonas takes care of all of his legal business and he said that Calder spends at least three weeks every year in Haiti, volunteering his time to work at some health clinic outside of Port-au-Prince. He knows a lot about who was who in Haiti during the Duvalier years. Jonas said that if anyone might know about this Ravel person, where he comes from, where he gets his money, it would be Jeremy Calder. And while I'm at it, it will be a perfect opportunity to ask him what he knows about zombification.' Another chuckle. 'As a matter of fact, Professor, now that I think about it, maybe the rumours about Eveline have some merit. Maybe she really is a zombie. Maybe we have the answers for Baird Labs right here under our noses.'

'Yeah. Right. And maybe I'm Jonas Salk. But seriously, Sylvie, you shouldn't be thinking about work right now. It's the least of your concerns.'

'Bull. You know that next to taking care of Edie, there's nothing I'd rather be doing than working on your project. So don't despair. I have a strong feeling that my cousin is wrong about her daughter. Even as a child Camille always believed everything she heard. And although she's adamant about this murder thing, she doesn't have any real evidence. She's reacting to whispered rumour and nothing more. In any case, if all goes well and my cousin *is* wrong, you'll see me bright and early on the fourth. But right now I've gotta go. Tell Galen I bought that Louisiana caviar she wanted. I'll deliver it when I pick up the cat. See you soon.'

'Right.'

'Bye.'

'Bye, Sylvie. And again, Happy New Year.' He dropped the receiver into the cradle.

'Did you get in touch with Sylvie?' Galen asked, coming into the room.

'I did.'

She reached for the phone, then stopped and stared hard at him. 'Is there something wrong?' A quick breath. 'It isn't Edie, is it?'

'No.' He told her about Sylvie's cousin.

'Sylvie shouldn't be messing around with this,' Galen said. 'If her cousin is right, and Eveline's death was suspicious, Sylvie is going to feel obligated to stick around, to give her cousin some help.' She frowned. 'You know Sylvie. She can't seem to bring herself to say no.'

'She will this time, Galen. Once Jonas gets the autopsy report, that will be that. Even if there is something going on down there, I'm not worried. Sylvie's a sympathetic lady but she has her priorities. One is Edie and the other is her job. She'll be back Monday morning come hell or high water.'

*   *   *

When Sylvie put down the phone she felt a sudden rush of panic. The same kind of bone-shaking panic she had experienced three days ago when she had seen the strange man lurking in the shadow across the street. But she hadn't seen him since that morning, so what in hell was the matter with her? Why was she suddenly feeling as if she were about to fall off a cliff? After all, she was only going out to dinner.

'Mama, you'd better hurry.' Edie came into the room. 'The cab driver is honking his horn like crazy.'

'I'm ready,' Sylvie said, giving Edie a quick peck on the cheek. 'You be a good girl and mind Jonas and I'll see you in a couple of hours.'

Edie nodded. On her way out the door, Sylvie blew her daughter another kiss.

When Sylvie arrived at Emeril's, a restaurant in the Warehouse District, Dr Jeremy Calder was already there, and Sylvie liked him from the first.

About as tall as she was, he was not especially good-looking: muddy blond hair going grey, horn-rimmed glasses, a rumpled suit. But such a warm smile, and behind the glasses a pair of deep blue eyes, full of genuine interest, that made Sylvie feel instantly welcome.

They spoke easily, like old friends getting reacquainted, without haste, neither one pressing the other for personal information. It wasn't until the coffee and dessert had been served that Jeremy Calder finally leaned back in his chair and said, 'Jonas tells me your mother came from Haiti. Have you ever been there?'

'Once, in the seventies. Right after I graduated from college. Never again.'

'Then I don't have to tell you what life is like there.'

'No,' Sylvie said softly. 'Which makes me wonder why you go back every year.'

He smiled. 'I suppose it's ego. In Haiti, no matter how little you give, it's far more than they expect, and they are eternally grateful to you. They treat you as if you were close to being a divinity. As a matter of fact, I'm headed down there next week. Want to come along?'

Sylvie smiled back. 'No, thank you. Deep down I am about as selfish as they come.'

'That must be why you're interested in Adrien Ravel. While he lived in Haiti he succeeded in turning selfishness into a pure art form.' He frowned. 'Selfishness, among other things.'

Sylvie watched him closely. 'How did you know him?'

He paused to stir his coffee. 'I didn't. But everybody who knew anything about the Duvaliers knew about Adrien Ravel.'

'What did he have to do with them?'

'He was high up in the Ministry of Economics back in the seventies, early eighties. But Ravel was always more a man of mystery than accomplishment. No one outside the inner circle really knew what he did.'

'Do you know where he is now?'

'No. People like him have a habit of disappearing without a trace when things get rough. I know he fled the country just before Baby Doc was deposed. But whether or not they both ended up in France I don't know.'

'Ravel didn't. He came to the United States. As a matter of fact he's living near a small town about fifty miles west of here. A town called Brancheville.'

A strange stillness came over Jeremy's face. 'That's not good news. I wonder what he's up to these days?'

Sylvie shrugged. 'As you said, a man of mystery. Nobody seems to know. He has a lot of money, that's for sure.'

'You've met him?'

'I have.'

'How'd you like him?'

'I only saw him for a few minutes but that was enough. I got the impression that he's a very powerful man – and not one you'd want to mess around with.' She told him about her trip to Shadow Hill with Camille and Edie. 'That's the reason I called you. My cousin believes that Ravel murdered her daughter.'

Jeremy didn't seem the least bit surprised. 'Adrien Ravel was feared and hated in Haiti for a good many reasons, not the least of which was murder. Although no charges were ever brought against him. Nothing about any of Duvalier's close associates was ever openly discussed. It was all rumour. Never fact.' He took a sip of coffee, then settled back in his chair. 'In the early nineteen hundreds there was another Haitian very much like Ravel. His name was Cadeus Bellegarde, a Voudou high priest gone mad. A specialist in the creation of human terror. No one was ever safe from Bellegarde, not even members of his own flock. In fact, it was the Voudouists themselves who finally denounced him in defence of their own religion. I don't know whatever happened to him, but back in the Duvalier years there was an eerie whisper floating around that Adrien Ravel was really Cadeus Bellegarde reincarnated.'

By the time she left Emeril's, Sylvie was convinced that Camille's suspicions about Adrien Ravel had merit.

Chapter Six

New York City, 3 January.

Galen felt a soft ball of fur, heard a faint purring, and she opened one eye. 'Hi, Mingo,' she said to the cat who had just curled up beside her on the bed. She didn't bother to move. It was only seven thirty on Sunday morning but she knew David had already gone. She had heard him leave early – five a.m. He had whispered something about a special shipment. Galen hadn't asked any questions. Today was one of the rare days when she wasn't on call and she had gone right back to sleep.

Now she burrowed under the covers, enjoying the warmth. A song her grandfather used to sing came into her head. Something about how nice it was to stay a-bed on Sunday morning. It certainly was true. She drifted off again but not for long. When the phone rang it was just eight o'clock.

She groaned. She wasn't ready to wake up. She reached over and picked up the receiver. 'Galen Wickliffe,' she said.

There was a pause, a staticky sound, then a woman's voice that she didn't recognize. 'Hello, Galen. Is David there?'

'Who's calling, please?'

'For Pete's sake, Galen, it's Sylvie.' Strained. Clearly upset.

Galen came wide awake. 'Sylvie? My God, it doesn't sound like you. Where are you?' A stupid question to ask. Galen knew perfectly well where her friend was.

More static crackling on the line.

'Sylvie? I can barely hear you. Call me back?'

'Yes.' There was a click, a buzz.

Frowning, Galen dropped the receiver into the cradle. Sylvie was calling, and Galen knew what that had to mean. Sylvie's cousin was in trouble. Sylvie wasn't coming home.

Minutes passed. Then the phone rang again. 'Sylvie?'

'Yes.' This time the line was clear. Still, Sylvie sounded far away.

'Don't tell me,' Galen said. 'It's bad news.'

'You said it. I have to stay in New Orleans.'

'Why? What did you find out?'

'It's so weird that I don't even understand it myself. Never mind knowing how to handle it. Last night Jonas heard from his friend in the Medical Examiner's office here in the city. As a favour to Jonas he went downtown to find out what the coroner's report on Eveline's death showed.'

'And?'

'That's just it. There was no autopsy.'

Galen didn't find that unusual. 'Perhaps there wasn't any need for one, Sylvie. Did Jonas ask about the cause of death? It has to be entered on the death certificate.'

'It was. Bronchial pneumonia, it says, signed by Eveline's doctor, Dr Aubin. No request was ever made for an autopsy.'

'I'm missing something here. If the doctor was

certain of the cause, and there was no evidence of foul play, in most cases there *is* no need for an autopsy. So what's the problem?'

'According to my cousin, Dr Aubin had no idea why Eveline died. He told Camille that he was going to call immediately and request an autopsy.'

'But he didn't.'

'No.'

'Have you spoken to him about it?'

Sylvie lowered her voice. 'That's one of the problems, Galen. Dr Aubin died the same day that Eveline died, on his way back from Shadow Hill.'

Galen felt a cold prickle crawl along the back of her neck. 'How?'

'An apparent heart attack. At least that's what his autopsy showed.'

'I think you should come home,' Galen said sharply. 'Right now. Today. Tell your cousin to request that her daughter's body be exhumed. She has that right. And then let the authorities take it from there.'

'Exactly what Jonas said.'

'So why are you staying?'

Sylvie didn't hesitate. She spoke with absolute certainty. 'Because I know there's more to this than what Camille told me. I had dinner Friday night with Jeremy Calder.'

'David told me about him.' A new consideration. Did Sylvie have another reason for wanting to stay in New Orleans? A personal one? 'Did you like him?'

'Very much, but that's beside the point. He told me some pretty scary things about Adrien Ravel. Jeremy knew the man only by reputation. Supposedly a high priest in some secret Voudou cult. A very powerful figure in Haiti at one time – and a very dangerous one,

Jeremy says. You can't imagine the hideous atrocities the man was suspected of committing.'

Again a statical interference, but through the crackle Galen could hear voices in the background. Then Sylvie came back on the line. 'I can't really go into it all now, Galen. I haven't time. The main reason I called was to see if you could pick Edie up at the airport today.'

'Sylvie, are you sure you're doing the right thing? I don't like the sound of this one bit.' Galen's voice shook.

'Galen, please calm down. This isn't anything for you to get upset over. I have some questions that have to be answered, questions that Camille is too afraid to ask. Jeremy Calder and I are going out to Shadow Hill this afternoon to get some answers. And then, if there seems to be a good reason, we'll put Camille in touch with the right people. A few days at the most and I'll be home.' She took a breath. 'So will you please pick Edie up?'

'You know I will. What's the flight number?'

'US Air 180. It gets into LaGuardia at four twenty-nine.'

Galen jotted it down. 'Got it.'

Sylvie lowered her voice. 'For a lot of reasons that I'll explain later, Edie is very nervous about all this. You know she hasn't been away from me for any length of time since she was eight, when she was in the hospital. But then, you were there for her, and you will be now, so she should be fine.' She paused. 'Okay?'

'Okay. But I still think you ought to get on that plane with Edie today, Sylvie, and come on home.'

'Don't fret, mother hen. I'll be very careful.'

64

'All right. But call me tomorrow, Sylvie. Promise.'

There was no answer. Only a soft click and the connection was broken.

Damn, Galen thought. Damn, damn, damn. For a minute she thought about getting Jonas' number and calling Sylvie right back. But for what? And she already knew the answer. Because for some inexplicable reason she was afraid for her friend, and she wanted her to come home. Today.

'I don't like this,' Galen said to Mingo. Without a doubt Sylvie's call had unnerved her. But why? Was it such a big deal? Surely there was nothing unusual about Sylvie wanting to help her cousin? She was going out to see Ravel but she wasn't going alone. So what possible harm could come to her?

Galen lay staring up at the ceiling. The weirdest thing about Sylvie's call, she thought, is the way I'm reacting to it. Usually reflective, cool, reasonable, Galen was wound up tight. But why?

She climbed out of bed, went into the bathroom, brushed her teeth, then took a shower. She was just stepping out when she heard Helen moving around in the kitchen.

Galen dressed quickly. She wasn't going to waste any more time wondering about Sylvie. Mulling and worrying weren't Galen's style. If something was bugging her she addressed it head on. No point in trying to make sense of it all by herself. She was going to get into a cab and go over to the University. Find David. It was Sunday and there wouldn't be many people around in the lab. She would be able to talk to him in private, see if he would be as disturbed as she was. Then they could decide if there was something they ought to do.

'I'm going over to the lab,' Galen said to Helen, gulping down her coffee. 'When Katy wakes up, tell her I'll be back in plenty of time to take her up to the Wollman rink.' It was something she and Katy did at least once every winter. They would spend an hour ice-skating, having the time of their lives laughing at each other wobbling across the ice, cursed as they both were by weak ankles. Then the horse-and-carriage ride through Central Park, followed by the grand finale: a hot fudge sundae at Rumplemyer's. Galen suspected that she looked forward to this outing even more than Katy did.

She grabbed a cab on Fifth Avenue and within minutes she was at the University building where David worked, heading up to the third floor.

When she walked into the lab David was in deep conversation with one of his staff and didn't see her. She waited until he was finished.

Surprise registered on his face when he saw her. 'What the heck are you doing here?'

'We have to talk.'

He frowned. 'What's the matter?' He took her arm, leading her into one of the outer offices.

'Nothing. I hope.' She sat down hard. 'You know me. I'm not a good worrier. I haven't enough patience. I can't stand to wait. Though to be honest, the more I think about it the more I think maybe I've freaked out over nothing.'

He sat down next to her. 'Let's have it. What's up?'

'It's Sylvie, that's what.' Galen told him about their conversation. 'Whether her cousin's suspicions have any merit or not, I think Sylvie ought to turn this business over to the proper authorities and get the hell out of New Orleans. And that's what she says she's going to do. But not today.' She exhaled. 'So. What do you think? Am I overreacting?'

The question hung in the air.

'David?'

'I don't like it either,' he said bluntly.

'Explain.'

'Sylvie is no private detective. She should offer her cousin her support, put her in contact with the right people, and come on home. What the hell is she going out to this place, this Shadow Hill, for? There are a lot of nuts in this world, and from what Sylvie told you, it sounds as if this Ravel person is one of them.' He smiled wryly. 'On second thought maybe *we're* the nuts. After all, this really isn't any of our business. Sylvie is our friend. We don't own her.'

A young man in a lab coat appeared in the doorway. 'Everything's all set, Professor.'

'Right,' David nodded.

Galen stood up and kissed him on the cheek. 'I'll get out of your way. We can continue to drive ourselves crazy later this evening.'

'You're picking Edie up?'

'I am. Katy and I will meet her plane. You'll be home for dinner?'

Again he nodded.

'Good. We'll all have a lovely Sunday evening together.' She paused. 'I'm sure Edie will be able to shed some light on this. Maybe set our minds at ease.'

They stared at each other.

For some reason neither one of them was at all convinced.

Chapter Seven

From the minute she saw Edie, Katy knew that something was wrong with her friend. Something worse than just coming home without her mother. But what? Edie wasn't saying. In fact she wasn't talking about anything at all.

On the way back from the airport Katy talked nonstop, trying to break the ice, telling Edie every detail of her own trip to her grandmother's. The new skis she got for Christmas. How much better she was doing on her traverses. The one run she had made down the Gun Barrel without a single fall. How she and her mother had gone to the Wollman rink but hadn't had time for their sundae because they had to meet Edie's plane. That was the wrong thing to say.

'I'm sorry I ruined your afternoon,' Edie said shakily. She sounded very nervous. 'My mother should've let me stay with her.'

'But school starts tomorrow. You always like school,' Katy said, trying to be upbeat.

'I don't care about school any more,' Edie said. 'My mother should've let me stay.' Then she fell silent again, and although Katy and her mother both tried to encourage her to talk, she didn't seem in the mood to discuss anything.

Determined to find out what had made Edie so upset, Katy followed her friend into the guest room, sat on the edge of the bed and watched in silence as Edie unpacked her suitcase and hung up her clothes.

Katy kept quiet. She knew better than to push. When Edie was ready to talk she would. And Katy was right. After all her clothes were put away, Edie sat down and began to talk in a hushed tone, almost as if she were talking to herself.

'I don't understand any of this. Two things happened while we were in New Orleans that scared me.' She took a deep breath. 'Things that I never imagined would happen.' She shook her head back and forth, her beaded hair making small clicking noises.

'Want to tell me?' Katy asked quietly.

Edie looked at her hard, then nodded. 'I have to tell someone, Katydid, and you're my best friend. I just hope it doesn't scare you the way it does me. First of all, I never got to talk to Ti Reine.' Her eyes filled with tears. 'We went to her house but I saw her only for a few minutes. I went downstairs to pick up her groceries, and when I got back Ti Reine had disappeared. My mother said she was sick but I don't think she really was. I think she and my mother had a fight about me and Voudou.' She shivered. 'We left Ti Reine's and we never went back.'

'But that doesn't mean you'll never see her again,' Katy said gently. 'She's like a relative. Your mother would never keep you from seeing her for ever.'

Edie's voice grew husky. 'I'm not sure what my mother would do if she thought I was becoming seriously involved in Voudou.' She got off the bed, walked over to the window and stood looking out over the city. 'I wish I were back in New Orleans.'

'Your mother will be home in a few days,' Katy

reassured her. 'And then everything will be back to normal. You'll see.'

'That's just it,' Edie said, coming to sit beside Katy on the bed. 'I don't know if anything will ever be normal again.'

'Why not?'

'A few days ago my mother and I went out to see her cousin Camille. And then we all went to a place called Shadow Hill. It was a beautiful place, Katy. You wouldn't have believed it. To get to it you have to drive a long way through acres and acres of swamps and stuff, but then all of a sudden there it is, all by itself in the middle of nowhere. A huge plantation house like something out of a movie, with nothing around it but dark marshy swamps. Sort of like moats around a castle.' Edie dropped her voice to a whisper. 'And there was something I saw inside the house that *really* scared me.'

'What . . . what was it?'

'A painting. I saw a copy of it years ago in a book. That's when I asked Ti Reine about it because I knew it had something to do with Voudou. And she said that the man who did the painting belonged to something called *le culte des morts*. The cult of the dead.'

Katy felt the colour drain from her face. 'The . . . the cult of the what?'

'The dead. It was a painting of corpses come back to life. Zombies. Ti Reine said it was an evil thing. Not to look at it ever again. And I didn't. Until I saw it hanging on the wall at Shadow Hill.'

Katy tried to keep calm. 'Maybe . . . maybe the owner doesn't know what it means. Maybe he just likes it.'

'He does like it,' Edie said. 'He told us he did. And

only a *bocor* could like such a thing. Only a *bocor* would have such a thing hanging in his house.'

'What's a *bocor*?' Katy asked, not sure she really wanted to know.

'A *bocor* is not a true priest, not a *papaloi* or a *mamaloi*. He is an abuser of the sacred Voudou religion. He serves only himself through the use of terrible black magic. He does not fight evil the way Ti Reine does. He embraces it.'

'You think one of them lives at Shadow Hill?'

Edie nodded. 'I do. His name is Adrien Ravel, and I don't know how I know, but I'm sure he's a *bocor*. And worse than that, today my mother is going to Shadow Hill to see him.'

'Why?' Katy gasped. 'Doesn't she know he's bad? Didn't she see the painting?'

'She saw it, but it didn't mean anything to her. My mother doesn't know much about the good side of Voudou, never mind the bad side.' She frowned. 'But Ti Reine does. If only I had been able to tell her about it she would never have allowed my mother to go back to that place. And certainly not without an *ouanga*.'

'A what?'

'An *ouanga*. It's a powerful charm made by a priestess to keep a person safe.'

'Did you tell your mother what you thought about Adrien Ravel?'

'No.' Edie began to cry. 'Because as far as I knew we were coming home today together. I didn't know she was staying until it was too late. Besides, even if I'd told her, she wouldn't have believed me. Not for a minute.'

'What if Ti Reine told her?'

71

Edie closed her eyes. 'I'm afraid not even then.'

'Maybe you should tell *my* mother. I bet she'd believe you.'

'Tell me what?' Galen appeared in the doorway.

Edie didn't answer, and then Galen opened her arms. 'Come here, sweet Edie,' she said gently. 'Dry your tears.'

For a moment no one moved, and then, like the frightened child she was, Edie went to Galen for comfort.

Katy was amazed. For the first time in her life she felt older than her friend.

Galen got up from her stool at the kitchen counter and poured herself a second cup of coffee. Not that she needed any more caffeine. She was jittery enough as it was.

She looked at the calendar: 15 January. Nearly two weeks had gone by without a word from Sylvie. Twelve days without a phone call, without a letter, without any news at all. Galen had called Jonas Beauchamp at least a dozen times to no avail. Sylvie wasn't staying with him any longer, he had said, clearly upset about it. She just up and left without a word, and although she had called him a few times to arrange pickups for her things, he hadn't seen her at all.

'Surely she has a number where she can be reached?'

'No. At least she wouldn't give me one. She has some business to attend to, she said. And she doesn't want any interference. Not from anyone.'

Galen had felt very uneasy. 'Is she involved with this friend of yours? Jeremy Calder?'

'No. It's not Jeremy Calder.' A pause. 'You aren't going to like what I tell you, Galen, any more than I liked hearing it myself,' Jonas had said. 'Sylvie is staying out at Shadow Hill, a guest of Adrien Ravel.'

Galen had been stunned. 'Jesus. Holy Jesus.' She hadn't gotten much information from Edie about the man except that he had frightened her. Galen had pressed for reasons but the more she had questioned, the more withdrawn Edie had become. In any case, when she added Edie's fear to what Sylvie had already told her about Ravel, it was more than enough to convince Galen that he was not someone to mess around with. 'But why is she staying? Sylvie and Jeremy Calder were supposed to go out to Shadow Hill, ask questions about Eveline Carne, and leave. So exactly what is going on?' She knew she sounded angry but she couldn't help it. She *was* angry. What the hell was Sylvie up to?

'I don't know any more than you do,' Jonas had said. 'I guess all we can do right now is wait.'

'Have you talked to Jeremy Calder?'

'I tried, but he left New Orleans on the fourth. He'll be in Haiti until the middle of the month.'

Galen had been incredulous. 'So as far as anyone down there is concerned, Sylvie has simply gone off without a word to anyone, to live with a man that nobody knows anything about. What the hell is the matter with you that you haven't called the police?'

'To do what?' Jonas had asked quietly.

'You're the lawyer,' Galen had snapped. 'Can't you think of something?'

'Short of kidnapping her, not a thing.'

Galen had forced herself to be calm. This was not Jonas' fault. 'Jonas, I'm sorry. I'm just upset. Will you

73

please go out to Shadow Hill yourself to see her? Please?'

Jonas had agreed. He would let Galen know as soon as he had anything new to report.

That was three days ago. Since then, nothing. Damn you, Sylvie, Galen thought. What the hell are you doing?

The sound of the doorbell brought her back to the present. 'Helen? Can you get the door?'

'I've got it.'

Galen took another sip of coffee. Time to go. She had a ten o'clock consultation. Tonight, when David gets home, she thought grimly, we're going to have to decide to do something about Sylvie. David was limping along in the lab, making do with a temporary assistant, but he was becoming more and more concerned. Not because Sylvie wasn't at the University doing her job; the loss of an assistant was one thing, the loss of a friend was quite another. Galen knew that David was just as worried as she was.

Helen appeared in the doorway. 'FedEx for you, Galen.' She held out an envelope.

Galen glanced at the return address. A post office box in Brancheville, Louisiana. Could it be from Sylvie?

Please God, she prayed, let it be some news. Any news would be better than none. She ripped open the envelope.

Galen,

I have decided to remain in Louisiana. I will be living at Shadow Hill until further notice. I have made all the necessary arrangements with the Sedgewick School for Edie to board for the rest of the term. She will join me at

the end of May. Our New York apartment has been
sublet. You may keep the cat or have him disposed of. As
you see fit. Many thanks for your kindness.
   Sylvie Valois

Galen was thunderstruck. Hand shaking, she read it
again. Impossible. But there it was: brief, to the point,
and brutal in its coldness, its finality. As if Galen and
David were casual acquaintances that Sylvie was glad
to be rid of. Not to mention the apparent unconcern
about a five-month separation from Edie. Impossible,
Galen thought again, staring at the letter. Absolutely
impossible. Something horrendous has happened to
her. The Sylvie she had known for seven years would
never never do such a thing. Abandon her own child to
live with a man she had already been warned was
dangerous? Abandon her work with David, her
friendship with both of them without a backward
glance? Never.

'Galen, are you all right?' Helen asked.

'Sylvie isn't coming back to New York.' Galen
heard herself say it. Slowly, distinctly, and yet she
knew it wasn't true. *Couldn't* be. Someone else was
controlling Sylvie. She just knew it. But how? Why?

'Well, that's a surprise,' Helen said. A pause. 'Isn't
it?'

'Please would you call my office?' Galen said. 'Tell
them there's an emergency. I won't be in.' She went
out into the front hall, a nervous Helen right behind.

'Galen, are you all right?'

Galen nodded. She threw on her coat. 'I'm going
over to the University.' Without another word, she
left.

*   *   *

75

Galen sat down and waited while David put through a long-distance call to Jonas Beauchamp in New Orleans.

'I know why you're calling,' Jonas said. 'I was about to call you.'

'Then it's true.'

'It is.'

'Have you talked to Sylvie?'

'Yes.'

'In person?'

'Yes. She phoned me yesterday and over her protestations I went straight out to Shadow Hill. Barged right in even though a very threatening servant tried to turn me away.' He paused. 'There's something about the place that makes my skin crawl. I don't know what it is. Like stepping into quicksand. From the minute you step foot on the grounds you know you've made a big mistake.'

'I'm not surprised,' David said. 'If Sylvie's cousin was right, Adrien Ravel is a treacherous man. Edie told us that he frightened her to death just meeting him. But then Edie is very young, very impressionable. What about Sylvie? How did she seem?'

Another pause. 'It's hard to say,' Jonas said finally. 'She seemed agitated, not at all pleased to see me. As if I were someone she would just as soon forget. I asked her if she had notified the University that she wasn't coming back and, can you believe it, she said no. That she didn't give a damn about the University.'

Galen picked up the extension. 'Jonas? I know you're as upset as we are about this. None of us understands it. There has to be something wrong with her. Do you think she's being drugged? Does she seem . . . sane?'

'I don't know. I didn't spend much time with her, but she certainly knew who I was and why I was there. And I didn't see any signs that would suggest she was on something. But I'm not a doctor. I suppose anything is possible, especially in that house. As a matter of fact, now that I think about it, if she is truly happy with Adrien Ravel then she *has* to be on something.'

'You don't like him?'

'No. As a matter of fact I think I hate him. Adrien Ravel radiates power. Absolutely *radiates* it. You're almost scorched by it. And yet at the same time he is the coldest man I have ever met. A brilliant intellectual. There doesn't seem to be anything he isn't an expert on, and he surrounds himself only with those things he admires. For example, he has a Napoleon obsession. A number of things in the house once belonged to Bonaparte himself – a treasury worth millions – and clearly Ravel patterns himself after the man. You know, the old "rise of the common man" thing.' Jonas took a deep breath. 'I hated Ravel from the first moment I saw him. I don't blame Edie. He frightens me, too. Just looking at him made me feel like I was alone in a Haitian jungle. I could almost hear the Voudou drums. Frankly, I think he's a madman. But a brilliant madman. There's something truly evil about him, Galen, truly evil.'

Galen felt weak. What had Sylvie gotten herself involved in? And more to the point, could they persuade her to get out?

'What about her cousin?' David asked. 'Does she know that Sylvie is living there?'

'I haven't been able to contact her. Her phone has been disconnected. After my trip out to Shadow Hill I drove into Brancheville to see if I could find Camille, but no luck. No one there wants to tell me anything about her.'

'What about Ti Reine?' Galen said. 'Have you spoken to her? She's a Voudouist herself, and like a second mother to Sylvie. Surely if anyone would know what Sylvie and Adrien Ravel are up to she would.'

'I doubt it.'

Galen frowned. 'Why do you say that?'

'Because just this morning a letter was delivered to my door from Ti Reine herself, enquiring as to Sylvie's whereabouts, with a request that I respond at once. Her messenger was told not to leave without an answer.'

'You mean Ti Reine didn't know anything at all about Sylvie's decision to stay in Louisiana at Shadow Hill?'

'No. But she does now. I gave the messenger a lengthy letter for her.'

'I'm going to call her,' Galen said. 'Does she have a phone?'

'None that I can find. There's nothing listed or un-listed. But if she does have one Edie might know the number.'

'Galen and I are coming to New Orleans,' David said suddenly. 'As soon as we can make arrange-ments.'

'I'd hoped you'd say that. If anyone can get through to Sylvie it'll be the two of you. Maybe you can find out why she's doing this. You'll stay with me, of course?'

'We will, Jonas. Thank you.'

'Will you bring Edie?'

'No,' Galen said, 'Edie isn't ready for this. Every

day she prays her mother will come home. I don't know if she can handle this latest development.'

'This is a tough situation for all of us to deal with,' Jonas said, 'never mind Edie. I did ask Sylvie about her plans for her daughter. She said she had made arrangements for her to board at Sedgewick.'

'That's what her letter said, but I'll be damned if I'm going to send Edie there to live. Edie is going to stay with us until we find out what really is going on. Maybe we'll be able to convince Sylvie to come home.' Galen took a breath. 'We'll let you know when we'll be arriving, Jonas. In the meantime, you try to contact Camille Carne, and I'll try to get Ti Reine's phone number. I think we're going to need all the help we can get.'

Chapter Eight

New Orleans, *16 January*.

The summons came just after two in the morning and Antoine Laval obeyed. The city was quiet, sleeping, but Antoine wasn't. He stopped for a moment at the end of Frenchmen Street, threw a nervous glance over his shoulder, then hurried on.

Antoine Laval was not happy. In fact he was filled with dread. Ti Reine rarely issued a summons, and when she did, it meant only one thing. Trouble.

With a last look to make certain he hadn't been followed, he ducked down the alley, through the unlocked side door and into Praline's Grocery.

The store was dark and quiet, closed for the night, but Antoine had no reason to turn on a light. He had been here many times and could find his way blindfolded. He moved to the rear of the store. Along the back wall was a wide display case filled with crates of fresh produce, and behind it, a door.

He paused to listen.

Still no sound.

Quietly he opened the door, stepped through and closed it behind him. Now the silence was broken by a low throbbing sound. Like distant thunder, steady, unhurried. The sound of drums.

At the far end of the dimly lit corridor was a closed door and Antoine knew what lay beyond: the sacred altar room where Ti Reine's followers congregated when she called down the Voudou spirits.

He walked quickly along the hall, opened the door and slipped in, careful not to attract attention.

Just inside the altar room, most of his spiritual brothers and sisters had already gathered, some sitting on the narrow benches, others standing in silent groups, waiting. Each one held a single lighted candle.

Along the far wall Antoine could see the altar, draped as was the custom in chalk-white cloth, set with multicoloured bowls containing offerings for the *loa*. At the centre the tall crucifix glowed bony white in the flickering candlelight.

But tonight there was something else on the altar, something that made Antoine stiffen. It was the sword of Ogou, the Voudou spirit of war.

He scanned the room. The snake staff, the *poto-mitan*, sacred symbol of Damballah, the most ancient of all the spirits, stood in the centre of the room, but tonight around its base a circle of thunderstones had been placed. The thunderstone – another symbol of Ogou. Clearly Ogou, the fierce warrior spirit, was to be summoned. But why?

Antoine shuddered.

Almost at once the drums stopped and the mystical chanting began. Antoine had only a vague idea what the words meant but he had learned to imitate, certain that in so doing he, too, was serving the spirits.

A sound from behind made him turn. The door had opened wide and the procession had begun. A long line of women robed in white, carrying lighted candles, came into the altar room. 'Damballah Oueddo,' they chanted. '*Nous p'vini.*'

Antoine knew what that meant. Oh, Serpent God, we come.

He took a deep breath, feeling the sweat begin to run down his sides. No matter how many times he had witnessed this ceremony – the crossing over of the spirits from their world to his – it never failed to frighten him. He always had to face the same danger, that for some cause or other he would be asked to serve, that he might be asked to do something perilous. Something that might cost him his life.

And then came Ti Reine, dressed from head to foot in flowing robes of scarlet, moving into the room to stand before the altar, her sacred *ason* held high above her head. Ti Reine, their *mamaloi*. All things to all people. Sometimes a healer, always a helper. Strong, all-knowing, gathering her wisdom around her like a cloak. As ancient a woman as the *loa* she served. Antoine guessed her to be at least two hundred years old, and because she was so old there was nothing Ti Reine couldn't do. She was the highest of the high, their Voudou priestess, who possessed all the power of the spirits themselves. And she used it. But always in pursuit of the good. Never the evil.

As she walked past him, Antoine was chilled to the heart at what he saw. Normally a tower of strength and purpose, Ti Reine seemed near death, her face a mask of pain. And her eyes, wide open, were filled with dread. But how could this be? Ti Reine was fearless, invincible.

With great effort she raised her bony arm and began to shake the sacred *ason*, and in a voice filled with terrible anxiety intoned the formal opening prayers. The litany of the spirits, naming them one by one. Damballah, Erzulie, Azaka, Gede . . . a long list that

Antoine knew by heart. And then came a final urgent plea to Papa Legba to open the gates. To let the spirits in.

Antoine had never heard such desperate sounds come from Ti Reine, and he was almost suffocated by a dire sense of foreboding, dreading what was coming. He never took his eyes off his *mamaloi*.

Ti Reine knelt before a bronze bowl on the altar and buried her face in her hands. Then suddenly she thrust out one arm, and on the instant the contents of the bowl were a blaze of liquid fire.

Again came the chant begging Papa Legba to open the gates.

Behind him Antoine heard someone shriek and fall to the floor but he didn't turn. Then another shriek. He knew what it meant. The gates had opened. The spirits were coming.

The air around Antoine's face grew still, ice-cold, a cold that was almost palpable. This was something he had never experienced before, and through the icy vapour he watched as Ti Reine jerked to her feet, her whole body trembling. Mumbling incantations that Antoine couldn't begin to understand, she managed to spread a small square of scarlet cloth on the altar. Then she pulled a leather pouch from beneath her robe and poured its powdery contents into the centre of the fabric.

Antoine caught his breath. He knew his Voudou priestess was making an *ouanga*, a powerful sacred amulet. But for what? For whom? For good? Or was someone to be punished?

Three times Ti Reine almost fell, and three times one of the other women caught her, held her upright. When she was finished she folded the square into a packet, tying it round and round with yards of scarlet thread, knotting it at the top. Then she staggered around to face the throng.

Now her eyes were wide, unfocused, as if she had suddenly gone blind.

All chanting, all sound faded.

There was nothing left but the deep pervasive silence.

For a moment Ti Reine stood motionless, then her head jerked forward as if she were being pushed violently from behind. Again, she stumbled, and again one of the robed women reached out to help her, but before she could, Ti Reine's whole body snapped up, rigid.

Antoine gasped. There was no doubt left. The possession was complete. Ti Reine was gone. Staring out from behind the old woman's eyes was the fearsome warrior spirit, Ogou.

For a moment no one moved. Then, arms trembling, one of Ti Reine's assistants stepped forward and draped a blood-red cloak over Ogou's shoulders. Ogou did not look at her. With piercing black eyes he scanned the crowd, searching, searching, his gaze finally coming to rest on Antoine.

Unable to flee, his mouth agape, Antoine could only stand and wait, the sweat rolling off his brow, down his cheeks, to soak his shirt.

Without turning, Ogou reached behind and picked up the *ouanga* Ti Reine had left on the altar. With a terrible face the warrior spirit moved across the floor, not stopping until he stood directly in front of Antoine.

Antoine stared into his blazing eyes, and Ogou, staring back, thrust the *ouanga* out in front of him.

'Servant of Damballah, take this!' he commanded in the dark fearful voice of the spirits. 'To protect yourself from the powers of black sorcery, from the evil of *le culte des morts*. You will need it!'

In total shock, Antoine uttered a single moan and fainted.

It was hot. A damp sultry heat.

Antoine lay on his back, staring up at the bunk above him. The other men in the room were already asleep, clad only in their white muslin pants, hoping for some relief from the oppressive heat. But Antoine was wearing the full uniform he had been given yesterday when he was hired to work at Shadow Hill as part of the kitchen staff. White muslin pants topped with a long white tunic with epaulettes.

He had not yet removed his tunic, not wanting anyone to see the scarlet *ouanga* that hung on a leather cord around his neck, the *ouanga* that Ogou had given him to keep him safe from *le culte des morts*. The cult of the dead. The name itself filled Antoine with abject terror, a name that he remembered from childhood nightmares, never spoken aloud, only whispered.

There were seven other men in his dormitory, three of them also on the kitchen staff. Antoine had no idea what the other four men did, nor did he want to know. He had one purpose here at Shadow Hill and one only. Ogou had sent him here to find Sylvie Valois. To talk to her if he could. To persuade her to leave this awful place. If she refused he was to give her the *ouanga*. That was his mission. Once completed he was to leave Shadow Hill and never look back.

Antoine had seen Sylvie only once at a distance, this morning, walking in the garden with Adrien

Ravel. And she had seemed content to be there. She wore no chains to prevent her from escaping.

But perhaps when he got close to her, Antoine would find a different Sylvie Valois, one who had fallen victim to some kind of dark sorcery, one who needed help. Antoine would do what he could, but he wasn't at all sure it would be enough. After all, Antoine was only a simple human being. He had no knowledge of black magic or spells. He could only do what Ogou commanded him to do. Find Sylvie Valois, try to persuade her to leave. Then leave himself. Nor did he want to stay here one minute longer than necessary, because there was something evil at work at Shadow Hill. Something that made Antoine quiver from head to toe.

Most of the people who worked here were Haitians, his own, his father's people. Ti Reine's people. But somehow these were different. They claimed to be Voudouists, but what fearful spirits did these men and women serve? Antoine did not know.

Last night, his first night at Shadow Hill, he lay awake, stiff on his bed, holding tight to his *ouanga*. In the distance he could hear a relentless, pulsing beat of drums, but it was not the familiar rhythm of his own Rada, dependable, even-tempered, calling down the friendly family spirits. It was the Petro drumbeat, a savage reminder of his own childhood spent in the mountain villages of Haiti, vengeful, unforgiving, signalling almost always a blood sacrifice.

He shuddered. Tonight he was hearing the drums again, and it was well past midnight before Antoine finally managed to fall asleep, for how long he did not know. It was still dark when Constant, the man who slept in the bunk above, woke him.

86

'Come, Antoine,' Constant whispered, 'take off your tunic and come. We have been summoned.'

Antoine's first instinct was to run as far away as he could, as fast as he could. But then reason took hold. He had not been threatened by anyone, he told himself. At least not yet. And all the rest of the men had been summoned too. They were already forming a single line at the door, preparing to exit.

Quickly Antoine pulled off his tunic, then realized that he would have to remove his *ouanga* as well. He slipped the cord over his head, tucked it under his mattress, and stepped into the line.

Outside, the night air lay heavy across the marshes. There was a sweet, fetid smell about it, like the odour of damp decaying earth.

Antoine followed the man in front of him along a path barely visible in the dense underbrush. On both sides the beards of moss hanging from the trees almost touched the ground. The moss parted as they moved through. A huge mosquito landed on his bare chest and he swatted it away, then realized that none of the others were moving anything but their feet.

Keep still, he told himself. Don't do anything that might attract attention.

As they walked, the sound of the drums grew louder and Antoine grew more terrified with each beat. Somehow he felt as if he were moving back in time, to the dark mysterious savage jungle of his ancestors. Breathing hard, he kept his eyes fixed on the back of the man in front of him, a man who, like Antoine, seemed filled with trepidation, quivering, shuffling along the worn path, looking neither to the right nor the left.

Antoine wished he had never come here, wished

Ogou had chosen someone else, someone less cowardly. But Antoine had had no choice but to obey. One could never defy the spirits and survive.

The air around him was moving now, set in motion by the steady rhythm of the drums. Like waves on the ocean, rolling relentlessly toward the shore. Boom. Boom. Boom.

But as the long line moved out of the forest into a small open clearing, the drum beats faded to a low pulse, then stopped altogether. There was silence. A silence so thick, so unexpected, so pervasive that it was even more terrifying to Antoine than the sound of the drums had been.

Afraid to turn his head even a little, Antoine rolled his eyes to the right. In the dim moonlight he could just make out the pale outline of a white marble structure with huge bronze doors. Two massive candelabras lit with dozens of candles marked the entrance. It was a mausoleum.

What are we doing here? Antoine thought wildly. Has someone died? Is someone to be buried?

As if in response, from out of the shadows stepped a man, tall and muscular, stripped to the waist, clad only in a pair of flowing blood-red trousers. It was Adrien Ravel. Around his neck on a heavy gold chain hung a huge circular disc, gleaming golden in the moonlight. Even at this distance Antoine could see that it was inscribed with intricate cabalistic signs, one of which he recognized. It was the mighty swirling serpent, Damballah.

Behind Ravel a second man appeared. No. Not a man. A gargantuan bald-headed giant, bare-chested like all the rest, but twice their size, with huge claw-like hands hanging limp at his sides. Standing together

88

in the flickering light, the impression the two made was mind-shattering.

These creatures cannot be human, Antoine thought, gasping for breath. Frozen with fear, he watched as the two, in perfect step, walked to the end of the line, stopping in front of the first man in the group.

Suddenly Antoine knew why they had all been summoned. Once, years ago in Haiti, Antoine had witnessed this kind of inquisition. Adrien Ravel was searching for someone. Someone guilty of a terrible secret crime. But which of them would be singled out. And even more terrifying, what would be the punishment?

Ravel took the golden disc in both hands and lifted it from around his neck. It hung suspended on its chain, inches from the man's face. There it dangled, motionless. Words began to flow from Ravel's mouth, dark mystical incantations that seemed to come from the very depth of his soul, words that Antoine could not understand, and yet somehow he knew that Ravel was commanding the disc to move, to identify the offender.

But it hung where it was. Motionless. Like the pendulum of a great clock that had stopped.

With the giant close at his side, Ravel moved to the next man in line, repeating the fearsome words, again holding up the disc.

Again the disc never moved.

Terror-stricken, his eyes starting from his head, Antoine followed their progress as they came slowly, deliberately down the line, closer and closer to the place where he stood, cowering.

And then they were there. Directly in front of Antoine. The golden disc of Damballah was raised, so close to his face that he could have touched the coils of the writhing serpent inscribed upon it with his tongue.

Again the disc did not move and, watching it, Antoine exhaled in relief. Like the others, he too had been found innocent.

But he had exhaled too soon. Before he could take another breath the disc began to swing, just barely at first, then faster and faster, gaining momentum with every second that passed.

What happened then had more horrific impact on those who witnessed it than it had on Antoine himself. In the next instant, with a single swift motion, Adrien Ravel took the disc in both hands and held it out in front of him as if it were a platter that he was asking to be filled.

And in response, the giant reached out with his huge claw-like hands and tore Antoine's pulsing heart from his chest, setting it down, still throbbing, on the sacred golden disc of Damballah.

It was almost midnight and the sky was dark, starless. So much the better for Ti Reine. Day or night she tried to go without being seen. Like the wind. Invisible. If you were invisible you were invulnerable. It was her way of keeping safe, she who had no confidence, no faith in any human authority. If she couldn't be seen by those in control, she couldn't be hurt. She had learned this secret of survival at an early age and it had never failed her. The only recipients of her trust were the *loa*, and sometimes even they could not be counted on. Nevertheless, they were the source of her strength. And like Ti Reine herself, they preferred to remain unseen.

Two days had passed now without any word from Antoine, and Ti Reine could wait no longer. With her straw *macoute* slung over her shoulder and her black overcoat covering all but her head, she hurried along the dark deserted road. She needed no light. She knew where she was going: to the crossroads.

She hadn't much time left, she knew. She had to be there on the stroke of midnight. And she was. For a moment she stood where the four roads came together, and lifted her head as if scenting the air. Then she lowered her *macoute* to the ground and took out a container filled with ashes, which she used to form a large circle in the dirt.

In the centre she made four crosses, and at the foot of each one she placed a single white candle. Then she knelt, struck a match and, intoning the same words over and over, she lit the first wick. Her depth of concentration was so intense that she never noticed the match flame burning lower and lower. Even as it charred the flesh on the tips of her fingers, she never cried out. She lit the last one, then drew back, weak, exhausted.

'I am calling you to me, ancient Masters,' she whispered. 'Acquaint me with Antoine Laval, I beg you. Tell me where he is at this very moment.'

And she waited. Waited for the spirits to bring the truth to her.

Gradually the air around her grew deathly still, and so heavy that all four candles were finally snuffed out.

Then with the return of darkness came the answer.

Ti Reine sagged.

The *loa* had spoken. Antoine Laval was dead, and Ti Reine knew what that meant. What she feared most had come to pass. An ancient enemy, a *bocor*, a monstrously evil sorcerer, had come to this land to work his magic, and in the process he would seek to destroy her family. His name was Adrien Ravel. An archfiend, a demon who used evil means to attain evil ends. Such monsters had always been, would always be far more powerful than she.

Filled with dread she dragged herself to her feet. She must not give in. She must act quickly. Ravel did not know about her yet, and that might give her a slim chance and the time she needed to set up her defences. To destroy him before he destroyed her.

Chapter Nine

New Orleans, 17 January

At the airport David hailed a cab and gave the address. It was raining and the taxi moved slowly, giving David a chance to gather his thoughts. He wished Galen had been able to come with him. It would have made this trip a lot easier. As a doctor, maybe Galen would have spotted something in Sylvie's manner that David might miss. But it couldn't be helped. Last night one of Galen's patients, Peter Vanek, had a relapse and was rushed to the hospital. Galen was still with him this morning.

So here David was, alone, riding through the rain-slicked streets of New Orleans on his way to Jonas Beauchamp's. He had always loved this city, and a visit here had been on his list of places to go with Galen but they had never managed it. What a cruel twist of fate, he thought glumly, that I would find myself back here without her. And worse, with Sylvie in God-only-knew-what kind of trouble. But together, maybe he and Jonas could get some answers.

The cab pulled up in front of a large brick townhouse just off the street, with narrow upper and lower galleries strikingly framed in wrought-iron lacework. David paid the driver, let himself in through a vine-covered gate and up the short walk to the front door. Before he could ring, the door opened.

'Come in, Professor. Get out of the rain.' A deep Southern accent.

David stepped inside.

'I'm Jonas Beauchamp.' Then a wry smile. 'Though I suppose you guessed.'

David held out his hand. 'I did,' he said, though to be truthful, for a moment he hadn't been sure. Somehow he had expected Jonas to be Sylvie's age, late thirties. In fact, the man was much older, tall, thin, with a pallid complexion and steel-grey hair. But his handshake was firm, his manner confident, full of energy.

'I'm glad you made it,' Jonas said affably. 'I was just about to have lunch. Will you join me? While we're at it, we can talk.' Before David could respond a servant appeared, and Jonas motioned. 'Cal, please take Professor Wickliffe's bag to his room.'

Jonas turned and led David to a wide gallery that bordered a courtyard at the back of the house. It was still drizzling but the gallery was sheltered and the table had been set for two.

'Galen phoned,' Jonas said, sitting down, dropping his napkin into his lap. 'Damned unfortunate about the boy.'

David nodded. 'Did she say how he was doing?'

'She said he was still in critical condition. She didn't have any time to talk. Just wanted me to know that you were coming alone.'

'So.' David took a deep breath and leaned back. 'What's the plan? How do I get out to Shadow Hill?' He spoke quickly, anxious to be on his way. Somehow he had the feeling that time was running out.

'We'll take my car. After Galen called I cancelled my afternoon appointments. I thought you ought to have company.'

94

David felt a rush of relief. The last thing he wanted to do was to go to Shadow Hill alone. 'What about Sylvie's cousin Camille? Have you been able to contact her?'

Jonas nodded. 'No. But as we're out that way, we can drive into Brancheville. Maybe we'll have better luck than I did the last time. Maybe we'll find her.' He poured David a glass of wine. 'I suggest you have some. I think we are both going to need some liquid reinforcement.'

'I have one major question,' David said, taking a slow sip. 'You're an attorney. Isn't there anything we can do legally about this?'

'Unless we can prove coercion, absolutely nothing. Sylvie is a consenting adult. To prove that she is a victim of some kind of crime is going to be damned near impossible. Unless of course she asks for help.' He frowned. 'I've made a lot of enquiries around town about Adrien Ravel.'

'And?'

'And nothing. Nobody in this city knows anything about him.'

'What about Jeremy Calder?'

'Still in Haiti. Though I did fax a letter to the clinic in Port-au-Prince. The response was that he was out in the countryside somewhere, isn't expected back in New Orleans until tomorrow.'

'Did Sylvie ever tell you anything about her dinner conversation with Calder?'

'Yes, and it makes these plans of hers seem all the more preposterous.' He poked at his salad. 'According to Jeremy, Adrien Ravel was a genius when it came to applying the science of the jungle, using ancient African skills for his own purposes, one of which was the accumulation of power.' He looked over at David. 'I'm talking about Voudou. Jeremy told Sylvie that even in Haiti nobody is really certain how many people actually practise the religion. And of those who do, no one knows how many follow the true faith, and how many others engage in acts of black sorcery. But one thing is certain: believers or not, most Haitians fear Voudou magic.'

'What do you mean, magic?'

'It's not what we think of when we hear the word. You know, rabbit-in-the-hat, sleight of hand, the illusion business. Not at all. Voudou magic, for good or for evil, is a science. According to Jeremy, in its purest form it can heal. It can mend relationships. It can bring hope. On the reverse side it can control minds and bodies. It can drive one mad. It can kill. Those experts who have studied the religion agree that there are mysteries even the most scientific minds cannot fathom.'

'What does all this have to do with Adrien Ravel?'

'Apparently while he lived in Haiti he was the best of the best. Or the worst of the worst, depending on your perspective. A man who learned from his father and his father's father all the secrets of Afro-Caribbean toxicology. In short, while he was there he learned how to poison with the greatest finesse, not necessarily to kill but to control. A brilliant man.' Jonas picked up his wine glass and studied it. 'A brilliant man,' he echoed. 'And from what Jeremy Calder told Sylvie, he is a born killer, a man without conscience.'

'Do you think he's using his knowledge to control Sylvie?'

Jonas looked at David. 'You know her. She is a smart lady. Does anything else make any sense?'

'But why? What does he stand to gain?'

Jonas shrugged. 'The pathology of madness has always been a mystery. Maybe Ravel is driven by some kind of sadistic curiosity. Maybe he is using Sylvie as some kind of human guinea pig to perfect his skills, the same kind of motivation that inspired the Nazi doctors to commit some of their monstrous experiments.' Now Jonas was angry. 'I know something is happening out there, David. I know that something *has* to be done. But I'll be goddamned if I know what.'

The road was little more than a path, cutting through a tangle of impenetrable green, and David felt a lump of tension come into his throat. He turned to Jonas. 'This place is really off the beaten track,' he muttered. 'I'm eternally grateful to you for coming with me.'

'I know how you feel,' Jonas said. They came to a deep rut in the road and he slowed the car to a crawl. 'The first time I came here I would've turned around in a New York minute and gone back, except that as you can see,' he waved his arm, 'there's no place to turn around on this god-forsaken track. Venture off it into the swamps and I'll guarantee you'll never be seen again.'

David nodded. 'Let's hope we don't get stuck.'

The farther they went, the more dense the vegetation became, the more fearsomely forbidding. David couldn't see any signs of life through the wall of green, and yet he had an uneasy feeling that they were being watched. 'How much longer?'

Before Jonas could reply, the question was answered. They crossed a small bridge and at once the marshes disappeared behind them. The narrow, nearly impassable road became a wide shaded avenue, and at its end, just as Edie had described it, stood the house Shadow Hill. Magnificent, David thought, truly impressed.

Jonas pulled around in front and stopped the car. For a moment they sat in silence.

'Jesus,' David said finally. 'This is quite a place.'

Jonas nodded. 'Wait until you see the inside.'

David followed him to the front door. Then Jonas stepped aside. 'It's all yours from here on in.'

David took a deep breath and rang the bell.

Why am I here? She remembered coming to Shadow Hill, but for what reason? To talk. But to talk about what? And to whom? The name Eveline drifted into her stream of consciousness but she pushed it back. It burned her brain to think of it.

She opened her eyes and through a mist of pain, Sylvie saw salvation. Blessed Adrien, she thought. So kind. So skilled. So able to help her escape from this torment. Though where the pain had come from she wasn't sure. But it came with relentless certainty whenever she was forced to remember. As she was being forced to remember now with the arrival of the two men outside, David Wickliffe and Jonas Beauchamp.

She was thirty-eight years old. Had she always lived with such torment, she wondered. It was as if one part of her brain that connected her to her past was diseased, being devoured by a huge malignant tumour, needing desperately to be excised.

She reached out and took the pills Adrien was offering. She had taken them before. She knew they would get her through this ordeal. Blessed Adrien.

He waited until she had swallowed them, then took

the empty glass from her trembling hand. 'This night-mare will be over soon,' he said softly. 'And then you will never have to think of these people again.' And he left her.

Sadness. Deep overwhelming sadness. And with it, anguish. Sylvie winced. Why were they here, David and Jonas? Did they hate her this much, that they were determined to make her remember them?

She looked down at the floor. Unaccountably she thought about a conversation she had had once with a professor of hers, about the required length of a term paper on Jacksonian Democracy. How odd that she would think of that just now when she had so much else to be concerned about. But then of late it was impossible for her to concentrate on anything.

'Sylvie?'

She turned. The door behind her had opened and there they were. Smiling, David held out his arms as if to embrace her. To embrace her? But why? And why was he smiling? How dare he smile when he was forcing her to remember him?

She looked away. Memories of that part of her life crowded in around her, trying to force their way in. She reached up to her face to see if her sunglasses were still there. Thank goodness, they were.

Another cruel voice intruded. Jonas. 'Sylvie, ma deah.'

Ma deah? What was that? She narrowed her eyes. What did he say? And what did he want? What did *either* of them want? 'Why have you come here?' she asked.

'To see you,' David said, a frown replacing the smile. 'To see how you are. To find out if you're okay.'

She felt a wave of revulsion. She didn't want to

talk to him, didn't want to look at his face. Her only peace came when she blotted out those years, those people from her mind. 'I'm fine, thank you.'

'And are you still planning to stay here? You aren't going back to New York?' That absurdity from Jonas.

'Of course I'm not going back to New York. I will never go back to New York.'

'But why?' David asked, taking a step towards her.

She backed away, a surge of panic bolting through her at the mere thought of physical contact with him. There was only one person with whom she wanted physical contact and that was Adrien.

'Sylvie, what's wrong?' David's expression was grim, and she felt like shrieking. Where was Adrien?

Satan, have pity on my long-drawn pain.

A pause.

David held out his hands. A pleading gesture? But what was he pleading for? And as Sylvie stared, for one instant the cruel mask covering David's face fell away and she saw her old friend standing there.

'David,' she whispered, stunned. She wanted to run to him, to cry out to him, to tell him how alone she was in this nightmare, how confused, how frightened, how she didn't understand, didn't know what was happening.

But like all of her other desperate impulses, this too was short-lived. Before she could move or cry out for help, the waves washed over her, drowning her in miserable anguish, forcing her to turn away. *You are not my friends, you are not my friends.* And that realization left her with nothing but a sense of overwhelming loss. 'I would prefer not to discuss this,' she said in a strangled voice, not looking at either one of them, unable to bear the sight. 'Please leave.'

'Jesus Christ, Sylvie,' David said. 'What in hell is going on here? Let us help you.'

Help? What possible help was there for her? Her brain wanted nothing but release from this torment. This confrontation with her past, this brutal collision with people she wanted so desperately to forget.

But David's voice kept on. 'We are not leaving here until we know what's happened to you.' A pause. 'And what about Edie?'

Edie! The name was like an electric shock. Sylvie drew back in horror, her eyes widening behind the smoky lenses of her glasses. Edie. Edie. Her baby. Her child. Again the searing pain of memory. But as she fought to forget, the name kept coming at her. EdieEdieEdieEdieEdie . . . Her shredded brain made a last desperate effort to understand what was happening. 'My God,' she gasped, 'what is wrong with me? How can I want to forget my own child? I must be insane, I have to be insane.'

'Excuse me, but I believe you must say goodbye to these gentlemen now, Sylvie, or we'll be late for dinner.'

She whirled around to see Adrien standing in the doorway. As always he had come to her rescue. The voice of reason, of salvation. Her saviour. He would pull her back from the brink of destruction. She rushed across the room to stand staring up at him in wonder.

'Go upstairs, Sylvie,' he said quietly. 'I'll show your guests out.'

Sylvie didn't look back. She raced across the hall and up the stairs, as if two demons from hell were after her. She darted into her bedroom, slammed the door, and stood leaning against it, sucking in great gulps of air. I am insane I am insane I am insane. Their faces –

David and Jonas's – floated towards her. With a violent swipe she obliterated them. But no sooner were they gone than another face came into her shattered mind: the face of her child. Edie. And no matter how hard she tried, she could not erase that sweet precious memory.

She fell in a heap on the floor, sobbing.

Satan, have pity on my long-drawn pain.

Adrien!

Chapter Ten

David Wickliffe was not a violent man. The only time he had ever inflicted physical pain on another human being was when he was in the third grade. When he hurt Spencer Charr. Every day at recess Spencer liked to bully him, and every day David took it, until the morning of 20 April 1943 when, driven beyond the limits of his eight-year-old patience, he had picked up a rock and had deliberately dropped it on Spencer Charr's foot. As a result Spencer had had to spend two weeks on crutches. And for those two weeks, every afternoon after school David had been banished to his bedroom.

David never knowingly hurt anyone again. But now as he stood staring at Adrien Ravel, he wanted to hurt this man. In fact he wanted to kill him. Before Ravel had appeared, David had been filled with anguish at seeing Sylvie. Whether she was being drugged or whether she was slipping into madness he couldn't tell. But clearly she was in deep trouble.

And then Ravel appeared and David knew without a doubt who was responsible for Sylvie's pain. Adrien Ravel. The man was a perfect physical specimen, moving with graceful, fluid motions, an impressive figure and handsome, until you saw the eyes. Feral, cold, the eyes of a natural predator, eyes that reflected not so much cruelty as utter indifference to human suffering.

To kill him would be a service to humanity, David thought. And certainly a service to Sylvie. He felt the blood rush to his cheeks. 'What have you done to her?'

Ravel's expression remained impassive. 'It was good of you to come,' he responded coolly. 'Please feel free to visit Sylvie any time. Any time at all. But now, as I'm sure you understand, we have other commitments.'

'We aren't leaving until you answer my question,' David said sharply.

Ravel never shifted his gaze but his eyes grew opaque, as if he had turned his attention to other more important matters. 'You will excuse me,' he said. 'I'm sure you can find your way out.' He turned and left them standing in the doorway.

'You haven't seen the last of us,' David said. 'We'll be back. And the next time we'll be taking Sylvie with us.' He said it quietly but he knew Ravel heard him.

Jonas started the car, threw it in gear and without a word the two were off down the gravel drive. 'Sweet Jesus,' Jonas whistled. 'What do we do now?'

'I don't know.' David shook his head. 'But we haven't much time. Sylvie is helpless. I don't know what he's doing to her but he's doing something. You're the lawyer. Let's hear our options.'

'I told you before, we have none,' Jonas said grimly. 'You have to have hard evidence to bring in the police. We don't have crap. As soon as we get back to the city I'll contact a colleague of mine in social services. Maybe there's a precedent on this kind of thing that I don't know about.'

'Bullshit on that,' David said sharply. 'We don't

104

have time to mess around with any state agency. What we really need is a hitman. I know what I saw. Ravel is a demoniacal madman.' He looked over at Jonas. 'What the hell do you suppose he wants Sylvie for?'

'I don't know. I told you earlier what Jeremy Calder told Sylvie. Ravel is a master in the art of mind control. At least he was with the Haitians. Perhaps now he has other more ambitious goals. Perhaps he wants to see if his brand of sorcery can control a bright, well-educated, modern-day woman like Sylvie. You should know better than I. You're the scientist.' Jonas down-shifted. 'In any case, I agree with you. Ravel is doing a damned fine job of destroying her.'

'When did you say Calder would be back? I'm sure he knows a lot that we don't.'

'According to his service, tomorrow. Meantime I know a good private detective who might be able to dig up something on Ravel. It's about all I can suggest. Unless we kidnap her.'

David glanced at his watch. 'Almost five o'clock. Is it too late, or should we drive into Brancheville and try to find Camille Carne?'

'It's worth a shot. If she's still living there she has to come home sometime. If we're lucky maybe we'll catch her. Maybe she'll be able to help us.'

The gate at the end of the drive was open. They drove through and slowly it closed behind them.

When they got to Camille's the house was dark, deserted. No sign of life.

'Damn,' David said, getting out of the car. 'Looks like another dead end.' But in the next instant a dim light came on in the back of the house.

'Someone's in there,' Jonas said. 'Let's go.'

They went up the walk and onto the porch. Jonas knocked.

The light went out and somewhere inside, a dog began to bark furiously.

'Mrs Carne?' Jonas shouted. 'My name is Jonas Beauchamp, a friend of Sylvie Valois. We'd like to talk to you.'

The only response came from the dog who continued to bark.

'Mrs Carne, we think Sylvie is in deep trouble. Please talk to us.'

The dog stopped barking. For a minute there was silence, and then a woman's voice, low, almost a whisper. 'What do you want from me?'

'We need your help,' David said, stepping forward. 'We really do.'

The door opened a crack and a pair of frightened eyes peered out. 'Who are you?' she asked warily.

'I'm David Wickliffe. Sylvie used to work with me in New York.'

The door opened wider. 'Used to?' Now there was alarm in the voice.

'Sylvie never came home after her trip to New Orleans. She's still here in Louisiana, living at Shadow Hill with Adrien Ravel.'

At that the door flew open and a stunned Camille Carne motioned them inside. The dog growled low in his throat but didn't move from his mat near the door. 'Be still,' Camille said sharply, then turned to Jonas and David and motioned them to sit. 'My cousin came here for the last time on January third,' she said. 'I remember distinctly because it was my birthday. She had been to see Adrien Ravel, had learned nothing, and was going back to New York. She told me there was nothing more to be done except to lay low, leave well enough alone.'

'Did she seem herself?' Jonas asked.

'No, she didn't. She seemed like she hated to be near me. Like she never wanted to see me again.' Camille's eyes filled with tears. 'She never even wished me a happy birthday. She just wanted to be gone. Back to where she came from.'

'She never went back to New York,' David said softly. 'She went to live at Shadow Hill.'

Camille sat down heavily and buried her face in her hands. 'I never should have asked her to go there with me. Never, never, never.'

'Tell us what you know about Ravel,' David said.

'I don't know anything about him except that he's going to do the same thing to Sylvie that he did to my Eveline,' she choked. 'He's going to kill her. Or worse.'

David reached over and touched her arm. 'No, he isn't, Camille,' he said quietly.

Her eyes were desperate, filled with tears. 'You don't know Adrien Ravel. He is a demon.'

For a moment there was a heavy silence. Then David said, 'I don't care what he is. If the three of us work together, I think there's a chance we might be able to get Sylvie out of there.'

Jonas was startled. 'How in hell do you propose we do that?'

And in the dim light of Camille Carne's parlour, David outlined his plan, simple, but which held the element of surprise. One that they all agreed might just work.

Chapter Eleven

The day that would end in disaster began on a note of optimism. Jeremy Calder was back in New Orleans. 'He left a message on my machine saying he'd be in his office all day if we want to see him,' Jonas said, taking a last sip of his morning coffee.

David took a deep breath. 'Finally, something helpful,' he said. He, Jonas and Camille were going to make an attempt to spirit Sylvie away from Shadow Hill, but one final problem had plagued them. If they did succeed, where would they take her? What doctor would be willing to examine her without her consent? And now maybe they had an answer. They would take her to Jeremy Calder. If anyone knew about Adrien Ravel, if anyone would understand their fears, if anyone would try to evaluate her condition without delay it would be Dr Calder. 'Let's get out to Brancheville,' David said, glancing at his watch, 'before Camille changes her mind.'

It had not been an easy task to convince Camille Carne to help them. At the mere mention of Shadow Hill she had become almost comatose with fear. 'If I become involved in anything like this,' she had whimpered, 'Adrien Ravel will have me killed too. Just like Eveline. Just like Dr Aubin.'

But Jonas and David had prevailed, promising that whether or not they got Sylvie out, they would take

Camille to the airport later today, send her to her family in Michigan. And finally she had agreed, still terrified at the thought, to go with them.

Now all they had to do was kidnap Sylvie.

At ten minutes after ten they pulled up in front of Camille's house. The windows were shuttered and padlocked. Even the hanging plants on the front porch were gone.

'Jesus,' Jonas whistled. 'Don't tell me she's backed out.' But in the next instant Camille appeared from behind the house, carrying one small valise. She came quickly. She never looked back.

Only once on the way to Shadow Hill did she speak, and then not to Jonas or David but to her God. 'Dear Lord,' she whispered, 'don't let me lose my mind.'

They drove along in silence and it wasn't until they were almost to the iron gate that David spoke. 'The more I think about it, the more impossible it seems. But maybe, just maybe, Ravel will be caught off-guard. In any case, let's review this one more time. Camille, you do nothing. You sit in the back seat and wait. You do not get out of the car. Jonas, you stay behind the wheel while I go into the house, ask to see Ravel. I will tell him that Camille is leaving the state and wants to see her cousin Sylvie one last time before she goes. If Ravel agrees then we're over the first hurdle.' David took a breath, then continued. 'Then I tell him that because her daughter died there Camille has vowed never to step foot inside the house again. And I ask if Sylvie is well enough to step outside to say goodbye. If Ravel's answer is no, then we're done. We leave. However, if his answer is yes, I'll take Sylvie out to the car, Camille will open the door, and hopefully the rest will be history. You, Jonas, will get us the hell out of there as fast as this machine will take us.' He paused. 'Does it all sound as stupid to you as it does to me?'

'It does, but maybe that's why it will work,' Jonas answered. 'Ravel would never think we'd do something like this. Besides, what can we lose?'

Another heavy silence.

'Right. What do we have to lose?' David echoed. 'The worst that can happen is that Ravel will say no, and we'll leave without Sylvie.'

As they approached the entrance to Shadow Hill, Jonas slowed the car to a crawl.

'Damn,' David said. He could already see that the gate was closed. Armed with miscellaneous tools, a wire cutter and a screwdriver, he got out and made his way across the road. He was going to have to disconnect the electronic device that controlled the gate, but before he had a chance to do anything the gate slowly swung open. David paused but only for a moment. Then he cut the wires and climbed back into the car. 'We sure don't want to be locked in,' he said to Jonas.

Jonas nodded and turned onto the drive. 'For better or worse,' he said softly, 'here we go.'

Along the way the sun shone through the trees in patches. A beautiful day, David thought, and yet the closer they got to the house, the more uneasy he became. Were they underestimating Adrien Ravel? Would he ever allow himself to be caught off guard? But no sense in wondering about Adrien Ravel, David thought. Their sole concern was to get Sylvie away from Shadow Hill.

Jonas pulled around in front of the entrance and switched off the ignition. 'Well?' he said to David.

'Wish me luck,' David said flatly. He got out of the car, walked up to the front door, rang the bell.

No response.

David paused, a small frown creasing his brow. He rang again.

Still no answer.

But this is impossible, he thought. Someone has to be here. He knocked, but the only sound came from behind him. Jonas had come up the walk and was standing at the foot of the steps. 'David? What's wrong?'

David turned and walked along the verandah, trying to see through the windows but all the curtains were drawn. 'There's no one here,' he said in disbelief. But how could this be? Shadow Hill was a huge plantation with a huge staff. Where were they? And more to the point, where in hell was Sylvie?

He went back to the front door and knocked again. 'Answer, God damn you,' he shouted.

Still nothing.

'I think we'd better go,' Jonas said nervously. 'I don't like this. Besides, I think Camille is about to have a stroke.'

'I don't blame her,' David said furiously, kicking the door. 'I'm about to have one myself.'

No one spoke as they made their way back along the drive towards the main road. Camille sat huddled in the back seat, sobbing quietly. David and Jonas were lost in their own thoughts. What next, David wondered. Was there anything else they could do? 'There is no justice,' he muttered. 'There is only the law, and the law stinks.'

'So does this car,' Jonas said. 'I think we have a flat tyre.'

111

He stopped and David got out. 'Shit,' David said. 'Flat as a pancake. Let's get to it while we still can.' The sky was clouding over, threatening to rain, and far off across the marsh David could hear the sounds of barking dogs. 'I hope they aren't heading this way,' he said, feeling a sudden chill touch the back of his neck.

Camille sat huddled where she was, stone silent now, struck dumb with fear.

Jonas got out, opened the trunk and took out the jack. 'This is going to be a bitch,' he said nervously. 'No way to find a patch of level ground.'

David took out the spare tyre, rolled it over to lean against the side of the car. He could hear the dogs clearly now, much closer. 'Maybe we ought to try driving on the rim to the main road,' he said.

Jonas had the same thought. 'Good idea.' He picked up the jack, and the next thing David saw was the Dobermann, teeth bared, a killing machine coming out of nowhere, knocking Jonas over, snarling, snapping, ripping at his face. Somehow Jonas managed to roll under the car.

The second dog came from behind, hitting David in the back with his front legs, driving him against the car door.

Blind with terror, David groped for the door handle but it was too late. The dog's powerful jaws closed over his wrist, crunching through skin and muscle and bone.

The third Dobermann tore out his throat.

Galen felt a blast of cold air on the back of her neck and she shivered. Damn, she thought. This heating system is for the birds. Either it's too hot in this office or it's too cold. She dropped Peter's report on the desk and punched the button on the intercom. 'Lily, please can you see about getting someone up here to adjust this blasted heat?'

'Too warm?'

'No. Too damned cold.'

'I'll see what I can do.'

Galen picked up the report and stared down at the numbers. Not good. She had hoped for a miracle for Peter Vanek but it wasn't there.

Another blast of icy air.

This time Galen turned around to see David standing by the window. She was stunned but she was so happy to see him. 'How the heck did you sneak in here?' she said, smiling. 'When did you get back? I wasn't expecting you until tomorrow.'

Behind her, the door opened. 'Galen, the heating man is here,' her secretary said.

Galen stood up and walked around her desk. 'Send him in,' she said. Then she turned back to David, *but he was gone*.

'David?' Galen blinked, then reached out her hand to steady herself. Impossible. He had been here only a second ago. So where was he?

She went into the outer office. 'Lily, did you see David just now?'

'No. Why? Were you expecting him?'

'You were just in my office. You saw him.'

An emphatic shake of Lily's head. 'Nope.' The phone rang and she picked it up. 'Dr Wickliffe's office.' A short pause. 'It's for you, Galen.'

Galen threw her hands up. 'I must be going nuts.' She went back into her office to answer the call.

It was a policeman.

David wasn't here with her at all. David was dead.

* * *

113

Galen closed her eyes. In her mind she could see him clearly. Her husband. In her mind he still lived. But in the world outside, he was gone. Dead.

But how? Why? She had listened to the police report. Heard words that were incomprehensible. A flat tyre? Guard dogs? Attacked? *Savaged?* A garble of meaning. What had they meant, savaged? And something about coming to New Orleans for identification purposes. Something else about Jonas Beauchamp and Camille Carne. But what?

Numb beyond understanding, Galen had said she would come.

Now she lay in her bed, a grief-stricken Katy close beside her on one side, a frantic Edie on the other. Katy had finally stopped crying, and Edie had stopped asking questions about her own mother, questions that Galen couldn't begin to answer. She still hadn't told Edie anything about her mother's decision to stay in Louisiana. Nor had she told Edie that arrangements had been made with the school to have her board there until the end of the term. And she wasn't going to. Not yet.

Yesterday morning, after David left for the airport, she had called the headmaster and told him that there had been a miscommunication. That Edie would be staying with the Wickliffes until Mrs Valois notified them to the contrary.

The headmaster said he could foresee no problem, but of course he would have to contact Mrs Valois for confirmation, to protect the school. Certainly Dr Wickliffe could understand. In any case he would get back to her as soon as he could.

Not that it mattered now. Tomorrow when Galen saw her, she would ask Sylvie directly. What did she *really* want for Edie?

Galen heard sounds of gentle breathing. Both children had finally fallen asleep. But Galen hadn't. How long, she wondered, would it take her? Would she ever fall asleep again? She had seen death many times before and she knew that somehow the people who are left behind survive. And she would, too. But how? How long before the pain dulled? The despair? She had no answer for that. David was gone. Vanished. So suddenly. So without warning. And she found herself groping around in a grey world of misery. She, who had counselled so many others in the first moments of shock and anger and disbelief, had no answers for herself except one: survive. She had Katy and Edie to think about. And in the midst of chaos other questions kept coming back to her. Why had Camille Carne been with them at Shadow Hill? What were the three of them doing? And what about Sylvie? Did she know about this horror? Of course she had to. *Didn't she?*

Galen took a deep breath, and through the cloud of despair a new emotion surfaced. Anger. Was all this Sylvie's fault? Certainly if David had never gone there, he would be alive right now. Galen wouldn't be forced to think about the unthinkable, never mind the simple things. Like where was she going to bury him? Had he really wanted to be cremated? He said so once but they never really talked about it.

Oh Jesus, why had he gone and left her?

Damn you, Sylvie. This is all your fault.

But was it? Or was it Galen's? If Galen had been more accepting of Sylvie's decision to remain in Louisiana, would David ever have gone to New Orleans? If Galen hadn't pushed? If she had told David not to go, not to worry about Sylvie, would he have insisted, gone anyway? Would she be flying to New

Orleans tomorrow to identify his body, sign the papers, make the arrangements, bring David home?

Eyes closed tight, she could still see him clearly, standing in the bedroom door. Saying goodbye. Kissing her. Yesterday morning. *Dear God, was it only yesterday?*

It was. And yet in terms of personal tragedy it seemed a hundred years ago. The tears and sobs came again and she rolled over and buried her face in the pillow so she wouldn't wake the girls. There was only one thing that would make her pain less acute. If Sylvie were really in trouble. If David hadn't died for nothing. If he had died trying to save her.

Tomorrow I'll see Sylvie, Galen thought numbly. Tomorrow I'll know.

Chapter Twelve

Edie came into the room and Sylvie held out her arms to embrace her. My child. How happy I am to see you.

Smiling, she opened her eyes wide to find herself alone, lying in the big canopied bed that belonged to Adrien Ravel.

Adrien Ravel. The name struck instant terror in her heart. But why terror? Why not joy? Wasn't Adrien the source of her rescue?

But rescue from what?

From the noise in her head? The searing, burning screaming hideous noise in her head that was there whenever she tried to think?

Think about what?

About why she was where she was.

Feeling her brain rolling around inside her skull like the little ball on a roulette table. Round and round. Until it stopped. Click. Fell into a slot. Red or black?

What difference when I don't even know who I am.

Of course you do. You are Sylvie Valois.

Sylvie who?

Don't answer. It hurts to think about it. She began to cry. Don't think about it.

But you *must*. You cannot forget yourself or you will forget your life. You will forget Edie.

Edie, Edie, Edie. And again the memory of the name split her head wide open and she pushed it away as hard as she could. And yet somewhere in her deepest soul she knew that even if her brain was burned to ashes, she would never forget Edie. *Must* never forget Edie.

She must fight. But fight whom? Adrien Ravel? Impossible. She loved him, *needed* him. He wanted her to forget the past and he was sure she would. He had promised it.

But in spite of his promises, still there was the memory of Edie. And again the stunning waves of pain washed over her, the pain that always came with remembering.

She threw the sheets off and jerked upright. What should I do, she wondered, caught up in a whirlpool of anguish. God help me, what *can* I do when I don't understand anything except this agony?

Concentrate. Don't give in.

But she couldn't help it. She bit down hard on her hand until it bled. Exchange one pain for another.

'Sylvie.' A ripple on the water. The sound of a voice that soothed her. 'How are you feeling this morning?'

How do I feel? How can I know? My brain is being pressed between two giant walls, one of fire, the other of ice. Help me oh help me oh help.

Adrien sat down beside her on the bed, his dark eyes watchful, taking careful measure of her. 'Tell me,' he said softly, 'did you sleep well?'

Sleep? Had she slept at all? She must have. Sleep. Blessed sleep, an escape from eternal torment. She nodded.

'Did you dream?'

She closed her eyes. 'I did.' She began to cry. 'I dreamed of Edie.'

'Why do you cry? With each day that passes your past is no longer of any importance to you. And as a result your pain is diminishing. Is that not so?'

'I don't care about my past,' she choked. 'I care about Edie.'

Adrien seemed surprised. 'She still matters to you?'

'I love Edie. I love her,' she groaned. Why was he asking her these questions? But she knew the answer. He wanted to help her. She was insane and he wanted to help her.

'You are a fascinating study, Sylvie,' he said, his eyes narrowing. 'I've never known anyone to cling to pain the way you do.' He leaned over and picked up her hand. 'Now I want you to listen carefully. You do not have to forget Edie. You simply have to stop caring about her. Then the torment will stop.'

She wrenched her hand away. 'I cannot stop caring about her! She is my child!' She fell back and began to howl pathetic animal howls.

Adrien stood up. 'You begin to bore me, Sylvie,' he said icily. 'I thought you were more intelligent than you really are. I dislike resistance. I assumed you would be quick to accept a new life, a new master. Apparently I was wrong.'

He turned to leave, then stopped, and when he turned there was a different look on his face, as if something new had suddenly occurred to him. 'This resistance I am encountering has nothing to do with Voudou, does it? Surely you are not part of that well-meaning but childish group of simpletons who believe in the *loa*?' His tone was full of derision. 'Fools who believe that their spirits can work miracles?'

Voudou? Sylvie forced herself to forget her pain, to pay attention to what he was saying. What had she heard before about Adrien Ravel and Voudou? Something. Something.

'Do you remember Ti Reine?' he asked.

An electric shock. Ti Reine. What had she to do with Adrien?

'Of course you remember her. I know she was like a mother to you once upon a time.'

'Did I tell you that?' Sylvie whispered.

'No. But there isn't anything in the Haitian community here in Louisiana that I don't know about. That includes Ti Reine and her Voudou family.' His smile was scornful. 'A simple old *mamaloi* who leads her group of innocents in their eternal quest to appease the Voudou spirits. She and her followers have retained all the superstitions of Africa, but they have lost the skills that make it all have meaning. I, on the other hand, have learned everything there is to know about how the ancient Africans controlled the human mind. Running along beneath the shadow of fear there must always be substance. A reason for that fear. Voudouists call it magic. I call it skill.

'But I digress. You are too intelligent to be a Voudouist. And perhaps I am misjudging. Perhaps it is your very intelligence that is telling you to resist.' He stood for a moment, silently surveying her as if she were some kind of creature he had never seen before. 'For some reason,' he said thoughtfully, 'you are fighting the drugs.'

The drugs? What drugs? Was she taking drugs? Of course she was. She knew that. She couldn't survive without them. The blue pills. The yellow ones. The ones that brought relief. She wasn't fighting the drugs. *Was she?* Unless . . . unless the pills weren't always the killers of pain. Unless sometimes they were its creators.

Another electric surge went through her brain, making her gasp for breath. 'Please, please help me. Help me. I know you can.' She reached out to him.

His eyes narrowed, considering. Then he nodded. 'I think it would add an interesting dimension to this experiment of mine if we send for Edie. A *ménage à trois*, if you will. You, me and my lovely young nemesis. I think when Dr Wickliffe comes to Louisiana to collect her husband, we will have some surprises waiting for her. One of which will be to send for Edie.' He smiled. 'Indeed, your Edie might be a delicious new challenge.'

Again the screaming pain. What did he mean, someone was collecting her husband? For what? And why at the mention of Edie, the one person she loved beyond life itself, did her brain convulse into such spasms of anguish? It was a question she couldn't begin to answer. But she wasn't alone in her confoundment. Apparently her continued pain was a mystery to Adrien as well. She squeezed her eyes shut and covered her face with her hands, trying to get through this single moment. But it was more than she could bear. Again she howled like a trapped animal.

And then she heard his voice, comforting, tender. 'All right, Sylvie. It's time. Let's try again.'

She dropped her hands to see his own, opening in front of her, outstretched. Holding round coloured bits of salvation.

She grabbed them, swallowed them down. 'Satan,' she whispered, 'have pity on my long-drawn pain.'

Numb, Galen left the hotel and gave the cab driver the address she had been given earlier by the police.

She was going to identify her husband. If she could, they said. If she could.

The driver's name was Royal and he talked steadily as they went. Was this her first visit? Was she looking for some great Cajun food at reasonable prices?

Galen didn't answer. Couldn't. But it didn't seem to matter to Royal. He kept talking. Even as she was paying him he never stopped talking. 'You need a driver while you're in the city, call me.' He handed her a card. 'Any time, any place, I'm your man.'

She nodded and got out. She stood still for a moment, trying to catch her breath. There was a sharp ache in her mid-section as if she had been running hard. It never left her, and with each step it grew more and more intense. She went inside the building and made her way to the pathologist's office. She followed his assistant down the corridor, into the elevator, down two floors and into the morgue. And as she stood waiting for him to pull the sheet back, the ache took on a life of its own.

The sheet was drawn back.

Galen stared. One side of David's face – the side that Galen could see – was untouched and peaceful. As if he were merely sleeping. But as she leaned forward she saw the other side. What was left of it. From his shoulder to the edge of his scalp his flesh had been shredded. The word she hadn't understood earlier she now understood in all its hideous meaning. *Savaged*.

She felt her hip strike something hard, the edge of the table, then she reached out to keep herself from falling the rest of the way to the floor.

'This is your husband?'

Galen closed her eyes and nodded. It used to be, she thought dumbly. It used to be.

The sheet was drawn up once again to hide the mutilation. 'Goodbye, David,' she said quietly.

The rest was a blur. Someone told her about the attack. Mr Ravel had been devastated by it, the man said, shaking his head. Somehow his dogs had broken loose. Of course they had been destroyed. Of course there would be a complete investigation.

Had there been an autopsy?

Yes. Without any doubt the dogs had been responsible.

And Jonas Beauchamp? Camille Carne?

Jonas was still hanging on. In critical condition at New Orleans General. But Camille Carne had been found in the back seat of the car. She was dead.

Had there been an autopsy on her?

Yes.

Results?

Heart failure.

Then there were papers to be signed. And arrangements for embalming, transporting the body back to New York.

Through it all, Galen sat numb, understanding in a new way what death meant looking from the inside out. How monstrously cruel that for everyone but David life would go on. The man sitting across from her would light another cigarette. Somewhere down the street someone would buy a theatre ticket. Right now someone was having a cocktail. Doing grocery shopping. Watering plants. Planning a trip. And as for Galen, she knew that, at least on the surface, it would soon be business as usual for her as well. She would board the plane and fly back to New York. Check her messages. Eat dinner with Katy and Edie. Go to bed. Get up in the morning and get on with her life. Business as usual.

But not yet. First she had to find out how this happened. And why.

'By the way, Dr Wickliffe,' the man said, shuffling through some papers, 'this note was left for you.'

Galen read it. *Please contact me regarding Sylvie Valois.* There was a phone number and a signature. Jeremy Calder. For a moment her mind went blank. Jeremy Calder? Who the hell was Jeremy Calder? And then she remembered – the doctor Sylvie had gone to dinner with on New Year's Day.

Galen stuck the note in her pocket. Before she left New Orleans she would phone him. Not that it would make any difference. There was only one person who could make any difference now and that was Sylvie herself. Galen had to see her face to face.

'Is there anything else I can do for you, Dr Wickliffe?'

'Yes. How do I get to Brancheville?'

At the gas station, a few miles outside the town, Royal, the talkative cab driver, stopped for gas and asked for directions. 'Is this the road that goes to Shadow Hill?'

The attendant seemed surprised. 'What you wanna go out there for?'

Royal shrugged. 'None of your business or mine either. I only do the driving.'

'It's tough to find is why I asked,' the attendant said. He began to talk with his hands and Galen tuned out. Not that she had had much to say to Royal. The shock and anger she had felt earlier had given way to a much deeper sadness that had silenced her altogether. But again Royal hadn't seemed to mind. He was perfectly content to carry the conversation all by himself.

Now as they headed west Royal grew quiet himself,

intent on the fog-shrouded road ahead, clearly taking heed of the warning given by the attendant. 'The bayous can swallow you up if you don't pay attention to where you're at.'

It began to rain. It made the way seem even more impassable. Dark wet tree branches hung low over the road, and dense underbrush pressed so close that in some places it scraped the side of the car.

Galen rolled up the window to keep out the rain and the fetid smell of swamp water. A terrible sense of dread had come over her, a dread so powerful that it dwarfed every other emotion. I shouldn't have come, she thought suddenly. Not now. I should have turned my back on all this and taken David home.

But she hadn't. What was done was done. There was nothing left but to see Sylvie face to face, find out once and for all if she and David had been right in their concern. Or if in pursuing Sylvie, they had made a terrible stupid mistake.

A mistake that had cost David his life, Galen her happiness, and Katy her father.

'*Sacré bleu*,' Royal muttered. 'I see nothing.'

And as if he had said some secret word, the trees suddenly drew back and through the rain Galen could see the house at the end of the long tree-lined avenue.

Startled by the sudden appearance of such a mansion, Royal slammed his foot on the brake and stalled the car. Cursing under his breath he turned to Galen, apologized, then restarted the engine and continued up the drive.

Galen fixed her eyes straight ahead. *I am afraid*. The words came clearly into her mind, unbidden, unexplained, but true all the same. *I am afraid*.

* * *

Ti Reine paused in the midst of her digging and looked up. Strange. She could have sworn a storm was building and yet the sky was still cloudless, a pale transparent blue. She leaned on the shovel and lifted one hand as if to wipe the beads of sweat from her brow, but her skin was dry.

At the edge of the oak grove, where the brooding marshes met the land, the water lapped impatiently around the roots of the cypress trees, urging her to hurry. To be done with it.

She stood back from the hole and took mental measurements. Her eye was good. There was no more reason to dig. She bent over and picked up the heavy ebony box. It had been years since she had put such a death box together. She prayed that it would do its work. That Ezili Danto, the mother of all children, defender of women, would accept it.

As she covered the death box with dirt, she sang in grieving tones.

'Seven stabs of the knife, seven stabs of the sword.
Hand me that basin. I'm going to vomit blood.'

When she had replaced all the soil, she covered the scar in the earth with chunks of turf and leaves and rotting humus, and when she was satisfied that no sign remained to mark the spot, she kneeled. 'Great Ezili Danto, mother of all children, you spare no effort to see that we are taken care of. And in return for all these years I have served you well, served you faithful and true. Now is the time for you to help your child, Sylvie. The evil one has come. Curse him as I curse him. Revile him as I revile him. By the fire of the night, by the strangled blackbird, by the jagged edge of his throat, by the blood on the ground, this curse be upon him. May he know no rest, no peace, no salvation. Nor can he hide. Waste him, scourge him, defile him, leave him to rot as the contents of this death box rot.'

Then Ti Reine turned and walked away, confident that she had accomplished what she had come here for, sure that through the great Ezili Danto she had marked Adrien Ravel for certain death.

Chapter Thirteen

New York City, 19 January.

Katy knew what death meant. Her mother had seen it happen a lot in her work and sometimes when one of her patients died she would talk to Katy about it. About how sad it was for the mother and father, but how brave they were. And how lucky the Wickliffes were that Katy was strong and healthy. And yesterday when she told Katy about her father's accident she had used words like 'peaceful' and 'heaven', but Katy hadn't cried until she heard the word 'dead'.

Katy had never realized before what dead really meant. Now she knew. It meant that her father was never coming home. It wasn't that he was just going to be late or anything like that. He wasn't ever coming home again. She would never see him again. Never hear him laugh. Never go to the movies with him, or ask him to make popcorn. Everything in her life would be different from now on. Nothing would ever be the same again.

She dealt out the last row of cards. She didn't really feel like playing. She felt like crying but she was all cried out.

'I think Helen has just made a pot of tea. Would you girls like a cup?' her grandmother asked. She had arrived this morning to stay with them until Katy's mother brought her father home. Poor Gram, Katy thought, looking up from her solitaire game. She was just like the people her mother had told her about. Very sad but very brave.

'Sure, Gram,' Katy said. 'That would be nice. Do you want some, Edie?'

'No, thank you,' Edie said quietly, then went back to her book.

Mingo jumped down from the window sill and walked across Katy's cards, making a big mess. Normally Katy would have yelled at him but not today. Today she didn't really care about her card game. It was just something to do to help get through the day. 'I wonder where they'll bury him?' she said almost to herself. The question had come out before she really thought about it, but now that it was out in the open, it took on sudden import. Where *would* they bury him? She had never seen a cemetery here in the city. Would they send him back to Utah with Gram?

She heard someone crying, a pathetic gagging sound but she didn't know that it was coming from her until Edie put her arms around her, hugging her tight. 'Hush, Katydid,' she whispered softly. 'It'll be all right. You'll see.'

'He can't be dead,' Katy sobbed. 'He just can't be dead.'

'He *is* dead,' Edie said soberly. 'That much is true. But it doesn't mean he doesn't exist any more. Souls never die. You'll see him again sometime, perhaps in a dream, perhaps in some other way.'

Katy stopped crying and stared wide-eyed at Edie. What was she saying? That her father was going to come back to earth? Like a ghost? 'That's impossible, Edie. Everybody knows that dead people go to heaven or to hell. No one except nuts think they come back to earth.'

'But Voudouists believe they never *leave* earth, Katy,' Edie said softly. 'They just exist on a different level. And sometimes, if you pray in the right way, the spirits will bring them back, allow them to cross over from the land of the dead to the land of the living.'

Katy gasped. 'You mean you think I can see my father again if I pray hard enough?'

Edie shook her head. 'No. It takes more than praying hard. You have to be able to call up the spirits. But if you are powerful enough, you can do it. In fact sometimes you can even call up the dead yourself.'

'Like Ti Reine.' It wasn't a question.

'Like Ti Reine,' Edie echoed.

A terrible thought suddenly occurred to Katy. 'Are you saying that my father is . . . is a zombie?'

Edie drew back, aghast. 'Of course I'm not. Zombies aren't dead *or* alive. They are just poor creatures who don't exist in the land of the living *or* in the land of the dead. They are trapped somewhere in between.'

'If that's true,' Katy said, breathing hard, 'if such things do exist, then how do you know my father isn't one? Didn't he get killed at Shadow Hill? And isn't that the place where you saw that terrible painting? The place where the evil sorcerer lives?' She burst into a fresh flood of tears.

Edie began to cry herself. 'Oh, Katydid, I'm so sorry. I didn't mean to frighten you. I was only trying to make you feel better and now look at the mess I've made. I can't do anything right.' She grabbed Katy's hand. 'Your father isn't a zombie,' she said, clenching her teeth. 'He *can't* be. Your mother is going to bring

130

his body home. That means he *can't* be a zombie. You'll see. There is nothing to be afraid of.'

Katy wiped her eyes with her shirt sleeve. She had been imagining the worst and now her friend was upset. 'It's okay, Edie,' she sniffed. 'I believe you.' She managed a teary smile. 'Don't cry. If Gram knows what we're talking about she'll really freak out. She's sure my father is in heaven.' And hearing herself say it, Katy decided to believe it. Her father *was* in heaven, for sure.

But in the back of her mind the terrifying image of Edie's painting still lurked. Only now there was a new addition to the scene. Her father, walking in line with the zombies.

Galen stared up at the painting and she was chilled to the bone. A primitive work at best, but there was something so sinister, so unnatural in its depiction that she couldn't help but shudder. You are out of your league, she thought suddenly. You don't know anything about Sylvie or this man she lives with. You are in way over your head.

'Dr Wickliffe?' A low velvet voice with a decided accent. Cultured.

Galen turned.

He stood in the doorway for a moment looking at her, and she thought she had never seen a more handsome man. Nor one half so frightening. There was no hostility in his expression. No evidence of dislike. What frightened her was his *lack* of expression. The cold brilliance of his eyes. The almost clinical detachment, as if she were a chair or a tree. And Galen remembered Jonas' words: *Just looking at him . . . I could almost hear the Voudou drums.*

131

He came towards her with a swift, purposeful stride but he did not extend his hand. 'I'm sure you know, Dr Wickliffe, how distraught I am over what happened to your husband.' He said the words, but she heard not a trace of remorse or even sympathy.

'I'm sure you are,' she said coolly, allowing no hint of emotion in her own voice. 'I've come to see Sylvie.'

'I'm afraid that won't be possible,' he said, sitting down behind his desk. 'However, before you leave, there is something we would like you to take care of when you get back to New York.'

Galen felt a surge of anger. She had come to New Orleans to collect her husband's body, her husband who had been devoured by this man's goddamned dogs, and he was telling her now that she couldn't see her friend, but could she do them a favour? She felt outraged, and she opened her mouth to tell him so, then closed it. A warning light had gone on inside her head, a light that kept her standing where she was with her mouth shut tight. Something told her to be very careful, that she was face to face with a very dangerous man. She drew herself up. 'I cannot see my friend?'

'I am afraid not.'

'I see. May I ask why?'

'Of course you may.' A silky response. Oil on water. 'She is feeling poorly.'

Galen nodded. 'I certainly wouldn't presume to interfere,' she said softly, 'but if she isn't feeling well, as a doctor I wonder if perhaps she shouldn't be in a hospital.'

A flicker of something in the dark eyes. Impatience? Or was it more than that? 'She has a physician, a highly competent professional. You needn't concern yourself, Dr Wickliffe. Sylvie is my concern now.'

He changed the subject. 'I understand from the people at Sedgewick School that Edie is staying with you.'

'She is. I thought the unexpected separation from her mother would be less difficult for her if she were to stay with us for a while. As I'm sure you are aware, Edie is a very fragile child. To be with friends would make the transition easier.'

'How thoughtful of you,' he said. 'In any case, it won't be necessary for you to inconvenience yourself any further. We would be most grateful if you would send Edie here immediately upon your return to New York.'

Galen was thunderstruck. Never had she anticipated such a request. 'I don't think I understand.'

'Sylvie and I have decided that Edie should not remain in New York any longer. We would like her to join us here at Shadow Hill as soon as arrangements can be made. Of course I realize that you have your own affairs to settle, so if you haven't the time, we can certainly contact the school.'

Galen could only stare. Send Edie here? To live at Shadow Hill? Never. But why not? What if Sylvie wanted it? In fact, as the shock wore off, Galen realized that it was precisely what Sylvie *would* want. To have her child with her. So why was Galen so appalled? She knew the answer, she was looking at the answer: Adrien Ravel. A man who for some reason made Galen quiver with fear. But what to say to him? How to respond?

She paused, fighting for calm, her mind churning. Don't be a fool, she told herself. Don't overreact. You know nothing about Adrien Ravel. Nothing but hearsay. Maybe he isn't what you think he is. Maybe Sylvie truly loves him. Maybe. But whatever you do, don't let him know what you are thinking. Let him believe that you are perfectly willing to send Edie here. She took a quick breath. 'Of course I'd be happy to make arrangements,' she said smoothly. 'And if time doesn't allow me to do it myself, I shall certainly have my secretary take care of the details.' She smiled. 'How nice for Edie. She'll be so pleased to be with her mother again.'

And then another blow that almost knocked her off her feet. 'Of course she will,' Ravel said, 'especially since Sylvie and I are to be married at the end of the week.'

This time Galen couldn't hide her shock. She jerked back as if she had been struck in the face. *'What?'*

'Sylvie and I have decided to marry.'

'When?' Her breath was coming in short gasps.

'As soon as arrangements can be made.' And as if Galen had been dismissed, he picked up a stack of papers from his desk and began to leaf through them.

Galen couldn't believe what she had heard. Edie was to be sent to Shadow Hill because Sylvie and Ravel were to be *married*. 'Monsieur Ravel,' Galen said, fighting to keep her tone level. 'I realize that if Sylvie is not feeling well she certainly doesn't want company, and under normal circumstances I would never force the issue, but since she is to be married I will be devastated if I don't see her. I need to wish her well. I shan't be in New Orleans again for a very long time. I would be most grateful if I could just peek in on her to say good luck and goodbye.'

Slowly he looked up. It was a full minute before he answered, and when he did his tone had changed.

Something she said had sparked some interest, though she was damned if she could imagine what. 'If it pleases you, Dr Wickliffe,' he said quietly, 'it pleases me. If you will wait here a moment, I will prepare her.'

Chapter Fourteen

Sylvie lay on her side, eyes closed, knees drawn up to her chest, drifting in and out of consciousness, sometimes aware of who she was, sometimes not. But that really didn't matter. What mattered was what was inside her skull.

It seemed to Sylvie that her brain was like the earth's crust, layered. The only people who existed on the surface were Adrien and Sylvie herself. And she existed there only to serve him. To worship him. To obey him.

The second layer was another world altogether, a sub-world, the one that contained all of her past life, all of her memories before Adrien. A simmering, bubbling mass of something resembling molten lava, lurking beneath the surface. And every once in a while it broke through the crust in a violent volcanic eruption, causing her such anguish that she wanted to scream and scream and scream just to blot it out.

Such an eruption had come yesterday with the sudden appearance of David Wickliffe and Jonas Beauchamp. A scorching burning agonizing explosion that would have destroyed her if it hadn't been for Adrien.

Blessed Adrien, putting out the fire, sealing the crack in the crust of her brain with his red and yellow and blue magic.

But there was one crack that Adrien couldn't keep

closed in spite of all of his efforts, one violent eruption that kept recurring and that eruption had a name. Its name was Edie.

EdieEdieEdieEdie.

Had Adrien said that she was coming here? And if so, could Sylvie stand the pain of seeing her?

Yes, she could. She could endure anything for Edie. Couldn't she?

Maybe she couldn't.

But she *would*.

She moaned low in her throat, 'Oh God, help me, if there is a God help me,' and with all her strength she pushed the memory of her child away. She would deal with it later. For now, all she wanted to think about was Adrien. Her only reason for living was to serve him, please him, obey him. All this in exchange for his round bits of magic.

She opened her eyes to see him standing by her bed. 'Adrien,' she whispered, holding out her hand.

He took it. 'Are you feeling better?' The voice of the master.

'I am now.' She smiled and kissed his hand. If she pleased him, maybe he would help her. Give her something.

'Sit up, Sylvie,' he said. 'There is something you must do for me.'

She did as he asked. Didn't she always? 'What is it? You know I'll do anything for you.'

'Galen Wickliffe is downstairs.'

The top layer of her brain cracked open. The lava flowed. She writhed in pain. *Galen Wickliffe*. She covered her face with her hands, trying to hide. 'I don't want to see her, I don't want to see her! I cannot, I cannot!'

'You can, and you must.' He pulled her hands down. 'Look at me, Sylvie.' Stern. Cruel. Commanding.

She stared at him. She had no choice. To disobey Adrien was not thinkable.

'I want you to see Dr Wickliffe, to speak with her. I want you to tell her how happy you are.' He paused. 'And I want you to tell her how much happier you will be when we are married.'

Married? Married? What new madness was this? 'Who? Who is to be married?'

'We are, my dear Sylvie. You and I.'

A monstrous tidal wave rolled towards her. Was this her moment of salvation? Or was it her ultimate destruction? 'But why?'

'I have decided that if the lovely Edie is to come to Shadow Hill to live, it would be best if you and I were married. With you as my wife and Edie as my daughter our privacy will be guaranteed.'

A whirring sound of a saw cutting through bone. Her bone? Her skull? She knew it had already severed her tongue because she could not speak. She could only stare.

'Therefore you must see Dr Wickliffe. Now.'

Another moan, low in her throat.

Adrien continued. 'When you see her, be polite, be calm, but keep your distance. The doctor is dangerous. She belongs to that part of your life that is gone forever.' He opened his hand. 'You will need these to give you strength.'

Frantic she reached out, but before she could take them he withdrew his magic. 'Am I not the centre of your universe?'

Sylvie managed to nod but she could feel the

hysteria coming up in her throat. She and Adrien were to be married. Edie was coming here. Galen Wickliffe was already here. All these things were happening *but she didn't care*. Right now the only things she cared about were hidden inside his fist. She closed her eyes. 'I need them, I need them, I need them.' But in spite of the need the old question came back into her mind, the question that in its complexity had already whipped her devastated brain into a frenzy. *With his magic pills was Adrien helping her to survive this madness or was he causing it?*

Sylvie couldn't stop herself. She screamed.

She felt him strike her across the face with the flat of his hand. Shock and fear drove everything from her mind – shock that he had struck her, but worse, much worse, fear that he was about to abandon her. Without him she knew she would die. 'I'm sorry, I'm sorry. Please. I'll do whatever you want me to do.'

'I hope so, Sylvie.' His voice cut like a whip. 'I don't like to be disappointed. I haven't the time or the interest. If it weren't for your daughter I would abandon you without a backward glance. You are still not reacting to treatment as I had hoped. In the beginning I thought you were a perfect test case – well-educated, bright, with a sophistication that all my other subjects lacked. And you piqued my interest. But now I am beginning to have my doubts. Perhaps you are never going to do well under my care.'

He was no longer speaking to Sylvie but to himself. Not that it mattered to Sylvie. She couldn't hear him because the sound of his voice was drowned out by the sounds in her head of her own silent moaning.

As for Adrien, he didn't seem to care whether or not she was listening. He was utterly self-absorbed. 'I know how to create zombies,' he said thoughtfully, 'creatures without will, without the ability to reason. And it has been a fascinating study. Not only am I able to eliminate my enemies, but no friend dares defy me for fear of becoming one of my living dead.

'But zombies make poor companions. I tire of their plodding brutishness. Nor can they be used for any profitable enterprise. They function well in a primitive culture, but they cannot function at all in this country, so I must keep them hidden.

'But you, Sylvie,' he turned to look at her, 'you were an inspiration. What if I could perfect my skills to the point where I could control the human will without destroying it altogether? What supreme power would be within my grasp? The possibilities are endless.'

He crossed to the bed and sat down beside her. 'You, my dear, are my first test case. I don't want to turn you into a mindless zombie. I want you to stay as you are, a magnificent female animal with a brilliant intellect who can think and discuss and function in society, all the while owing absolute immutable allegiance to one person. Adrien Ravel.' He frowned. 'But perhaps there is no middle ground. Perhaps a mind cannot ever be only partially controlled. Perhaps it is all or nothing.' He stood up. 'In spite of my successes I must admit that mine is an imperfect science. I will just have to wait and see.' He paused, as if waiting for some response.

Adrien put one finger under her chin and lifted her face. 'I see you haven't absorbed what I have said. But then perhaps it's just as well.' Again he opened his hand.

Sylvie still didn't hear, but she saw the bits of

magic. With a low moan, she grabbed them and swallowed them down.

The room was so overwhelming in its ornateness that it was almost suffocating. On three sides, the windows were draped in deep scarlet velvet with black tassels; gilded furniture carved with elaborate images of swans and griffins and open-winged eagles filled every inch of floor; the ceiling was a hand-painted masterpiece illuminated by four immense gold and crystal chandeliers. On the fourth wall a huge tentlike canopy supported by tall marble columns covered a gilded bed that looked like something borrowed from a French museum.

At first, staggered by the ostentatious display, Galen didn't see Sylvie, who stood in shadow, almost hidden by an enormous free-standing mirror set up just to one side of the bed. 'Sylvie,' Galen said, taking a quick step forward, instinctively holding out her arms, 'I am so happy to see you.'

Sylvie did not respond. In slow motion she turned away and walked to the window.

Galen froze. 'Sylvie?' Did her friend not know she was here? Hadn't she seen her? Heard her speak?

'Why did you come?' The words were muffled, as if Sylvie had something covering her mouth.

Galen stood where she was. 'I came to see you, of course.'

She heard Sylvie take a quick breath. 'That was kind of you. But I'm afraid I'm not up to the task. I have a touch of something or other. But thank you for coming.' The voice was clearer now, but still lacking any emotion. Not even a hint of curiosity. A kind of robotic indifference.

Galen felt an urge to yell: *Sylvie! For God's sake, look at me!* But she didn't. Something was drastically wrong here. 'Will you be coming home for the funeral?' she asked quietly. Galen wasn't even sure there would be a funeral but she needed to see how Sylvie would react to the question, if Sylvie reacted at all.

Sylvie did. Slowly she turned around and for the first time Galen saw her face. A devastation. Even with the dark glasses hiding her eyes, Galen could see utter devastation. The hollow cheeks, the skin stretched tight across bone, the lips drawn back in what seemed like a horrible grimace. 'What funeral?' Sylvie whispered.

Galen stared at her. Clearly Sylvie had not been told about David or Camille or Jonas. And yet the anguish Galen saw in Sylvie's face was more than enough to convince her that her friend was in deep trouble. But how? Why? Was she ill? And suddenly for Galen none of those questions mattered. What mattered most to her right now was to get Sylvie out of here, away from Shadow Hill.

'A friend has died,' Galen said quietly. 'But now that I think about it, I don't believe you knew him.' You did know him, Sylvie. You just don't know that he is dead. You don't know that Camille is dead. You don't know that Jonas is fighting for his life.

Why didn't she know? Hadn't Ravel told her? Obviously not. But judging from Sylvie's condition, perhaps he had good reason. Perhaps Adrien Ravel had a genuine concern for Sylvie. Perhaps he knew that in her present state she wouldn't be able to handle such news. Perhaps.

Sylvie turned away. 'Thank you for coming,' she said again. Again, the tone of dismissal.

I have to do something, Galen thought, but what? Sylvie needed help, that much was certain. But what to do? And how to do it? Clearly Ravel wanted no interference.

'I'm worried about you, Sylvie,' she said, choosing her words carefully. 'I wish you would talk to me. Tell me how you feel.'

Sylvie didn't answer, but Galen saw the tremor take hold of her thin shoulders and work its way down her back until her whole body was shaking.

'Sylvie, you know I love you.' Galen took a few quick steps forward and held out her arms. 'Please. Let me help you.'

'I think the best way you can help Sylvie is to allow her to rest.'

Galen turned to see Adrien Ravel standing in the doorway, and she felt a sudden urge to grab Sylvie by the hand and run away from this place as fast as she could.

He stood watching her in silent concentration, as if he were assessing her, trying to decide whether she was friend or foe.

Don't be a fool, she told herself. Don't jump to conclusions. Sylvie is in bad shape, but if this man is responsible for her condition, he would never, never have let you see her. He would have turned you away at the door.

But in the back of her mind were still questions that had no answers. Did Sylvie really love this man? Was she here because she wanted to be? Was Ravel providing medical help for her?

Tread cautiously, Galen. Don't let him know what you are thinking. 'Of course, you're right, Monsieur Ravel. She does need rest.' Galen crossed the room

143

and moved past him into the outer corridor. 'Goodbye, Sylvie,' she said over her shoulder. 'Take good care of yourself.' Then she turned to Ravel who had followed her out of the room. 'I'm grateful to you for letting me see her,' she said. 'I only wish I had more time to spend with her but as you know I have urgent matters to attend to in the city.'

He didn't respond. Together they walked in silence down the staircase and across the foyer.

A white-smocked servant was standing at the front door and as she and Ravel approached, he opened it. Galen breathed a sigh of relief when she saw Royal standing in the driveway beside his cab. She turned. 'Goodbye, Monsieur Ravel,' she said and extended her hand.

He took it. His own hand was cool and dry. And incredibly strong. 'You will let me know what arrangements you make for Edie?' His voice was as cool and dry and forceful as his grip.

'Of course,' Galen said. She withdrew her hand and headed across the wide verandah to the steps. And suddenly every nerve in her body told her to run. The way a child wants to run up the stairs at bedtime to escape the clutches of the bogeyman.

But she didn't allow herself to panic. She walked slowly down the steps, taking in the landscape, trying to give the impression that she was sorry to be leaving. It wasn't until she was tucked safely into the back seat of Royal's cab and well out of sight of the house that she began to breathe normally. But why had she felt so threatened? What was there about Adrien Ravel that unnerved her so? Certainly Sylvie was in terrible shape, but was it his fault? Perhaps he did have a doctor looking after her.

And then she remembered David. Only yesterday her husband had been here at Shadow Hill. Had he been as upset by what he saw as she was? She would never know. David was dead. So was Camille Carne. But there was still Jonas, a glimmer of hope in an otherwise desperate situation. Galen had to talk to him, find out if he had been afraid for Sylvie, too.

What a powerful force fear is, Galen thought, taking a deep breath. If it's strong enough it can make all else seem irrelevant. Even grief. In the face of what she had seen at Shadow Hill she had put her grief aside. She couldn't think right now about her loss. About David. She could think of only two things: what was happening to Sylvie and what was about to happen to Edie. She couldn't imagine Edie coming here alone, not with her mother in such a terrible state. But what could Galen do? What *should* she do?

The first person she knew she had to see was Jonas. If she couldn't see him, Galen would go to Ti Reine. And as a last resort, she thought, feeling inside her pocket for the crumpled note, she would get in touch with Jeremy Calder.

Ti Reine took a long time to answer the door. So long that Galen almost lost her nerve, though why she was so uneasy about this visit she wasn't sure. She knew very little about this woman except that she was a Voudou high priestess. Perhaps it was because the thought of asking for help from such a person in twentieth-century America bordered on the absurd. What could this woman possibly do that the authorities couldn't? Galen would have felt much better if she had talked to Jonas, but he was still not being allowed any visitors.

Galen knocked one last time and was about to turn

away when the door opened a crack. A very old woman peered out. A small, frail creature, her face a web of wrinkles, her hair iron grey, pulled back, knotted at the back of her head. 'Ti Reine?' Galen asked tentatively.

A nod.

'I am Galen Wickliffe. A friend of Sylvie Valois.'

Again Ti Reine nodded but she didn't open the door any wider.

'I would like to talk to you about her.'

'There is nothing to say,' the woman answered.

'Do you know where Sylvie is?'

A shrug.

'Do you know that Sylvie is in deep trouble?'

The answer caught her off balance. 'I have taken care of it,' Ti Reine said flatly.

Galen frowned. What was this woman talking about? 'I was at Shadow Hill this morning,' she said angrily. 'I saw Sylvie but I saw no evidence that she was being helped. On the contrary, clearly she is in the grip of some kind of mental breakdown.'

The woman's expression remained impassive. 'I have taken care of it,' she repeated, then made an effort to close the door but Galen leaned against it.

'Do you know that Sylvie is to be married? That I am to send her daughter Edie to Shadow Hill immediately?'

There was a long moment of silence. Then slowly Ti Reine shook her head. 'That will not happen.'

'And why not? Sylvie may marry whomever she pleases. And as for Edie, it is the law that she go with her mother.'

'I have no concern for your law, Dr Wickliffe. Edie will not go to Shadow Hill.'

'And who will stop her?'

'I will.'

And in spite of Galen's efforts to keep it open, the door slammed shut.

Galen dropped the phone back into the cradle. Another dead end. Jeremy Calder was in surgery. Try again tomorrow.

Galen felt sick. She was desperate to talk to someone, *anyone*, about Sylvie, about Edie, about Adrien Ravel, but she couldn't. There was no one left to talk to who would understand the insanity of what had happened, the insanity of what was still to come. All she could do now was to wait, pray for tomorrow so she could go home. Safe home. Maybe there she would find some help.

Chapter Fifteen

It wasn't a funeral. Certainly not like the ones Katy had ever read about or seen in the movies. It was what her mother called a memorial service. It wasn't held outside in a cemetery. Everyone had gathered in a small chapel near Greenwich, the place where her mother and father had been married. The place where he was going to be buried.

Katy stared at the dark wooden coffin with the blanket of white roses on the top. The lid was closed. It had been all along except for that quick minute earlier when her mother had lifted it so Katy could see him.

Ever since Edie told Katy that maybe her father would come back to see her, Katy's fears kept resurfacing. What if he really wasn't in heaven like her grandmother said? What if he was going to come out of the grave even after he was supposed to be dead? What if he was a zombie?

Katy hadn't dared mention such a thing to her grandmother, nor had she brought it up again with Edie. But it was a fear that she couldn't handle by herself so she had asked Helen about it. Helen had been horrified.

'That's nothing but silly superstition, Katherine. You'd better not mention such nonsense to your mother. She's upset enough as it is.'

And yesterday when her mother came home from New Orleans Katy tried to keep her mouth shut, but in the end she couldn't keep quiet. She told her mother what Edie had said, told her how afraid she was.

Her mother had taken it all very calmly. Edie was right, she said. Zombies were not supernatural creatures. They were living human beings who had been poisoned and were in a state of suspended animation. They didn't come back from the dead because they had never really died. 'But your father isn't one of them, Katy,' her mother had said softly.

'How do you know?'

'Because the authorities in Louisiana performed an autopsy. That means that all his vital organs have been removed. He really is gone, Katy,' her mother had said. 'He really is.' And Katy had seen new tears in her mother's eyes.

She began to cry herself. 'Can I see him?'

At first her mother had been very upset at the thought. 'He doesn't look good, Katy. Not good at all.'

'But, Mom, don't you understand? I want to see him with my own eyes. It may sound stupid but I want to see him one more time. Please.'

Galen hadn't said any more, but this morning, when she and Katy and Edie and Helen had gone to the chapel, before the mourners had arrived, her mother had lifted the lid on the casket. And Katy had seen her father. It was the most awful moment of her life, but at least she knew he was there, and he was really truly dead. He wasn't going to be a zombie.

Now, standing beside her mother, listening to the minister praying, she closed her eyes tight. Maybe like Edie said, Katy would see him again in a dream or something. Tears began to trickle down her cheeks.

The fear really was gone. Now there was nothing left but awful aching sadness. She squeezed her mother's hand tight. At least she still had her. And Edie. At least she wasn't alone.

There were many, many people. Friends of his, friends of hers, old colleagues, staff members, some seated in the rows of chairs behind her, others standing in the rear. The chapel was too small to hold them all. Too small, she thought, and in her mind she heard David agree. *You should have held this in Carnegie Hall.* She fought a sudden hysterical urge to laugh. Please God, please help me through this without making a scene. It wasn't until Helen reached over and handed her a tissue that she realized she was crying.

The eulogy was short. Or was it? Galen didn't know. She heard words but only through a fog, didn't have any idea what was said, didn't care. Her mind was numb. An overload. She felt nothing but despair, abandonment. No David to help her any more. How cruel, she thought, that now when she needed him the most he was gone.

She turned to look at her daughter. Katy's fears about zombies had been put to rest, but now her child seemed to be lost. Galen knew she would have to spend a lot of time with Katy, at least for a while. Give her a chance to heal. Get her sense of security back.

But thoughts of her child's grief and her own feelings of devastation were pushed aside when, out of the corner of her eye she saw Edie. What the hell was Galen going to do about her?

Yesterday, when Galen had first heard what Edie had said about the dead coming back, she had been angry. No wonder Sylvie had been so opposed to her daughter's involvement in Voudou. She remembered Sylvie's objections. 'It might be a sacred faith to some,' Sylvie had said. 'But there are too many unanswered questions about the religion. Too much secrecy.' Not that Sylvie hadn't understood the need. Voudou had been a much maligned religion from the first moment the white man encountered it, and for the Voudouist, secrecy had become his only protection, preserving the religion but also creating an aura of fear. An elemental kind of fear that had no logical explanation.

Galen had always understood Sylvie's concerns about Voudou, but until this encounter with Ravel, she herself had been uninvolved. Now she too was concerned. According to Sylvie, Ravel had been a Voudou high priest at one time. And she couldn't help but wonder. If Ti Reine had been a powerful influence in Edie's life, what effect would Adrien Ravel's brand of Voudou have on her?

After she had calmed Katy down, she had taken Edie aside. She had decided to find out everything Edie knew about the religion, but at the first mention of the word Edie had burst into tears.

'I told Katy what Voudouists believe about people not really dying because I thought it would make her feel better. I never meant to frighten her. I never imagined that she would think I was talking about zombies.'

Galen had hugged her tight. 'Katy is young, Edie. Sometimes she imagines too much. Especially now. Losing a parent is very, very hard.'

'I know,' Edie had nodded. 'I feel as though I've lost my own mother.' She paused. 'You saw her. Do you think she is ever going to come home again?'

In the face of those fearful, frightened eyes, Galen

had decided that now was not the time to question Edie about anything, nor the time to tell her the truth about her mother. Too much had happened to Edie too soon. Too much had happened to them all. Galen hadn't had time to straighten out her own thoughts, her own turmoil, her own problems, never mind Edie's. So she had lied, told Edie that her mother was coming home very soon.

The look of undisguised relief on Edie's face had been worth the lie, but Galen knew it would vanish as soon as Edie found out that Sylvie wasn't coming home at all – that she was to be married. That, in fact, Edie was to be sent to Shadow Hill to live.

But I won't tell her yet, Galen thought grimly. Not yet. First they had to get through this memorial service. Tomorrow Galen had an appointment with Deke Fareau, her attorney. She had already talked to him about Sylvie and Edie. He had said that without some evidence of wrongdoing there was nothing to be done about Sylvie, but he was going to see what could be done legally, if anything, to keep Edie in New York. He had not been encouraging. Parental rights and all that. But since Galen was Edie's doctor, she might be able to buy a little time, but only a little. Ultimately, if Sylvie Valois wanted her daughter with her, Edie would have to go.

Galen felt a tug on her sleeve and looked down to see Katy staring up at her, and she realized that everyone else was kneeling.

She knelt. Dimly she heard the words. 'Grant, we pray you, God of the living and the dead, eternal rest to the soul of David Wickliffe.'

Everyone stood, and suddenly Galen panicked. What next? What in God's name do I do next?

'Come on, Mom,' Katy said softly, taking her hand. 'We can get through this. We still have each other.'

'Everything is going to be just fine,' Edie whispered.

With Helen following close behind, the three of them walked down the aisle and out into a cold grey drizzle.

Far away, in an old country graveyard, quite a different ritual of death was taking place. Here, no minister was eulogizing the dead, no mourners bowed their heads in prayer. Here, even the cemetery itself was different. Most of the people had been buried in whitewashed tombs above the ground.

And here, there was a low sound of drums and a steady rhythmic chant. 'We stand as one united family, Baron Samedi. We are threatened.' They were praying to the Lord of all the dead, the guardian of the cemetery, asking for his permission, his help in what they were about to do.

The messenger stood at the edge of the graveyard, watching, waiting. He did not join in the chant nor did he move inside the circle. That was not his role. He was merely the messenger, the one who would take whatever the *mamaloi* gave him, and deliver it according to her instructions.

The night was dark. The only light came from the rows of tapered candles, but he could see well enough to count the number of people crouched inside the circle. He counted ten. Just enough for the death *ouanga* ritual.

The *mamaloi*, cloaked in a scarlet robe, her head crowned with the traditional headpiece of black and scarlet ostrich feathers, lay prostrate before the white wooden cross, her arms outstretched, her hands open, palms up.

On her right, one assistant holding a large white dove kneeled. On her left, a second assistant broke a small biscuit into pieces, then placed the crumbs in the open hand of the *mamaloi*.

The dove was released but it didn't take flight.

The *mamaloi* lay motionless until the dove came close and pecked a single crumb from her hand. In that instant she seized it, leaped to her feet, and with a sudden twist she tore off its head.

Its blood gushed out over the base of the sacred cross.

Then the *mamaloi* turned and with one motion gave the command.

Two men stood and, moving silently between the tombs, picked up their tools. The *mamaloi* waited, watching. The two men crossed in front of her to stand like statues on either side of a large whitewashed vault, waiting for her to waken Baron Samedi, beg for his permission to open the tomb.

She lifted the two round polished thunderstones from the base of the cross and with a crashing sound brought them together three times.

The tone of the chanting changed, became desperate. 'We beg you, Baron Samedi, grant your consent. Allow us to do what must be done. Do not become enraged. Sleep sweetly, Baron Samedi.'

Still on their knees, the company fell silent, swaying back and forth to an ancient secret rhythm.

The final signal came when the *mamaloi* set the stones down beside the sacrificial dove at the base of the cross. The men began their work. They were strong. Within minutes they had moved the heavy marble cover, lowering it quickly to the ground. Working with deliberate, almost dance-like movements, they attached their ropes to the iron rings on each end of the coffin and began to pull.

A scraping, screeching sound filled the night as the heavy wooden coffin came up out of the vault.

The next sound was that of metal striking metal as the edge of a spade hit the latch on the coffin, smashing it to pieces.

The two men stepped back.

The *mamaloi* was a thin frail old woman but she lifted the heavy lid as if it were weightless. Then she leaned over the yawning cavity and peered into its terrible darkness. The messenger saw her arm rise high over her head, the glint of steel, and the sudden swift descent of her knife. The *mamaloi* was taking what she needed.

When she turned, she held it in her hands, gleaming white in the flickering candlelight. A fleshless human skull.

Holding it out in front of her she glided across the graveyard and stepped outside the sacred circle.

The messenger took what she was offering. He knew what he had to do with it: deliver this death *ouanga* to Adrien Ravel. Beyond that, his only remaining task was to wait. The messenger had no idea how Ravel was to die. But he knew he would. The *mamaloi* had decreed it. Once Ravel was dead, the messenger would cut his head from his body. And as Baron Samedi, the Lord of the dead, demanded, he would return it here to replace the one that the *mamaloi* had taken.

* * *

Sylvie stood at the window. It was a glorious sunny day and yet to her the world outside looked grim. As if she were seeing the clear blue sky reflected in a dark murky pool. It was her wedding day and she was supposed to be feeling euphoric. No anguish. No fear. Adrien said so.

But he was wrong. She didn't tell him that the screaming pain was still there. That in spite of his magic it kept coming back. She didn't tell him because there was still a little something left in her battered brain, a speck of intelligence that told her not to speak of it. Something – a last survival instinct perhaps – that told her to be afraid. Afraid of Adrien. Because of something.

But what? Was it something he had done? Or was it something he had said?

Yes. It was words. But what were they? She couldn't remember, but the words had clouded her image of him, covering him with a dark film so she could no longer see him clearly. Not that she ever had. From the beginning Adrien had appeared to her in shadow. Only his magic had colour. Red, blue, yellow.

In her hand she held four bits of magic he had given her this morning. But she hadn't taken them yet. Something held her back. The echo of a question. *Was he playing with her mind?*

She turned away from the window. What difference did it make? She was already destroyed, living in absolute fear of the present, dread of the past, and despair for the future. And suddenly it came to her that she should kill herself, that she should put this Sylvie-thing out of its misery. Its brain was suffering endlessly. Should she not kill its body, end its torment? Shouldn't she? *Could* she?

But what about Edie?

She fell to her knees, driven down as if by blows from an invisible hand. She had to kill herself. She *had* to. But how could she leave Edie behind? Edie was coming to Shadow Hill. Adrien said so. And yet what good was the Sylvie-thing to its child when it couldn't even bear the thought of her?

She felt the bits of magic still clutched in her trembling hand. Should she take them? Again, were they helping her? Or were they destroying her?

The Sylvie-thing heard the knock on the door but she didn't answer.

The door opened. 'Monsieur Ravel would like you to come down to the library,' the servant said. 'The judge has arrived. Everything is ready for the ceremony.'

Numb, she nodded and got to her feet. She crossed to the night stand, picked up the glass of water and in one gulp she swallowed the pills. She was no longer certain about their magic. She only knew that without them she would kill herself. She would die without ever seeing her child again.

From a blissful distance she watched the Sylvie-thing take its place beside Adrien. The words were a blur but the meaning was clear. Sylvie and Adrien were being married.

But wasn't *she* Sylvie?

Well, no matter. Perhaps she was, perhaps she wasn't. It really didn't matter. She didn't feel at all like Sylvie. She felt dreamy, euphoric. Adrien had been right after all. Nothing really mattered, not even this wedding because it didn't involve her. She was simply an observer.

When she first came into the room they asked her to sign some papers. She had been curious about that. How could she sign anything? She had no arms, no hands to hold the pen. But somehow she must have managed because they stopped asking, and the ceremony began.

'I will,' someone said.

'I now pronounce you husband and wife. You may kiss the bride.'

But Adrien did not kiss anyone. At the sound of breaking glass he had turned to stare at the rock that had shattered his great mullioned window, the rock that now lay in the centre of his magnificent Aubusson carpet.

But was it a rock?

The Sylvie-thing squinted.

No. It wasn't a rock. *It was a gleaming human skull.*

The judge's eyes grew round in horrified disbelief. The servant standing by the door pulled back in sheer terror.

For a moment Adrien stood silent. And then he began to laugh. 'Let us be thankful,' he said softly, 'for the simple fools like the old *mamaloi*. But for them the rest of us could not succeed.'

Chapter Sixteen

New York City, 23 January.

Thank God it was a Saturday and the girls were at home. It gave Galen a chance. Not much of a chance, but at least it was something.

The phone call had come at precisely nine a.m. from the headmaster at Sedgewick School. His tone had been cool, all business. He had finally made contact with Mrs Valois, he had said, and he had made all the necessary arrangements. Edie would be picked up by the school van at one thirty this afternoon. Departure from LaGuardia Airport, four o'clock. All her belongings should be packed and ready for pickup at one thirty. 'I realize that you have had your own tragedy to deal with, Dr Wickliffe,' he had said, 'otherwise I'm sure you would have notified me that Mrs Valois was anxious to have her daughter with her as soon as possible.'

Galen had uttered a few noncommital words, then had hung up. They were coming to take Edie away without any warning, leaving Galen no time to fight.

Now, she picked up the phone, punched in Deke Fareau's home number, her hand shaking so hard she could barely hold the receiver. 'Is Deke there?' she said. 'Galen Wickliffe calling.'

She waited.

'Hi, Galen.'

She was breathing hard. 'Deke, what did you find out about the Valois situation? Can I do anything to keep Edie here?'

'Unless you can prove abuse, the answer is no. Can you? Has the school ever had any problems with Mrs Valois? Have any complaints ever been registered?'

'No.'

'Galen, I hate to say this.' He sounded suddenly uneasy. 'I know you're under terrific stress right now because of what has happened to David.' A pause. 'Do you think maybe you are overreacting? I know you are very fond of Edie, don't want to see her go. But it's not unreasonable for her mother to want her with her. And Edie's young. She'll adjust.'

Galen felt suddenly hot beads of sweat standing out on her forehead. Could he be right? Was she not thinking rationally? Her mind was churning. Maybe she was way off base. Maybe David's death had triggered an imbalance in her own mind. Maybe all Sylvie really needed right now was Edie. Maybe, maybe, maybe . . . And as for Ravel, short of second-hand hearsay, what *did* she know about the man?

'Thanks, Deke. I'll be in touch.' She dropped the phone into the cradle. Right or wrong she needed time to think, but time was running out. One thirty and Edie would be gone.

In a flash of inspiration it came to her. It wouldn't buy much time but at least it would give her a chance. A chance to do what, she didn't know.

Galen stepped into the elevator and went directly to her office. Across the street at the hospital they would be calling Sylvie right now, telling her that Edie had been admitted to the emergency room by Dr Wickliffe because of fear of a possible strep infection. And Sylvie would tell them to do whatever was necessary. Sylvie knew that strep was something that had to be avoided at all costs for anyone with a history of rheumatic heart disease.

As for Edie, she had been through this kind of thing before and she always took it in her stride. This morning, after Galen made her decision, she had gone into the kitchen where Edie was having breakfast, had checked Edie's throat. 'The school infirmary just called,' she had said casually. 'Some strep going around.'

The phone call had come as no surprise to Edie. In the past the school had always notified Sylvie when there was any cause for concern.

After Galen had checked Edie's throat, just to be on the safe side, she had admitted her to the hospital for tests.

Now Galen walked into her empty office. Saturday. No one around. Good. She needed some time alone to try to get control of herself, to make some sense of all this. But first she had to call the headmaster at Sedgewick.

He was concerned about Edie's health. He knew her history, but he took the news calmly. Should he call Mrs Valois or would Dr Wickliffe prefer to contact her directly?

'The hospital is contacting her,' Galen said. 'But I suppose I should, too. Do you have the number? I know it's unlisted but I'm in my office and don't have access to my personal directory.'

With a sick lump in her throat she made the call. Her last hope was that somehow when she talked to Sylvie, Sylvie would sound normal, excited about seeing her daughter, anxious to be reunited. And then Galen would stop worrying, send Edie happily off to start a new life.

Someone answered on the first ring. 'Shadow Hill.'

'Sylvie Valois, please. It's Galen Wickliffe calling.'

A pause. 'Mrs Ravel is unable to come to the phone.'

Mrs Ravel? Galen stared at the receiver. Of course, Mrs Ravel. Adrien had not wasted any time making arrangements for the wedding. Sometime during the past few days he and Sylvie had been married.

Galen gripped the phone tight. She was not going to be able to talk to Sylvie, find out how she was. Her concern about Edie's future was not going to diminish one bit. 'Then is Monsieur Ravel available? This is extremely important.'

Another pause. And finally the dark familiar voice. Smooth as glass. Chilling. 'Dr Wickliffe, I was expecting your call. I have just spoken to someone at the NYU Medical Center. What seems to be the problem?'

'You know, of course, that Edie has rheumatic heart disease?'

No response. But surely he must know. Galen thought. Surely Sylvie has told him. 'Edie is being tested for streptococcal infection,' she continued, 'a simple condition for most people, extremely dangerous for a rheumatic.'

'I assume you will have results within the hour?'

'Most probably.'

'And if they are negative, she will be flying to New Orleans as planned?'

Galen felt her heart sink. Why had she tried to avoid the inevitable? She knew there was no hope of keeping Edie in New York. Even if there were something wrong with her daughter, Sylvie would insist that she be transferred to a hospital in New Orleans as soon as possible.

'Dr Wickliffe? Are you still there?'

'I am,' Galen said dully. 'If the tests are negative, I see no reason to keep her here.' Her next words were so unexpected that she couldn't believe she was saying them. 'Edie is a very special patient, Monsieur Ravel. She needs constant medical supervision. I would like to accompany her to Shadow Hill and stay with her for a few days, in a professional capacity, you understand, to discuss her case history with a cardiologist in your area.'

There was a long silence. Not that it was unwelcome. Galen couldn't have responded even if Ravel had asked her a question. The suggestion that she go to Shadow Hill had rendered her speechless. Deke was right, she *was* going off the deep end.

And yet what choice did she have? To send Edie there alone was unthinkable.

Again the satin voice. 'I see no reason for you to inconvenience yourself, Doctor. We have excellent specialists here. I will see to it that Edie is well taken care of.'

The same way you are taking care of her mother? Galen pushed the thought back. 'Very well,' she said. 'If the tests are negative I will see to it that new arrangements are made for Edie. Perhaps tomorrow.'

'Not perhaps, Doctor. Absolutely. Edie's mother would hate to be disappointed again.'

'I will be in touch,' Galen said sharply, and before he could respond one way or another she hung up. After a moment she stood up, then sat back down hard. What had she done? Was she going crazy? But how could she tell? She had no one to talk to.

'You *have* to talk to someone,' she said to herself. 'Anyone who might understand the hellish world you're about to step into.' But who?

And then she remembered. Jeremy Calder. She reached into her pocket. Wrong jacket. No note. She dialled information and after a few minutes got through to his service. 'This is an emergency,' she said, breathing hard. 'Please have Doctor Calder get back to me at once.'

And he did. Moments later the phone rang. 'Doctor Wickliffe? Jeremy Calder. Thank goodness we finally made contact.' A low gentle voice. Concerned. Anxious. Yet at the same time oddly comforting. For the first time since this nightmare began Galen knew there was someone she could trust.

Without hesitation she told him everything she knew about what had happened at Shadow Hill, about Sylvie, about Adrien Ravel. And finally about what was going to happen to Edie.

'I think we have a very dangerous situation on our hands,' Jeremy said finally. 'Let me tell you what I know.'

We, Galen thought, feeling a huge rush of gratitude. I'm not in this alone any more. He's in it with me.

And like comrades in arms they made their plans.

'Edie, I have to be straight with you.' Galen sat down on the edge of the hospital bed. 'You are only fifteen years old, and if I had any other option I would never tell you about this mess we're in.' She took Edie's hand. 'But I know you're a fighter. You've come through hell and you will again. I have absolute faith in you.'

Slowly Edie nodded. 'The tests were positive.'

Galen shook her head. 'No, they weren't, Edie. You don't have any infection of any kind. If that was all we had to worry about we'd be in great shape.'

Edie's brown eyes widened. 'What, then?'

'It's a long story.' Galen paused, took a deep breath and continued. 'It's about your mother.'

Edie drew back, alarmed. 'Is she hurt? *Dead?*'

'No. She isn't hurt or dead. But she's in trouble.'

'I knew it. I just knew it. She hasn't talked to me or written to me or anything since I left New Orleans.'

'You remember Adrien Ravel.'

Edie nodded.

'He and your mother have been married.'

A gasp of disbelief. 'No way. My mother would never marry without telling me.' Tears welled up in her eyes. 'How could she marry him without telling me?'

'I don't know, Edie. That's the problem. I just don't know what's going on. But something is.' Galen handed her a tissue. 'Here, blow your nose.'

Edie did. Her next words were reproachful. 'You told me that when you saw her she seemed just fine.'

'I know. I had hoped that time would fix things, that Sylvie would come home. But the truth is that your mother isn't ever coming back to New York. When I saw her she seemed in terrible distress. But she isn't coming home. It was crystal clear that she didn't even want to see me.'

Edie was silent, and Galen could see the delicate muscles tensing up along her cheekbones. Galen had seen this with Edie before – her way of gathering herself together. During those long battles with her illness, when Edie was in real pain, she never cried. She simply tensed up. 'Do you . . . do you think my mother has gone crazy?'

'I don't know, Edie. Maybe *I'm* the one who is crazy, but we'll soon find out. She wants you to go to Shadow Hill to live.'

Edie's immediate reaction was one of sheer joy. 'I'm going to be with my mother!' But before Galen could even nod, reality took hold. Edie's expression changed, became anxious. She shuddered. 'Shadow Hill?'

Galen nodded. 'I'm not going to pretend that the move is going to be easy for you. I know very little about Adrien Ravel. And without knowing what state of mind your mother is in I'm nervous about you going there. To say the least, I'm *very* nervous. But we aren't alone in this. We have a friend in New Orleans, your mother's friend Jeremy Calder.'

Edie didn't seem to hear. She squeezed Galen's hand tight. 'I want to be with my mother more than anything else in the world,' she said softly. 'But I'm scared. I don't know why but I'm so scared.'

'I know you are, Edie,' Galen said firmly. 'And that's why you can't go alone. That's why, whether Adrien Ravel likes it or not, I'm going with you.'

Katy was stunned. Her mother and Edie were leaving tomorrow for New Orleans. Edie was going for good, to live there for ever. And Katy's mother was going with her, to be with Edie until a new doctor could be found.

Katy was more than stunned, she was devastated. She was going to lose Edie, her very best friend. She had just lost her father and now she was losing Edie, too. But worse, her mother was going with her *and they were leaving Katy behind*.

Katy stared down at her plate. 'You . . . you mean you're going without me?'

'Your mom will be gone only a few days,' Edie said quietly. 'And you don't want to miss any more school. You know how hard it is to catch up.'

Katy looked from Edie to her mother and back. Neither was looking at her. They were looking at each other. Neither seemed to care whether Katy was here or not.

'I can't take you with me, Katy,' her mother said. There was an edge to her voice. 'I don't want Edie to go, I don't want to go myself, and I certainly don't want you to go.'

Katy couldn't speak. She was too choked up. She had never felt so alone, so frightened. What had she done wrong? She looked down at the piece of apple pie on her plate but she didn't touch it. Silent tears dripped off the end of her nose onto the plate.

And then she felt her mother's arms around her. 'I'm so stupid, Katy. I need to have my head examined. I should've thought about how awful this would be for you.' She brushed the tears from Katy's cheek, then held her close. 'Cheer up, sweetheart. Of course I won't go without you. We'll all go together. We'll go sightseeing. We'll eat lots of praline cookies and Cajun shrimp. We'll even take a boat ride on the Mississippi. And before we come back to New York we'll make sure that Edie is safe and sound and happy. How does that sound?'

Katy looked up at her mother, her eyes still brimming with tears, but these were tears of relief. 'It sounds . . . it sounds like you love me.'

'I do love you, Katy. More than anything.'

'I love you too, Mom.' She smiled over at Edie. 'I love both of you. And I just know we're all going to have the time of our lives.'

Chapter Seventeen

Quickening darkness. Outside, the streetlights had come on. Inside, the candles that had been burning all day on the altar had finally extinguished themselves, leaving the room in shadow. But Ti Reine sat where she was.

From time to time the *mamaloi* jerked upright as if she were awakening from a troubled sleep, only to fall back in the chair into semiconsciousness.

This morning, for the first time in her life, Ti Reine had come face to face with the full forces of black magic. A power far greater than hers had surfaced, was poised to strike against her. The straw basket that had been left on her doorstep sometime during the night contained evidence of that power.

This morning when she found the basket, she had opened it without hesitation, assuming that it held the usual offering for the *loa* from one of her Voudou family. But when she saw its contents she was seized by a deep, primitive fear, a fear that had been born to Ti Reine's ancestors centuries earlier in the heart of the jungle. A fear that was as much a part of Ti Reine as the colour of her hair.

Inside the straw basket was a death *ouanga* far more lethal than the one she had prepared for Adrien Ravel. The fleshless skull she had taken two nights ago from the tomb stared up at her, but it was not

168

alone. Cradled next to it was the severed head of the *mamaloi*'s messenger, eyes bulging, mouth agape, stretched wide in a hideous silent scream.

Numb with horror, Ti Reine sat down in her chair beside the altar and took refuge in the dream world of the *loa*, hoping that there she would find some direction. Many times in her life Ti Reine had made contact with the spirits in her dreams and had found the answers she needed.

But this time, nothing. Ti Reine, despairing for Sylvie, fearful for Edie, stripped of her own self-confidence, drifted in and out of the spirit world, but the *loa* were silent. She had implored them to help her but they had not responded. She had failed.

For Ti Reine the silence of the spirits was a death sentence. This horror, this curse named Adrien Ravel was someone she did not know how to fight. She was skilled only in the healing rites of pure sacred Voudou, a simple *mamaloi*. She had always known that evil sorcerers lurked in the high mountains of Haiti, but she had never been forced to confront one. Now she had. His name was Ravel.

Ti Reine's breathing became more and more laboured and she knew her end was near. She was no longer of any use to her family. The energy of her soul would soon return to the earth.

But just before dawn, just as she was about to breathe her last, Damballah Oueddo and Ayida Oueddo came to her in a dream. Arched together over the sea they called to her, and in a flash of inspiration Ti Reine heard their instructions.

She sat erect, bathed in sweat, then sprang to her feet. She knew what she had to do. If she were to save herself, if she were to destroy the *bocor*, she had only one hope. She must go home to the high mountain, to the Voudou mountain of her homeland. She must go back to Haiti, and if he was still living, she must find Papa Sudre. If he was still alive, Papa Sudre would tell her what she must do.

As soon as they claimed their baggage, and a yowling Mingo in his cat carrier, they left the main terminal at the New Orleans airport. Just outside the entrance, Galen saw him, a slender black man in a white uniform holding the sign: VALOIS.

Well, here goes, she thought. 'Come on, girls,' she said. She took a deep breath, walked up to him, and set her bag down. 'Excuse me. You are here to pick up Edie Valois?'

He nodded, but his attention was focused more on the cat carrier and its angry occupant than on the three of them.

'Wonderful.' Galen picked up the suitcase. 'Where is the car?'

For a moment the driver seemed hesitant, then he shrugged and motioned for them to follow. When they got to the car the driver opened the trunk and they threw their bags inside. Again he looked unsure, but he said nothing. It wasn't until he opened the back door and Katy and Edie hopped in with the cat that he held up his hand. 'Wait a minute, lady,' he said to Galen. 'My orders were to pick up only one passenger.'

'A change of plans,' Galen said smoothly. She smiled and slid in beside Edie.

The driver stared for a moment. Then he shrugged, got behind the wheel and they were off.

Galen could see that Edie and Katy were both full of nervous excitement. Katy because she had been included in what she saw as a great adventure, heading off with her mother and Edie to Shadow Hill; Edie because she couldn't wait to see her mother. If the memory of Adrien Ravel filled her with an uneasy kind of dread, the thought of being reunited with Sylvie more than made up for it.

As for Galen, she didn't know *how* she felt, except that one thought kept her going. She wasn't alone in this thing any more. There was Jeremy, too. Together they had agreed that for now this was the best course of action, but what was Ravel going to say when he saw her? What if he refused to allow her to stay until Edie was settled? For some reason Jeremy didn't think that would happen. Ravel would be surprised, Jeremy said, and certainly angry, caught off balance, but he would be cautious. Adrien Ravel would never do anything he hadn't thought out well in advance.

Galen leaned back against the seat and closed her eyes. She was tired. Exhausted, in fact. Running on sheer guts and instinct, and within minutes the motion of the car had lulled her to sleep.

She dreamed that she was with David and hundreds of dogs were chasing them. When she woke up, for a minute she thought she was still dreaming because she could still hear the howling dogs. Mingo could, too. Edie had let him out of the carrier and, growling deep in his throat, he had crawled under the front seat of the car.

'We're here,' Edie breathed.

'You'd better get Mingo,' Galen said.

Somehow Edie managed to get him out from under the seat and back inside the carrier. With Katy holding Galen's hand and Edie holding the caged cat, they went up the steps to the front door.

'Yikes,' Katy whispered. 'This is awesome.'

Galen turned to Edie. 'You ring,' she said, still holding tight to Katy's hand. Be calm, she told herself. Ask to see Sylvie. Remember what Jeremy said. You have the element of surprise in your favour. Don't blow it.

The door opened but before Galen had a chance to speak, the servant said, 'He's expecting you.'

They were led to the room where both Edie and Galen had first met Adrien Ravel, but this time he was already there, sitting behind the massive mahogany desk, writing.

He looked up when they came in, his gaze steady, evaluating, but not at all surprised, as if he really had been expecting all of them. 'Dr Wickliffe, we meet again.' He turned slightly in his chair, this time to stare at Edie. 'Mademoiselle Valois.' Now his voice was velvet, almost hypnotic in its softness. 'Even more lovely than I remembered.'

He never really looked at Katy. His gaze simply skimmed past her and back to Galen. Almost as an afterthought he said, 'Your daughter, I presume.'

'She is.'

'And what may I ask is in the cage?'

'My cat,' Edie said. 'Mingo.'

'I see.' He leaned back in his chair. 'Well, Dr Wickliffe?'

Galen drew herself up. 'I came with my patient, Monsieur Ravel, because as a physician I have certain responsibilities. Having spoken with you only briefly about her condition, I had to assume that you do not understand the risks involved when caring for a rheumatic. I, on the other hand, know how precarious her situation is, and as her physician I could not in good conscience send her off without making certain that a

172

competent knowledgeable staff is in place to care for her.' All this was said in the crisp, clinical, no-nonsense tone of Dr Galen Wickliffe, eminent paediatric cardiologist. 'Of course I cannot stay here at Shadow Hill any longer than is absolutely necessary,' she added. 'I have other patients who depend on me as much as Edie does. Therefore I would appreciate it if you would give me the names of the doctors with whom you have discussed her case, so I can set up appointments with them.' She made a quick motion with her hand. 'I've brought with me a list of recommendations of my own. The best people in the field. If you like, I'll be happy to share it with you.'

The whole time she was speaking his gaze never wavered. His concentration was complete. Even after she was finished he sat motionless, clearly considering his options.

Galen was quaking inside but she never looked away. She met his gaze with one of equal intensity. She *was* concerned about Edie, and she *was* determined to settle her here safely.

'Very well, Dr Wickliffe,' he said finally. 'Certainly I want Edie to remain in perfect health. By all means set up your appointments as quickly as possible. In the meantime I assume you'll want to stay here at Shadow Hill. Unless you would prefer to go back to the city and find a hotel?'

Edie took a small step forward. 'I would like them to stay here at Shadow Hill,' she said quietly. 'But now, may I please see my mother?'

'Of course you may,' Ravel said. He stood up and held out his hand. 'Come along, *ma chère*, she's waiting for you in the garden.' At the door he motioned to a servant. 'Take Dr Wickliffe and her daughter to the green room. And the animal out to the servants' quarters.'

Edie uttered a weak protest. 'But Mingo always sleeps with me.'

'Perhaps in New York,' Ravel said coldly. 'Not at Shadow Hill.' He turned to Galen. 'I'm sure you have no objections to Edie seeing her mother alone?'

'Certainly not.' In truth Galen did, but she had pushed as far as she dared. She and Katy were going to stay here at Shadow Hill with Edie. At least she had accomplished that much. What came next remained to be seen.

The sunshine on her face was warm but the air chilled her to the bone. What was she doing out here in the dead of winter? If she remembered anything it was how much she hated the cold. She wasn't in New York. She was in Louisiana. The Deep South. But it didn't matter. In January, even here it was too cold. If it was still January.

She wasn't sure.

She looked around. Why was she outdoors in this garden? And then she remembered that Adrien had told her that something was happening today.

Something.

Never mind, never mind. A dozen or more pills had finally turned off the pain.

Oh look. A small yellow butterfly had come to rest on the tip of a branch just beside her chair. She shivered. Was this poor creature as cold as Sylvie was? If she held it in her hands would it feel warm? Safe? Happy? The way Adrien said she should feel?

But I don't, I don't, I don't.

She waved her hand. Fly away, butterfly. Escape while you still can. Don't stay here.

But why not? Wasn't this the most beautiful garden on earth?

The gnawing fear stirred inside. And the pain.

But wasn't the pain gone? Hadn't Adrien said so? Where *was* Adrien? What *was* happening today?

And without warning the answer came to her: Edie. *Edie was coming*.

High-pitched wails filled the garden.

But hush, Sylvie-thing. Don't let him hear you cry. Don't let him know you still care about her. Don't let him know that you can never let go of your child. If he knows that then he'll know that *nothing* he has done is working. That he isn't the centre of your universe.

Through the mist of tears she saw him approaching. Heard voices. His. And another, a soft lyrical sound that ripped her heart with its sweetness.

'Mother,' the voice called.

Sylvie shrank back, trying to melt into the chair. What little brain she had left told her that somehow she must stay away from this child. Keep her distance. Be cold. Care only about him. Adrien.

But in spite of her fear, suddenly she found herself running through the grass, throwing her arms out wide, feeling other arms around her.

Someone was trembling. Was it Sylvie?

And for one instant her mind cleared. She knew she was in trouble and she began to scream. 'Help me, oh God, my precious child, *help me!*'

She felt him pulling her from the arms of her daughter, dragging her across the lawn. She saw his face. A contortion of rage. 'I must apologize,' he was saying to Edie. 'As you can see, your mother is ill.'

'Mother!' A high-pitched wail.

And in the midst of the storm Sylvie was stricken with a blinding flash of truth. Adrien Ravel *was* evil. It was Adrien who was destroying her!

'Get away from here, Edie!' she screamed. 'Run for your life!'

She tried to break free but he held her in a vicelike grip. He dragged her, kicking, clawing, screaming, back to the house.

Chapter Eighteen

Even before Katy stepped foot inside the house she was nervous. But when she saw Monsieur Ravel she went from nervous to downright scared. Not to mention how she felt when Edie whispered to her to look at the painting, the one of the zombies. No wonder Katy's mother hadn't wanted to bring her here. No wonder she didn't want Edie to live here. There was something awful about Shadow Hill. Katy didn't know what it was, but it scared her to death.

She and her mother followed the servant up the wide staircase to the second floor. The room that was to be hers was like all the others Katy had seen in this house: overwhelmingly ugly. Next door, her mother's room was just the same, filled with pieces of furniture that looked as though they belonged in a museum, crowded so close together that there was barely enough room to move.

Galen helped Katy to put what few things she had brought with her away. There was no lack of drawer space, that was for sure. There were chests of mahogany and chests with brass pulls and chests with carved lions for feet. Once they had both unpacked there was nothing left to do but wait.

'I wonder what will become of Mingo,' Katy said, sitting down beside her mother on an ugly velvet-covered sofa. 'He isn't going to know how to protect himself if they let him loose. He's always been an indoor cat.'

'He's a smart cat, Katy. He'll learn,' her mother said. 'Besides, cats have nine lives.'

'They do not. And he isn't going to learn either. Mingo doesn't have a clue about enemies. Like the things that live out there.' She pointed towards the window and shivered. 'Out there in that dark eerie swamp.' Katy ran her finger along the carved arm of the sofa. 'Gross,' she said in a whisper. 'I feel like we're in someone's attic.' She wrinkled her nose. 'It even smells like an attic. Old and musty.'

Her mother nodded.

'Monsieur Ravel sure does like Napoleon,' Katy said, pointing to the portrait hanging over the mantel. 'Did you see the huge painting of him on his horse at the end of the hall downstairs? It covers the whole wall.'

Again her mother nodded but she didn't say anything. She seemed preoccupied.

There was a long silence while Katy considered whether or not she ought to ask the next question. If she did, would she be getting Edie into trouble?

She decided she had no choice. 'Did you see that other painting?' she asked in a hushed tone. 'The one in Monsieur Ravel's office?'

Galen frowned. 'What painting?' But Katy knew from the uneasy tone of voice that her mother knew perfectly well which painting she was talking about.

'The one over the mantel,' Katy said. 'The one with the zombies.'

Her mother was quiet for a minute. 'Katy, why do you think they are zombies?'

Katy hesitated, then forged ahead. There was something scary about Shadow Hill, and her mother really

178

ought to know everything there was to know about Monsieur Ravel. 'Edie told me. She saw the painting the first time she came here. She said it was an evil thing, that whoever owned it was a *bocor*. That's the Voudou word for evil sorcerer.' Katy glanced over at her mother but Galen had turned towards the window, her head tipped to one side, listening intently as if she were hearing something barely audible.

And then Katy heard it, too. A distant sound at first, but it was unmistakable. The sound of someone screaming.

Galen jumped up, crossed to the wide doors that led out to the upper gallery and threw them open.

The next series of screams were ear-splitting.

Katy ran to her mother's side. 'What's happening? Who is it? It isn't Edie, is it?'

Her mother shook her head. 'I don't know, but I'm going to find out.'

Together they flew out of the room and ran to the top of the stairs, but that was as far as they got.

A servant was on his way up, holding a frantic, sobbing Edie by the arm.

It was dark.

Sylvie came to consciousness slowly, drifting back and forth between sleep and waking, not certain which was which. But whether asleep or awake, it was dark.

Have I gone blind?

But how could she know? She wasn't sure if her eyes were open or closed. Nor could she lift a hand to feel.

Paralysis. Absolute paralysis.

What had happened to her? Had she been in an accident? But what? When? She tried to sort out her thoughts but it was difficult. So difficult. She felt as if she were lost in a thick enveloping fog, not knowing how she came here. But one thing she knew. *The pain was gone*. Bits of memory, places, the faces of people she had known came slowly, but without pain.

Lying so still, unable to move, not knowing why or how, she tried to make some sense of it. It seemed as if there must have been a terrible accident that had injured her brain, but now it was recovering.

Slowly she began to remember, to reconstruct her life. New York. Edie. Galen. Her work with David. And then the picture narrowed, focused on her holiday trip to New Orleans. Camille. Jonas. Jeremy Calder. *Adrien Ravel*.

Little by little it all came back, bits and pieces, finally ending with the most recent memory of her darling precious girl running towards her through the garden. And in the midst of their embrace she remembered *Adrien*.

Adrien Ravel. The master of destruction with his coloured bits of poison. A fiend who somehow had found a way to control her mind. To destroy her ability to think, *to remember*. Until this very moment.

But how could this be? How could she remember now without the scourging pain, when yesterday she had been able to remember nothing? Why was she thinking rationally now, when for so long her mind had been unable to comprehend anything beyond those coloured bits of hell?

And where *was* Adrien? Had something happened to him? Was that why she was able to think clearly?

Please God, let him be dead.

And in the midst of the whirling maelstrom that was blowing through her mind, cleaning out the debris, suddenly she heard his voice.

'Ah, Sylvie, my dear. How tragic for you that I have been forced into this sorry impasse.'

She felt his cold hand caress her cheek. *Don't touch me!* But it was a silent scream. Nor could she pull away. She lay motionless.

'I don't have to ask you how you are feeling, do I? I know the old pain is gone because I have taken it away. Part of my genius is that I can cause pain. Another skill – I must admit a skill I rarely use – is one where, if I choose, I can take that pain away. And with you, I decided that it would be the kindest thing. I have given you the antidote, an incredible potion that almost instantly erases the pain. You will now re-member your past life without anguish.' He lifted her hand and pressed it to his lips. 'Can you feel me smiling?' he asked softly. 'Of course you can. I *am* smiling because I have done you a great service. I have released your mind from the dungeons of scalding pain and deep despair. A trade, if you will.' Gently he set her hand back down and moved away. 'I have released the mind in exchange for the body.'

Now all Sylvie could hear was his breathing, but somehow she sensed a change. Now there was malevolence in the room.

'You have disappointed me, Sylvie,' he said. 'I made a mistake in choosing you. I thought you were the perfect subject for my experiment. I was wrong. I *hate* to be wrong.' The tone was still soft but now it was full of menace.

Sylvie knew that he had come close to her again because she felt the movement of air against her skin. 'I had hoped that when you saw your daughter you would reject her, you would realize that I was the only one who meant anything to you. You would become

181

content, placid, a brilliant companion whose only desire would be to please me in all things. But alas, you turned against me. In your ridiculous outburst in the garden you became a threat to my very existence, so I was forced to sedate you. And then I had to decide what to do with you.'

Now she could feel his warm breath against her cheek. 'At first I was inclined to kill you. The way I always kill, quickly, efficiently, without ever leaving a trace. Of course, your dear friend Dr Wickliffe would have demanded an autopsy and I would have agreed.

'I have nothing against autopsies. They present no threat to me because I have elevated the art of killing to a science. I leave no footprints in the sand.'

His voice became pensive. 'The only time I ever resist such medical invasions is when they threaten to destroy one of my own creations, as in the case of your cousin's daughter, Eveline. Dr Aubin wanted to cut her up, find out why she had died so suddenly. And in that case I had to intervene. A zombie cannot survive without its organs, so I was forced to dispose of Dr Aubin before he could arrange to have her dissected.'

There was a long moment of silence, then he exhaled. 'Well, enough meandering. Back to the issue at hand. If I kill you, your doctor friend will see to it that they cut you, piece by piece, searching for a clue, a cause. And in the end they will find no evidence of any wrongdoing. Nothing but a case of simple heart failure. But after they have finished with you, you will be truly dead, and where will that leave me? All the time I have spent with you, wasted. Such a tragic waste.'

She felt him pull the sheet away from her body, felt the pressure of his hand tracing a pattern lightly over her breasts. 'They will cut here. And here. And here. And that will indeed be tragic. In spite of your mental resistance, you are a magnificent physical creature, Sylvie.'

Her revulsion was complete. And yet she couldn't move away, couldn't escape.

His hands still moving over her body, he continued. 'I have decided to put your fate in the hands of your friend Galen. She is a skilled physician. She will make every attempt to save you, but within the hour she will declare you dead. Should she demand an autopsy, as she most probably will, I will not object. And then she, not I, will be your executioner.'

Sylvie felt his hand tighten on her breast. 'However,' he continued, 'if by some rare stroke of luck she does not believe that anything can be gained by such a move, and if within two days she goes back to New York, leaving your poor lovely body here at Shadow Hill for burial, then I will bring you up out of the grave, give you another chance. Not to live independently, mind you. If I am able to bring you back it will be as a zombie.'

His hands left her and he moved away. 'But you have only two days left. After that, autopsy or not, you will be dead. It is Dr Wickliffe's decision to make, my dear Sylvie. Let us see what kind of friend she truly is.'

She heard the footsteps going away, the opening and closing of the door.

Sylvie was left frozen, suspended in a state where the only active thing was the horrified mass that was her mind.

Help me, Galen! Please help me!

*   *   *

Furious, Galen left Edie and Katy together in Katy's room. She had spent almost an hour trying to calm Edie down. Now she was going to find Ravel, demand that Sylvie be hospitalized at once or she would call the police. Edie's description of what she had seen in the garden had been devastating, and Sylvie's words to her daughter had been even more appalling. *Get away from here, Edie! Run for your life!*

As far as Galen was concerned, whatever else Ravel was guilty of, to keep Sylvie here in this condition *was* a criminal act. And whatever had triggered Sylvie's outburst, Ravel had made a terrible mistake in allowing Edie to see it. He had given Galen a reason to bring in the authorities. Unless he killed Galen, Ravel would not be able to prevent her from getting help, and she didn't think even he would be so foolish as to kill her. Ravel didn't know about Jeremy Calder, but he did know that other people knew where she was and why she had come to Shadow Hill. On that score Galen felt safe.

The lower hall was deserted, as were all the rooms on the first floor. A thick silence had descended over the house, no sound but the echo of her heels tapping on the marble floors.

Galen retraced her footsteps, trying to remember the first time she had come to Shadow Hill, trying to remember where Ravel had taken her to see Sylvie.

In her mind she could picture a small landing at the end of one of the corridors and then a short flight of steps that had led to a suite of rooms. One of them had been Sylvie's.

She walked quickly in that direction, driven by a sense of outrage, and now, more than that, a sense of urgency – a deep gnawing fear that something terrible had happened, or was about to happen to Sylvie.

After covering what seemed like endless miles of corridor she finally came to a landing that seemed familiar. And there she stopped abruptly. Barring her way stood a huge black man with a brilliant golden pendant hanging from a thick chain around his neck. He had no hair, no eyebrows and small reptilian eyes. 'I demand to see Sylvie Valois,' she said fiercely. 'Step aside.'

The man didn't move but, coming into view behind him, she saw Adrien Ravel.

'I've been looking everywhere for you, Dr Wickliffe,' Ravel said sharply. His face was no longer a granite mask. He seemed visibly shaken. 'I need your help. Quickly. My wife has had some kind of seizure. I've phoned for the doctor and he is on his way, but I'm afraid for Sylvie. I've never seen her like this before.'

Outside the door to her bedroom he stopped and looked hard at Galen. 'I never wanted you to come to Shadow Hill, Dr Wickliffe. But now, if you can help her, I will be eternally grateful.' He opened the door.

Galen stepped inside. The heavy velvet drapes had been drawn and the room was in semidarkness. Sylvie lay on her back in the middle of the bed, eyes closed, a light sheet covering her body.

Galen rushed to her side and put her fingers on Sylvie's neck, checking for a pulse. It was quick, intermittent. Her pupils were constricted. Her breathing was short, laboured, and there was clear evidence of cyanosis. Even her fingernails were purple. Beads of sweat stood out on her forehead. Sylvie was showing all the signs of rapid progressive heart failure.

'Jesus Christ, help me!' Galen shouted, motioning to Ravel.

Together they lifted Sylvie off the bed and lay her flat on the floor. Galen tilted her head back, then put her mouth to Sylvie's and began to respirate. 'Get an ambulance!' she gasped between breaths. 'She's dying!'

With one frantic glance over his shoulder, Ravel rushed from the room.

Again Galen felt Sylvie's neck for a pulse.

Only a faint fluttering.

'Oh God, Sylvie,' Galen begged. 'Don't die.'

Another mouth to mouth, then cardiac compression. She began counting. 'One thousand, two thousand, three thousand.' Galen was so intent on resuscitation that she never saw the other doctor come in.

He didn't speak. Like Galen, he knew precisely what to do, quickly positioning himself to take over the cardiac compression.

Without skipping a beat Galen nodded at him, blew two short breaths into Sylvie's mouth, then checked her pulse.

Now nothing. No pulse at all. Galen checked the pupils. Dilated. 'Jesus,' she whispered.

The other doctor never looked up. 'Blow,' he said softly.

She did. And silently she said a prayer of thanks. This man *was* a doctor. A good doctor. He knew what had to be done and he was doing it. Working together maybe they could save her. If they could keep her going until the ambulance arrived maybe she would survive.

Maybe.

Chapter Nineteen

'Is there anything I can do?' Katy asked helplessly.

Edie shuddered and shook her head. 'I just hope your mother can do something,' she said tearfully.

Katy stood up and crossed to the window. She stared out across the garden. If only she could think of something to get Edie's mind off the terrible thing she had just witnessed with her mother.

In the centre of the garden she could see a gigantic tree with huge branches, growing so low they almost touched the ground. A true climbing tree, Katy thought. A tree you could climb almost to the sky. And as she looked up, following the curve of the great trunk, she saw him, crouched in the V of one branch. 'Edie, come here quick!' She pointed. 'There's your cat! There's Mingo!'

Edie jerked her head up. 'Mingo?'

Katy nodded. 'Right out there in the tree.'

Edie rushed to the window and stared out.

'Let's go get him,' Katy said, breathless. If anything would make them both feel better it would be to have Mingo with them.

'Let's go. Quickly.' Edie grabbed Katy's hand and together they went out through the double doors onto the upper verandah.

Inside, the house had been dark and gloomy, but outdoors the sky was a brilliant blue, and Katy had to squint to adjust her eyes to the bright sunlight. 'I hope Mingo stays put,' she said, racing to keep up with Edie.

They ran the length of the gallery, down the stairs and across the lawn to the edge of the garden. They had no trouble finding the tree. It towered over the whole landscape.

'Mingo,' Edie called, clambering onto the lowest branch. 'Come here, kitty.'

Above, Mingo saw her but he didn't move. He crouched where he was, tail flashing, ears laid back.

'Do you think maybe he doesn't know who we are?' Katy panted, climbing up after Edie.

'He must. But maybe he's so scared he doesn't dare come down.' She pulled herself up onto the next limb and reached out. 'Come here, Mingo,' she crooned softly.

For one moment Katy thought the cat was going to let Edie get closer. But he didn't. In the next instant, claws unsheathed, he was off through the branches, down the trunk of the tree and across the lawn to vanish into the swamp.

'Mingo!' Edie wailed. She and Katy jumped to the ground. 'Come on, Katy,' Edie said. 'We have to catch him.'

They ran to the edge of the grass where the swamp began, hesitated for a moment, then plunged ahead.

Once into the dark marshy swampland they moved single file, neither saying a word. They picked their way along, hopping from grassy mound to grassy mound, following a narrow path, trying to catch sight of Mingo, catching only glimpses of dark still water on either side. Katy was frightened. It was as if she had stepped over the line into a strange misty world where everything was slimy green, reeking of something wet and sickly sweet, a smell that she couldn't identify. There were sounds of hundreds of little frogs peeping. High above the thick green canopy she heard a bird cry out, but she couldn't see it.

'I think we should go back,' she whispered, but Edie paid no attention, clearly intent on finding the cat.

At one bend in the path she stopped and pointed. 'There he is, Katy. Come back here, Mingo, you bad cat.' And she hurried on.

Katy squinted but she couldn't see anything except trees and hanging moss and dark pools of murky water. As much as Shadow Hill frightened her, this swamp *terrified* her, but she didn't dare go back alone. She had no choice but to continue on, following Edie.

Suddenly the curtains of green parted and she and Edie found themselves in a small clearing. But it wasn't just a clearing, it was a cemetery, unlike any cemetery that Katy had ever seen before, because here, all the graves were above the ground – rectangular white marble tombs with elaborate carvings and brass markings.

At the far end was a beautiful square building with marble columns across the front and huge earthenware vases on each side of the entrance. 'It's a mausoleum,' Edie whispered.

'Who do you suppose is buried in there?' Katy asked in a hushed tone.

'I don't know. But I think we ought to get out of here. Right now. Let's go back to the house.'

Katy needed no encouragement. She took Edie's hand but before she could take one step, she heard the sound of people splashing through the swamp. 'Come on,' Edie said, pulling Katy with her. 'Hide.'

They ran around one side of the mausoleum and crouched down, as close to the cool white marble as they could get, scarcely daring to breathe.

The first person they saw was a giant black man, the most terrifying man Katy had ever seen. Around his neck hung a shining golden disc.

Beside her, Katy felt Edie stiffen. Coming into view behind the giant, five more people appeared. Three women and two men, shuffling painfully along as if the simple act of walking, just lifting one foot and placing it in front of the other, was a terrible ordeal. They looked neither to the right nor to the left, nor did they make any kind of sound. As they passed through the cemetery they came close enough for Katy to see their faces, and what she saw frightened her beyond tears, beyond shrieking out, beyond everything. She could only stare, open-mouthed, gaping.

These five creatures were not living human beings. Their faces were frozen masks, expressionless, their eyes polished lumps of coal, wide, staring, but seeing nothing, like the eyes of life-size dolls. These were the same creatures that Edie had described to her. Corpses walking in the sunlight, trapped between the world of the living and the world of the dead. Zombies.

Katy felt Edie pull her close and she buried her face against Edie's chest so she wouldn't have to look any more.

The two stayed where they were, locked in fearful silence, hoping that they would be able to keep quiet, stay undiscovered, until this parade of horror passed by.

Floating high above the floor. Watching with a queer sense of detachment. Somehow removed from it all.

Who was lying there on the floor?

Why Sylvie, of course.

Galen was there, too, kneeling beside Sylvie's head. And someone else, a man, leaning back on his heels, shaking his head. 'There's nothing more to be done,' he was saying.

Sylvie saw Galen's face, frantic, incredulous. 'There has to be something we can do.'

The man again. 'No. She's gone.'

Sylvie saw his hand reach out, but somehow now it was right in front of her. Then gently he closed her eyes.

Utter darkness.

And suddenly the truth hit her. She wasn't floating at all. She was here on the floor, trapped inside her own body. She heard Galen moan, felt Galen touch her on the neck, then take her by the shoulders and shake her. 'It can't be. It can't be. Oh Jesus, Sylvie, you can't be dead.'

But I'm not! You are a doctor, Galen! Surely you must know that! My heart is still beating!

And then from somewhere across the room, Adrien's voice, anxious. 'The ambulance is here.'

'Too late,' the man said sadly.

Too late? But surely this must be a nightmare. Surely I will wake up. Nothing so terrorizing, so hideously terrorizing can be real.

'No pulse,' Galen said flatly. 'No nothing.'

And then Sylvie felt hands on her body. Someone lifting her up off the floor, laying her down again on the softness of the bed. Faintly she could smell the scent of almond on the bed linens. But how could she smell when she wasn't even breathing? When she had no pulse? When she could not speak?

The same way you are hearing, she told herself. The same way you can still feel. Adrien has paralysed you. He has robbed you of mobility, but he has left you with your senses. The better way to torment you, Sylvie. You should know him by now.

'She is dead?' This from Adrien, full of anxiety. And yet Sylvie knew he was play-acting.

'She is.' Again, the other man's voice.

Nothing from Galen.

'What happened?' Adrien. Accusing now. Angry. More play-acting.

And sometimes even as the truth terrorizes, it can also infuriate. Sylvie was suddenly outraged. *You* know what happened, Adrien, she screamed silently. *You* have done this to me. I am helpless, unable to open my eyes, or speak or even show that I am still breathing. And standing beside me, you *know* all this. You *know* I am hearing you speak. *And you are pleased.*

There was no way now that Sylvie could disappoint him. Adrien had trapped her as she had never imagined possible. He had perfected a method of torture so exquisite, so flawlessly exquisite that there was no way to fail. And for Sylvie there was no escape. No hope.

Hopeless. Hopeless.

'Heart failure.' The man's voice again.

'Heart failure,' Galen echoed.

Sylvie felt Adrien take her hand, press it to his lips, felt his tears burn her flesh. And she was filled with revulsion.

A throat burning with bile, but unable to vomit.

A voice box, but no way to scream.

Hands, but no way to tear Adrien to pieces.

Help me, Galen. Dear God, help me.

'I'd like to be alone with my wife for a moment.' Adrien's voice, overcome with grief. 'You understand.'

She heard the sounds of footsteps going away. A pause. The opening and closing of the door.

Suffocating silence. But Sylvie could feel his eyes watching her. And then she heard him exhale. 'Ah, Sylvie,' he whispered softly. 'What do you think your doctor friend is going to do now? Let me tell you what I think. When Dr Wickliffe returns to your bedside she will refuse to sign the death certificate. Your death was untimely, she will say. She will not consider leaving you here to be buried. Not for a moment. She will insist that your remains be taken to New Orleans for an autopsy. I, of course, will not protest. After all, the ambulance has already arrived. The paramedics are here. Why send them away empty-handed?'

A long silence.

'Within days,' he mused, 'perhaps only hours, someone will begin to cut.'

Hearing those words, the terror in her soul was complete. Dead meat, she thought dully. Dead meat.

But even as she realized that everything Adrien was saying was true, there was something in her soul, a spark, a tiny element of the human spirit that kept her praying. Maybe somehow Galen would sense that something was wrong. Or maybe she would see the futility in looking for evidence to find Adrien guilty. Maybe she would go back to New York and leave Sylvie to be buried here at Shadow Hill.

But then what?

And the answer was clear. Adrien will raise you from the grave. You will become a zombie.

Thoughts like bits of broken bone rattled through her mind. What *was* a zombie? A thing without will? Without hope? Was it a state worse than death? Sylvie knew only what had been whispered to her as a child. That for Voudouists, to be a zombie was to be trapped in a state of perpetual hell. They believed that the human soul was better off dead, returned to the spirits of the earth.

But Sylvie was not a Voudouist, and in her mind, she began to weep. Because no matter what others believed, she didn't want to die. If Ravel made her a zombie, no matter how fearful, how cruel, how torturous the path, at least she would still be alive. And someday maybe someone would find her, know how to cure her. Bring her back.

For Sylvie, the worst horror of all was death.

Oh please, Galen. Please. Don't let them kill me.

But was there anything Galen could do? In order to fight Adrien Ravel's demonic magic, she would have to understand its source, the secret cults of Africa. And except for Ravel himself, did anyone have that knowledge? Galen certainly didn't. Nor did David. Only one person Sylvie knew, had ever known, might be able to save her now. That person was the *mamaloi* Ti Reine.

The road curved upward, the thick green forest rising up on one side, on the other the steep drop to the sea. Ti Reine left the bus and continued on foot.

Early this morning, without speaking to anyone, she had left Port-au-Prince, heading for the high mountain and the remote village of Jean Rabel. She had no time to reacquaint herself with old friends. She knew she had no time to lose.

Her straw bag slung over her shoulder, she trudged on, pausing only to catch a breath. The sun had risen high in the sky and the heat had risen with it, but Ti Reine never stopped for more than a minute. Past small thatched huts and small fields of cotton clinging to the sides of the hills, she walked quickly.

Once she was forced to stop and ask for a drink of water. It was given willingly, along with questions. 'Where do you come from? Where are you going?'

But Ti Reine had time for only two words in creole. *'Moi aller.'* I go. With a quick nod of her head she was off again on her search for help. Her search for Papa Sudre.

It was almost dark when she reached the village, no more than a cluster of mud huts set in the middle of a small clearing. Exactly as she remembered it.

In the distance, far across the ravine she heard a dog bark. She paused to wipe the dust from her face, then made her way to the closest dwelling.

Outside the hut a cooking fire was burning. An old woman sat on a small chair beside it, grilling coffee beans. She glanced up, then went back to her work.

'Bonswa, Celie,' Ti Reine said softly.

The old woman looked up again, squinting in the fading light. For a moment she looked dazed, as if she were hallucinating.

'What you see is real, Celie,' Ti Reine said. 'I am your sister.'

'It's been a long time since you come,' Celie said sadly, shaking her head.

'I know.'

'Why now?'

But before Ti Reine could answer, another woman emerged from the hut, a much younger woman in a faded cotton dress, with a dark red bandanna wound tightly around her head. Ti Reine knew she was Celie's daughter, but the woman looked at Ti Reine without recognition and without interest.

'*Moi aller, Maman,*' she said to Celie. 'It is time.'

Faintly, like far-off thunder rumbling across the gorge, Ti Reine heard the sound of the drums begin, the call to assemble for the *Petro* sacrifice. It was a sound she had never forgotten and it was the reason she had come. To answer the summons to the sacred Voudou mountain. 'I must go with you,' she said to the young woman.

A questioning glance passed between Celie and her daughter, and then Celie nodded.

Without another word, Ti Reine followed the young woman into the hastening gloom.

Standing outside Sylvie's door, Galen heard the clock strike six but time had lost all meaning. Is it possible, she wondered numbly, that only this morning we were in New York? Can it be possible that David has been gone only six days? Can a normal life change so catastrophically in so short a time? Hers, Katy's, Sylvie's, Edie's, David's? She suddenly felt without substance. As if the smallest eddy of wind could blow her away.

'Are you all right, Dr Wickliffe?' If Dr Walsh hadn't reached out to hold her up she would have collapsed.

'I'm all right. It's just that I can't believe that Sylvie Valois is dead. That we couldn't save her.'

'I know. But we tried our damnedest. We did the best we could.' He sighed.

She looked at him hard. 'Did we?'

'You are a cardiologist, Dr Wickliffe,' he said quietly.

'I am a simple country doctor. You should know the answer to that question better than I.' He sounded very tired. But he was right. Galen knew that they had done their best. 'Did you ever treat Sylvie Valois before?'

He shook his head.

Somehow Galen wasn't surprised. Dr Walsh was a good, a competent physician. Had Sylvie been his patient he never would have left her here at Shadow Hill in her condition. But what difference did it make now? Sylvie was dead. The only question left unanswered was why. What had happened to her?

The bedroom door opened and Adrien motioned them inside.

Galen went in. How much despair can the human mind stand, she wondered, staring at the still form of her friend, lying lifeless in the middle of the canopied bed. At some point is there mental meltdown? Can grief become so overwhelming that the brain simply stops functioning, leaving the body to continue on alone? Was that happening to her now?

And then she remembered Edie. Dear God, what was she going to say to Edie?

Maybe you shouldn't say anything at all, she thought suddenly. Maybe you ought to take the girls back to New York right now, tonight. Wait until you have her safely away from here before you tell her anything. And all at once she was desperate to talk to Jeremy, hear the sound of his voice, understanding, telling her what to do.

Dimly she heard the sound of Ravel's voice, words without meaning. And then she heard Dr Walsh.

'Dr Wickliffe is the authority here, Monsieur Ravel,' he was saying. 'I defer to her.'

'Well?' Ravel asked. 'Why did she die?'

The question was not unexpected. It was the way he asked it that brought Galen up short. It was as if he was *mocking* her, and underneath her sadness and despair she felt a current of anger. 'I don't know, Monsieur Ravel,' she snapped. 'Perhaps you are in a better position to know the answer to that than I.'

For a moment Ravel stood motionless. Then he turned and walked slowly across the room to stand looking down at Sylvie's body. 'I suppose we would all like to know why,' he said.

'I certainly would,' Galen said, her tone still sharp. Adrien Ravel was a fool if he thought for one moment that there would be no autopsy. 'I have every intention of finding out what killed her.'

Ravel reached down and ran one finger along the curve of Sylvie's jaw. 'Do I understand correctly, Dr Wickliffe?' he asked softly. 'Are you suggesting that there should be an inquiry?' Now his tone was unmistakable. He *was* mocking her, daring her to challenge him. Did he possibly think she would back down?

'Make no mistake, Monsieur Ravel, there will most certainly be an autopsy,' she said quietly.

Ravel didn't look at Galen. Instead he bent over and kissed Sylvie on the lips. 'Poor darling,' he said, shaking his head. 'I'm afraid we must do as Dr Wickliffe says. She is, after all, the expert. Wouldn't you agree, Dr Walsh?'

'I would.'

'Then so be it.' Ravel turned to meet Galen's stare, his eyes brilliant in their intensity.

Galen was shocked. Incredibly Adrien Ravel had the look of a man who was well pleased.

Chapter Twenty

Please God, don't let them find us. Please God.

Katy's legs had begun to tingle and she moved them a fraction of an inch. Just enough to keep them from going to sleep altogether.

For a long time she and Edie stayed huddled together, afraid to move at all. Because *they* had never gone away. They were doing something to one of the graves, but what, Katy had no idea. She could hear the scraping sound of stone on stone, hear the terrible rasping of their breathing, hear their footsteps shuffling across the gravel.

And then there was a long agonizing time when there was no sound at all, but she and Edie were both still too terrified to look. Minutes dragged by and finally Edie moved. Inch by inch, on her hands and knees, she crawled over to the corner of the mausoleum and peeked around, then motioned for Katy to follow.

'Let's get out of here,' Edie whispered. 'They are nowhere in sight. Let's run while we still can.'

Warily, Katy got to her feet, and together she and Edie edged around the mausoleum until they could see the path that led into the swamp. Then Edie grabbed Katy's hand and they fled, feet barely touching the ground, back the way they had come, into the deepening shadows of the marshland.

It's a trick, Katy thought as she ran. They are hiding out there somewhere, waiting for us! When we show up they are going to catch us!

Stumbling over roots, crashing through the under- brush, sometimes ankle-deep in mucky water, they ran on, not knowing whether they were going in the right direction, knowing only that they had to get away.

Once Katy lost her footing and fell, but Edie pulled her to her feet. 'We have to keep going,' she said, panting hard. 'We're almost there.'

But they weren't almost there. Katy didn't know *where* they were. Panic-stricken, she just kept follow- ing until suddenly Edie stopped.

'What . . . what's the matter?' Katy whispered, try- ing to catch her breath.

'We're lost,' Edie moaned and sank down on a slip- pery tree root.

'Lost?' Katy blinked. She looked around. The shad- ows had lengthened and now the marsh seemed even more threatening, its trees closing tight together, making it impossible to see through their tangled branches. Not only that, but from where she stood she could make out very little dry ground. Only dark pools of stagnant water that gave off the foul rotten smell that made Katy's stomach turn. She felt hot tears sting her eyes and impatiently she brushed them away. She couldn't behave like a baby. It wasn't going to do them any good at all. She was terrified, but so was Edie. 'What . . . what do we do now?' she stammered.

Edie's own eyes were full of tears. She shook her head. 'I don't know.'

Katy sat down beside her. 'If we stay where we are, will they find us?'

Edie hesitated for a minute. 'Who do you mean, *they*?'

That question startled Katy. 'I meant my mother or Monsieur Ravel. I wasn't even thinking about the zombies.' She began to tremble. 'They *were* zombies, weren't they?'

Edie shuddered. 'They were.'

'Do you think they are looking for us? Do you?'

Edie glanced nervously over her shoulder. 'I think we'd better try to find our way out of here.'

Katy jumped to her feet. Now she was really scared. 'Me, too. But which way do we go?'

Edie stood up. 'I don't know.'

Katy felt another surge of panic but she forced herself to stay calm. 'I think we have to keep moving, Edie,' she said gravely. 'We have to try to find our way out of here now. Before it gets any darker.'

For a minute they looked hard at each other. Then Edie took a few hesitant steps forward, changed her mind, reversed direction.

Katy sucked in her breath and followed.

They hadn't gone a hundred yards when suddenly they heard something way off in the distance. The sound of a siren wailing. Like a police car or an ambulance. 'We're saved!' Edie shouted. 'If we go toward the sound we'll find the road, and then we'll be saved.'

Together they began to run.

Dreaded butchery.

No hope to live, not even as a zombie. Two days, Adrien had said. If I do not bring you back within two days' time you will die anyway. One way or the other, certain death.

But if they butcher me, where will they cut me first? And which of their hideous incisions will kill me?

Not that it mattered. Sylvie knew she would feel all of them. Every single one. Right to the last.

Even as she had felt the gentle touch of Galen's lips brushing her cheek.

Even as she had felt the silken sheet being drawn up to cover her face.

But why had Galen allowed them to take her away?

And where was Edie? Was she never to hear her child's voice again?

She knew that the answer was no.

But my blood is still pumping through my veins! My mind is still intact! I am alive!

But no one knows. And they never will *until they have killed me*!

She had felt them lift her from her bed, strap her onto the stretcher, carry her down the stairs. She had felt the rush of fresh air just before they placed her in the back of the ambulance. And just before they slammed the door shut, she heard Adrien whisper. 'Goodbye, dear Sylvie. Sweet dreams.' And then she had heard the engine start.

In any other circumstance she would have been ecstatic to be leaving Shadow Hill for ever. Ecstatic – if it hadn't been for the terrible dread of what was coming.

And now she was being borne away, and there was nothing to do but wait.

As they drove from Shadow Hill, Sylvie was suddenly aware of what it would be like to be waiting in a cell on death row. Except that she couldn't beg for forgiveness or cry out for compassion or pray for a reprieve. She could do nothing but lie silent, her mind trapped inside her own skull.

Unable to endure the horror another moment she fled into memory. She thought about Galen, her friend, her anchor. Why had Galen failed her? Why couldn't she see that Sylvie still lived? Galen was a doctor, a heart specialist – didn't she know that Sylvie's heart was still beating?

And what about David? Where was he? Back in his lab in New York, working? If only Sylvie could see him, tell him about Adrien's private storehouse of knowledge. If only he knew what secrets Adrien Ravel possessed. Oh David, she thought sadly, if only you knew.

And Edie, her poor pathetic child. Who would care for her now? Would Galen? Would they all leave Shadow Hill today and fly back to safety?

Please Galen, take Edie home.

Please God, let me sleep.

And as the vehicle rumbled east, carrying her towards certain death, her prayer to God was answered. She fell into deep dreamless oblivion.

Numb with grief, Galen stood alone on the verandah and watched until the ambulance disappeared over the bridge. She still couldn't believe that Sylvie had died, but she had, and Galen had to find out why. Somehow she had to get in touch with Jeremy.

But first things first. Right now Galen had to figure out how to tell Edie. Her first instinct had been to find Edie immediately, tell her that her mother had died, bring her to Sylvie's side, and let her say goodbye. But after a moment's thought she had changed her mind. She needed time to talk to Edie, prepare her for this devastation, and time was not something she had much of. The medics had said that if they were to take Sylvie's body all the way to New Orleans, they had to leave Shadow Hill as soon as possible.

Galen had stood beside Sylvie's bed, looking at the still, lifeless face of her friend. And then she had looked over at Adrien Ravel. His face was a steel mask once again, but there was something in his eyes that still angered her. Amusement? Mockery? Or was it something more? Did he know how Sylvie had died? Had he poisoned her? And if he had, did he know that the traces would disappear with time? Was that why he wasn't concerned about an autopsy? Did he think that Galen would keep the body here until Edie was told? Would that delay make the difference between proving his innocence or his guilt?

She had made the decision. Take the body now, she had said. She had watched while they covered Sylvie with a sheet, lifted her onto the stretcher, wheeled her out. She is dead, Galen had thought, but why? Hearts of thirty-eight-year-old people in good health didn't just stop. But had Sylvie truly been in good health? Or had there been something wrong with her all the time?

The sound of footsteps behind her brought Galen back to the present. A servant had come through the front door. 'Monsieur Ravel would like to see you,' he said.

'Not now,' Galen answered sharply. 'Monsieur Ravel will have to wait.' She took a deep breath. There was no way she wanted to see Adrien Ravel now. Her only concern was to think of a way to break the news to Edie. Prepare her first, then break the news.

Heartsick, she turned and went back inside the house. How can this have happened? she wondered dully. How can our lives, so normal only a few weeks ago, have become so fragmented, shattered into a million pieces?

She headed across the hall and started up the stairs. She knew she couldn't call Jeremy. They had both agreed that it would be a fatal mistake if Ravel were to discover that she knew him. Not that it mattered any more. It was over now. The only thing left to do was to find out why Sylvie had died. Then she would go home.

Galen supposed she ought to call the hospital again, see how Jonas was. Not that there was much point in talking to him now. If he is able to talk, she thought grimly, I can knock him flat again by telling him that Sylvie has died.

And what about Ti Reine? She should be notified, poor old woman. Galen remembered what she had said, how confident she had been that she had fixed everything – and how foolish, how mistaken. But that was then. This was now. Someone would still have to tell her.

But first you have to tell Edie.

'Right,' she whispered to herself. 'First I have to tell Edie.' A hellish task with one saving grace. At least Edie would not have to stay here at Shadow Hill. Tomorrow they would all go home together.

Slowly, bone-tired, she walked down the deserted hallway. No sign of a servant and, thank goodness, no sign of Adrien Ravel. She hoped she would never have to see him again.

Somewhere far down the corridor she heard the tinging of a clock. Seven bells. Impossible. She glanced at her watch. It *was* seven o'clock. They had been at Shadow Hill only five hours. The nightmare of a lifetime crammed into five short hours. No matter what, she thought miserably, the next five hours can never possibly be as bad.

Just outside Katy's bedroom she paused. Oh God, give me strength. Somehow let me help Edie get through this new nightmare in one piece. She opened the door.

The room was empty. Impossible. When she left them she had told them to stay put. Even if she hadn't, they were far too nervous to go anywhere. 'Katy? Edie?'

No answer.

Oh my God, where are they?

She was about to go back into the corridor and scream for help when her eye caught a sudden movement across the room. A breeze from outside had stirred the curtains, and Galen realized that the doors leading out onto the upper gallery were open.

She rushed out and leaned over the railing. 'Katy!' she shouted. 'Edie!' A wave of panic hit her. Where the hell were they?

And as she scanned the horizon, far off in the distance, across the bridge, she saw a flicker of movement. Someone was coming. *Oh please God, let it be the girls.*

And it was. Edie and Katy came flying up the gravel drive and across the lawn as if something from hell was snapping at their heels.

Galen ran the length of the gallery and down the stairs to meet them.

*   *   *

They're going to catch me! Katy thought wildly. The zombies are going to catch me! She could feel their hot steaming breath on her back but she was running as fast as she could. In front of her the only thing she could see was the back of Edie's legs, her sneakers kicking pieces of gravel up into the air. 'They're coming!' Katy gasped. 'They're going to get me!'

And then they were off the driveway and across the lawn, but still Katy didn't dare look back. She knew they were right behind her, *gaining on her with every step*. Panic-driven, tears stinging her eyes, she flew across the grass, and at the very last instant, just as she was about to be grabbed from behind, she saw her mother running, arms outstretched to save them.

And save them she did.

When, from the shelter of her mother's arms, Katy finally dared to look around, no one, *nothing* was there.

Chapter Twenty-One

Katy was terrified. Kneeling in the grass beside her, Galen could feel her shivering. And the child couldn't talk fast enough. The words just tumbled out of her mouth, all mixed up together. 'Mom you know that painting you know the one in his office it was them it was them it was them the zombies.'

Galen hugged her tight. 'Hush, sweetie. Slow down.' Oh God, she thought, what fresh hell is this? She stood up, pulling Katy with her. 'Let's go inside and you two can tell me everything.'

'We'd better hurry,' Katy said, throwing a fearful glance over her shoulder. 'If we stay out here until dark they'll get us for sure.'

As for Edie, Galen could see that she was just as shaken as Katy. 'We really saw them,' Edie mumbled, shivering as they went. 'We really did. Wait until you hear. Shadow Hill is everything I was afraid it would be. Oh, I'm so scared. We have to get away from this place. We have to get my mother and get out of here.'

They didn't go through the front door. The last thing Galen wanted was to run into Adrien Ravel. Quickly she led them back up the stairs to the upper gallery and once inside the room Galen closed the double doors and locked them.

It wasn't until the three had settled themselves on the sofa that the colour began to creep back into Katy's cheeks, but for several moments no one spoke. Finally Galen said, 'First, are either of you two hungry? It's after seven, you know.'

They both shook their heads. 'I don't think I'll ever eat again,' Katy said fiercely. 'I was that scared.'

Galen looked from Edie to Katy and back. Clearly both girls had been badly frightened, but by what? The best course of action, she decided, was to hear them out. Then she'd know what and how much to tell Edie about her mother. If anything at all. Perhaps she would even wait until morning, until Edie had a chance to recover from this fright. 'Okay,' she said softly. 'Let's hear it. What happened?'

It was a story that under normal circumstances Galen would have dismissed as impossible. Zombies? Never. If she were back in New York she would have chalked it up to the ghoulish imaginings of two very vulnerable children. But not here. At Shadow Hill the real world seemed very far away. Galen found herself actually considering the worst – that the story about the zombies could be true.

Remember what Jeremy told you, Galen thought. At Shadow Hill with Adrien Ravel, *nothing* is impossible. She shivered. It wasn't cold in the room. The chill was in her bones.

As the ghastly tale unfolded, Galen's mind raced back to other stories, stories David had told her about Sylvie's cousin, about rumours that Eveline Carne hadn't really died. That she was a zombie. Sylvie had laughed when she told David about it. Galen had laughed when David repeated it. They had all considered it ridiculous. But sitting here on the sofa at Shadow Hill it didn't seem funny any more. Was it possible that one of the creatures Edie and Katy had seen was Eveline Carne?

And then Galen remembered Sylvie's own description of Adrien Ravel: *a high priest in some secret Voudou cult.*

And Jonas. *I hated Ravel from the first moment I saw him . . . He frightens me. Just looking at him made me feel like I was alone in a Haitian jungle. I could almost hear the Voudou drums. Frankly I think he's a madman. But a brilliant madman. There's something truly evil about him, Galen, truly evil.*

Truly evil.

Truly evil.

And putting all those stories together with what Jeremy had told her made Galen weak with fear. What *had* the girls seen?

Wide-eyed, Katy moved closer. 'What's the matter, Mom?'

Galen shook her head. 'Nothing, Katy. It's just a scary story, that's all.'

'Do you . . . do you believe us?' Edie asked.

Galen couldn't answer. She had to clear her mind first, try to make some sense of this.

'Tell her what you told me before,' Katy whispered to Edie.

Edie shook her head.

'You *have* to,' Katy pressed. 'The stuff about Monsieur Ravel. About being a *bocor*.'

Galen took Edie's hand. 'Don't be afraid. I need to know.'

'It's . . . it's about the painting,' Edie said in a hushed tone, 'the one downstairs in his office.'

Galen nodded. 'I know the one.'

'I saw it once before. In a book about the dark side of Voudou, about sorcery, and Ti Reine told me then that it was an evil thing. A painting of corpses walking in the sunlight. Zombies. She said that only a *bocor* would own such a painting.'

'What's a *bocor*?' Galen asked with a sinking feeling. 'Something to do with Voudou?'

Edie nodded. 'A *bocor* is an evil sorcerer. He uses black magic to control people's minds. Sometimes even to kill them.' Her voice grew faint. 'And he has the power to bring people back from the dead, turn them into zombies.'

A wave of horror swept over Galen. Too close to what Jeremy had told her. Too many pieces falling into place. 'How do you know this, Edie?'

'Ti Reine was my teacher. There is nothing Ti Reine doesn't know about Voudou. Both the good and the evil.' Edie's voice cracked. 'If Ti Reine were here she would know how to stop Adrien Ravel. But she's not, so we have to get away. We have to get my mother and get away.'

Get my mother and get away. Oh, Jesus. Filled with a new sense of desperation, Galen leaned her head back against the sofa and closed her eyes. What the hell am I going to do?

And the answer came in a rush. Do just what Edie says. Get the hell out of here now. Take Katy and Edie and go. Now. Tonight. What are you waiting for? For Adrien Ravel to trap you? To kill you? Don't tell Edie about her mother. Don't answer any questions. Just go. To the airport. To Jeremy's. Any place safe. Now is not the time to deal with Sylvie's death or zombies or anything else. Now is the time to run!

In a sudden burst of energy Galen sprang off the couch. 'You two wait right here. Don't you move. Don't answer the door. And for God's sake, don't go looking for Mingo. I'll be right back.'

*   *   *

Galen opened the door to the library. Adrien Ravel was sitting on the far side of the room in front of a low fire, sipping brandy from a crystal snifter. 'You wanted to see me?' she asked.

Slowly he looked over at her. His face was a bronze sculpture. Cold. Utterly disinterested. As if she were a wisp of dust blowing across the floor. 'I did. Before. Not any more.' He turned away to stare once again into the fire.

'There is no longer any reason for us to remain here at Shadow Hill,' Galen said curtly. 'The girls and I have packed our things. We will be leaving tonight. As soon as you can arrange transport into the city.'

He shrugged. 'As you wish.'

Galen felt a powerful rush of relief. Not that she had expected resistance – she knew that Adrien Ravel would be only too happy to see her go. She also knew that getting out of here within the hour was only the first step in their flight from an incredible nightmare. She still had to tell Edie about her mother, but she would do that later.

She turned away and was almost to the door when she heard him speak. 'Whenever you are ready, you and your daughter will find my driver waiting outside.'

'Fine,' Galen said.

'You know, of course, that Mademoiselle Valois will be staying here.'

Galen stopped in her tracks. His words were so ridiculous that she almost laughed out loud. The man *is* mad, she thought, slowly turning back to stare at him. He is absolutely mad. 'I beg your pardon?'

'Edie will be staying here at Shadow Hill.'

Keep calm, Galen told herself. No point in exploding. Just tell him like it is. Then get the hell out. 'I am afraid you are mistaken, Monsieur. Edie won't be staying here,' she said coolly, shaking her head. 'By the terms of Sylvie's will, I am Edie's legal guardian. I am taking her back to New York.'

Ravel swivelled his head around and returned her stare with one so scorching that she felt her cheeks burn. 'I am afraid *you* are the one who is mistaken, Dr Wickliffe. By the terms of my wife's will, signed and witnessed here at Shadow Hill, I am Edie's legal guardian. And it is my wish that she remain here with me.'

The room grew deathly still. The only sound was the hammering of her own heart. Galen stood thunderstruck. This could not be true. She dug her fingernails into the palms of her hands until she drew blood. *This can not be true!*

A faint smile appeared at the corners of Ravel's mouth. 'I see I have taken you by surprise,' he said softly. He stood up, picked up something from the library table, and crossed the room to stand in front of her. He held out the folded document.

For a moment Galen stood transfixed. Then, trembling with disbelief and a sense of absolute outrage, she reached out and snatched it from his hand. Through a red haze she read it. The last will and testament of Sylvie Valois Ravel. It was brief and to the point. In the event of Sylvie's death, Adrien Ravel was to be Edie's guardian!

Struck dumb by what she had just read, Galen stared down at the paper in her hand. Was there anything, *anything* in this world, in her wildest imagination, in her worst nightmares to equal this? Now her mind was racing out of control. Was sanity about to leave her?

But no. At the last moment, at the very edge she pulled back. If Galen had learned anything in the course of practising medicine, from years of dealing with other people's pain and death and horror, she had learned how to pull back. How to survive. First rule: never lose control.

Slowly she looked up. Ravel was watching her with his usual air of detachment, but this time it was tempered by a spark of curiosity. He wanted to see how she would react. To see if he had destroyed her defences.

She took a deep breath and handed him the will. 'If this was Sylvie's wish, then so be it.' Her voice was as detached as his had been. 'However, since Edie won't be coming back to New York with us, I'm afraid we are back to square one. She still needs a competent physician, one who knows her history. Especially now that her mother is gone. So Katy and I won't be needing transport into New Orleans tonight. In the morning I will have to go into the city and make some appointments.' She started to turn, then paused. 'I would appreciate it if you would arrange to have a plate of sandwiches sent to my room. The girls haven't eaten anything since noon and I'm sure they are hungry. As for me, I'd like a large pot of coffee.'

He looked surprised, as if he had expected something more from her than this. Certainly not this quiet calm. He nodded.

'And one more thing,' she said. 'I haven't told Edie yet about her mother and I would prefer to wait until morning, until she has rested. I'm sure you can understand. She is a very fragile child. This is going to be very difficult for her.'

He shrugged, then turned away. Galen had been dismissed. He went back to his chair by the fire.

As she watched him, a thought came suddenly into her head that in its savagery shocked her: I am a doctor, but if I could kill you right now, Adrien Ravel, no matter how cruel or inhuman the method, I would do so without a moment's hesitation.

Katy and Edie crawled into Galen's bed and within minutes fell into a sound sleep. But Galen sat where she was, sipping coffee to help her stay awake. Before she dared drag her body into bed she had to think this through, decide what her options were.

First, the most nagging question. Had the girls really seen human beings that were neither dead nor alive but trapped somewhere in between? Impossible for a doctor to believe such a thing – almost. In her profession Galen had seen incredible phenomena of science and equally incredible phenomena of nature, so why not this?

All right, she reasoned, suppose there is a drug that can destroy the will. Not hard to believe. She knew what toxins could do. So the notion that Adrien Ravel might possess a formula whereby he could control a human mind was not so preposterous. Hideous, diabolical, but not impossible. The concept of a creature, brain-drugged, robotic, was something Galen could accept.

But with that same creature, a zombie, it was what came *before* mind control that puzzled her most.

According to Edie, Voudouists believed that zombies were human beings who had died but had been brought back from the grave by an evil sorcerer, to live for ever trapped somewhere between the world of the living and the world of the dead.

So, Galen told herself, if a *bocor* decides to create a

zombie, he must first convince the world that the subject has died. He must place the victim in some kind of state of suspended animation and after everyone is convinced that he is dead, after they perform a mock burial, the *bocor* applies the antidote that revives the poor creature. In effect, he brings the dead man back from the grave, creating the illusion that he possesses supernatural power. In an unenlightened society, fear of the supernatural would make a *bocor* invincible.

But as Galen thought about it, there was more here to fear than the supernatural. A *bocor* would have to possess an incredible knowledge of toxins and their effect on the human body.

Was Adrien Ravel such a man?

Had Adrien Ravel created such creatures? Zombies, incapable of thought? Human beings that lived on even though medical science had declared them dead?

Suddenly Galen was stricken with the most horrible possibility of all. Had Adrien Ravel intended to use Sylvie for such a hideous purpose? Could it be possible that Sylvie was still alive?

She felt a wave of nausea. No, she thought wildly. Impossible! If Ravel had had any such intention, he would never have allowed Sylvie's body to be sent to New Orleans. *Would he?*

She stood up and began to pace from one side of the room to the other. 'Think,' she said, clenching her teeth. 'You are not stupid. Think. Is this possible?'

If Sylvie were still alive, paralysed, trapped inside a useless, motionless body, waiting for him to apply the antidote, why would Adrien Ravel not fight to keep her here? Why had he allowed Galen to make the decision that would most certainly kill Sylvie?

She answered her own question. Because whatever his original intention, now he is playing a game with you. You represent science that stretches toward the twenty-first century. You are the omniscient physician. You know everything knowable about the human body. And yet you could not save Sylvie. Nor do you know what killed her. You suspect Adrien Ravel and now you want to prove him guilty.

Galen moaned low in her throat. Dear God, this cannot be true, because if it is, in order to prove Adrien Ravel guilty, I have condemned Sylvie to certain death. And all the while, he sits back and watches, smiling to himself, knowing what he has accomplished, knowing that no twentieth-century physician would ever consider such a thing possible.

She sat down hard. But what if it is? *What if, inside that seemingly dead body, Sylvie is still alive?*

And she knew she had only one hope. Somehow she had to get away from this place, get to Jeremy before it was too late.

The moon was full, the air strangely still and cool. Ahead, the mountain was bathed in patches of light and dark. Black as pitch at the bottom of the gorge, three thousand feet below, almost day along the high mountain path where Ti Reine walked, following Celie's daughter.

They walked with a natural rhythm, as steady and unhurried as the sound of the drums that echoed through the ravines and up the side of the mountain to the very pinnacle. As always, the sound transported Ti Reine back to the jungles of her ancestors, to a world inhabited only by others like her, those who embraced the mysteries of Voudou.

217

Lanterns hanging in the trees along the way flickered and hissed as they passed, and ahead, in the middle of a plateau jutting out high above the valley floor, Ti Reine could see the circle of fire, throwing flames high into the air, the sacred *poto-mitan* in its centre.

A large number of people had already assembled, some standing, some sitting on the hard-packed ground, but all were silent, waiting for the ritual to commence. The blood sacrifice for which Ti Reine had come so far.

As they entered the outer circle the drums ceased and the chant began. 'Damballah Oueddo, we come.'

And it was then that Ti Reine saw him, the one person in the world who might help her. The most powerful *papaloi* of them all. The possessor of all ancient Voudou truths.

Papa Sudre.

Old beyond years, the man was unchanged. Tall, thin, his face smooth, unlined, his eyes hooded, unreadable like dark fathomless pools, he stepped from the shadow into the light, a blood-red turban wrapped around his head, his shoulders draped in a scarlet robe. With sacred cabalistic signs drawn in the dirt, he sealed the entrance to the inner circle. Then he turned and, holding the *ason* high above his head, he addressed the congregation. 'Where does the sun rise?'

The chorus of voices answered. 'It rises in the east.'

'And where does it set?'

'It sets in Guinea.'

'Guinea,' Ti Reine echoed. The only true name for the place of their origin. Mother Africa.

And then the procession began.

The large black bull draped in white, his horns wound tight with snake skin, was led in from the forest. The voices sang to him in wailing tones: 'Forgive us, O Lord. For what we are about to do, forgive us.'

The response was a terrified bellow from the throat of the bull, and Ti Reine, caught up in the current of frenzy, began to chant with the rest. 'Come to our aid, O Spirits. If sacrifice is demanded, we will obey.'

And like the rest of them, she was filled with fear. Like the rest, she prayed that the offering would be accepted, that the *loa* would be pleased. That they in turn would help their children.

And as the tide of fear rose up, Ti Reine felt it, became a part of it. Was what they were about to do enough? *Damballah, I am trying to find you. Is the road barred?*

And suddenly a young woman, a *mamaloi*, appeared beside Papa Sudre. She was dressed in the scarlet robe and headdress so familiar to Ti Reine, and she began to pray to Ezili for intercession. 'Will this beast please the mighty Damballah? Or must we find one without horns. A human beast.'

There was a low moan from the assembly.

And then the preparation for the sacrifice began.

A coffin-shaped trough was carried to the centre of the circle, set down before the dazed bull. Then came two women clothed all in white, carrying the sacred sword high above their heads. All was done quickly, without sound. Four strong men followed, each taking his place beside the straining bull, each laying his hands on the quivering hide, holding the bull in place.

Papa Sudre took the sword but before he could

raise his arm to complete the bloody ritual Ti Reine leaped forward into the inner circle. For a moment she stood eye-to-eye with the sacrificial bull. Then she turned and fell to her knees before Papa Sudre, spreading her arms in supplication, speaking to him in pure creole. 'The black bull is not enough,' she said strongly. 'The need for spiritual help is too great, the enemy too powerful. My family is sick. I have cried out, but the *loa* have not heard me. So in order to heal my family, I who am not sick *must die*.'

The *papaloi*'s face grew rigid and his eyes began to glow with an intense hypnotic fire. He stared through the eyes of Ti Reine and into her soul. And suddenly time stopped.

Nothing moved.

No sound.

And then solemnly Papa Sudre nodded. 'Damballah calls you.'

He raised the sword in both hands and placed its tip against Ti Reine's throat. And in the next instant he whirled around and plunged the blade deep into the heart of the bull.

An anguished bellow split the air and the bull sagged, but the men held it upright.

From the shadow came the young *mamaloi*. She rushed forward and without a word handed the large wooden bowl to Ti Reine.

Ti Reine turned and caught the spurting river of blood, filling the bowl to overflowing, transferring its contents to the common trough.

In a frenzy of ecstasy the crowd surged forward, leaping, dancing, pressing into the centre, finally drinking of the sacrificial blood.

And Ti Reine, still kneeling, knew that the *loa* had

finally heard. She had offered herself to them on the altar and the offer had been refused. They had diverted Papa Sudre's hand.

But what did it mean? It meant that the *loa* had decided; the battle lines were drawn. Ti Reine would have to meet Adrien Ravel, face to face.

For better or worse, a fight to the end.

Chapter Twenty-Two

'I want to see my mother!' The scream of a wounded animal. Tears streaming down her cheeks, Edie ran. 'You can't stop me,' she shrieked at Galen. 'Nobody can. If it's the last thing I ever do I'm going to see her before they cut her to ribbons!' She threw the bedroom door open and raced down the corridor, screaming for Adrien Ravel to help her.

Galen flew after her but before she could catch her, Ravel appeared at the top of the stairs.

Edie threw herself, sobbing, into his arms. 'Please, Monsieur Ravel,' she choked. 'Help me! My mother is dead and Dr Wickliffe sent her away before I had a chance to say goodbye!' She was almost incoherent with grief and rage, but Galen heard her next words clearly. 'Dr Wickliffe has destroyed me. She has allowed my mother to die.'

Galen stood where she was, staring helplessly. 'I had no idea this would happen,' she whispered, spreading her hands in a gesture of absolute disbelief.

Over the top of Edie's head, she saw Ravel smile. *This is exactly what he had hoped for. My destruction.*

'I think Dr Wickliffe has done you a terrible injury, Edie,' he said softly.

'Please. I have nowhere else to turn,' Edie pleaded, looking up at him, her lovely face bathed in tears. 'I have to see my mother. Do you understand? Will you help me?'

'Most assuredly.' He glanced over at Galen, a look of triumph on his face. 'Had it been my choice I would have kept your poor mother here for a quiet dignified burial. But Dr Wickliffe decided otherwise. She sent your mother away without a moment's hesitation.' Gently he ran his hand along the side of Edie's cheek. 'Dry those tears, *ma chère*. I would take you myself this morning but time will not permit it. Instead I will see that my driver delivers you to see your mother without delay. He will wait until you have said your farewells, and then he will deliver you safely back to Shadow Hill.'

Watching his performance, Galen stifled a violent urge to rush to Edie's side and pull her away. 'Am I to be allowed to go with her?' she asked, heart hammering.

'No. My driver will take you and your daughter to the airport. I don't believe you have any further reason to stay here. Unless, of course, Edie thinks otherwise.'

'I have no wish to have anything to do with Dr Wickliffe,' Edie said vehemently. She turned to stare at Galen. 'I will never forgive you for what you have done.' Then she turned and walked back to her room, closing the door firmly behind her.

Thirty minutes later Galen and Katy left the house and headed for the car. The morning was cool, but Galen's face was burning. Dear God, please let this be over. Please let us leave this place safely and never have to come back.

With Katy close beside her she opened the car door. Katy slid in. Then Galen. Edie was already there, huddled in the corner next to the window.

'Edie,' Galen said softly, feeling the tears sting her eyes.

Edie didn't look at her. Instead she kept her eyes fixed on Adrien Ravel who was standing at the edge of the verandah.

The driver received his last instructions, then got in and started the engine. Slowly they went down the driveway to the little bridge, crossed over, and within minutes Shadow Hill had disappeared in the distance.

Time passed in stony silence.

And then, without moving her body, without turning her head, Galen reached past Katy and took Edie's hand. She squeezed. Good work, Edie, you poor baby. A brilliant performance so far.

Edie didn't turn. She kept her eyes averted, staring out at the passing landscape. But she returned Galen's squeeze. No words were exchanged. They didn't dare speak to each other. Without question Adrien Ravel had ordered the driver to listen to everything that was said, and not to let Edie out of his sight. But once we make it to our final destination, Galen thought grimly, this man will never see any of us again.

Drained of what little strength she had left, Galen closed her eyes. All through the night she had agonized about what to do. And about how many of her fears should be shared with Edie and Katy. Just before dawn she had wakened Edie, leaving Katy to sleep. And she had told Edie what had happened to her mother.

Edie had reacted exactly as Galen had known she would. Grief-stricken, lost, bewildered. And then angry. Why? she had gasped. Why had her mother died? Why hadn't Galen saved her?

Galen told her everything. About Adrien Ravel.

About what she feared he had done. About how she was going to try to stop the worst, the autopsy, from happening. About how maybe Sylvie was really still alive.

Edie had listened to it all without making a sound, the only evidence of pain the familiar tensing of her muscles. She listened to everything Galen had to say. And at the end she simply nodded. 'My mother may still be alive,' she said gravely. 'I know that zombies are real. The problem is . . . ' she began to tremble violently ' . . . do you know how to bring her back?'

'No, Edie. I don't. But maybe someone might.'

Edie began to cry. 'Adrien Ravel does.'

And then for a long time Galen sat with Edie, rocking her in her arms, trying to soothe her. But with each passing hour, Galen knew that time was running out, and she still had to tell Edie the rest: that by the terms of her mother's will Edie was to remain here at Shadow Hill.

It was almost dawn when Galen finally told her, but not before she had the plan for escape all worked out in her mind. First they had to convince Ravel that Edie was devastated by what Galen had done, hated her for it, and that she was desperate to see her mother one last time. But would he allow it? No. Not unless he thought it would serve some sadistic purpose. Would seeing Galen accused, dismissed as Edie's doctor, be enough? It was their only hope.

'Whatever happens,' Galen said, 'we have to get away from here. And if we do, I'm going to take you back to New York with me. If we have to hide for the rest of our lives, so be it. We are never ever coming back to Shadow Hill again.'

Adrien Ravel had taken the bait. He had allowed

Edie to go. Step one. Now Galen had to call Jeremy, get him to stop the autopsy. And then what? Galen didn't know.

In what seemed an endless ride in silence they finally arrived at the airport. Without a word to Edie, Galen and Katy got out of the car. They stood on the sidewalk and watched until the Mercedes had disappeared. Then Galen found a phone and placed a desperate call to Jeremy Calder.

Somewhere she could hear the ticking of a clock, but beyond that, nothing.

Thoughts came and went. Slowly, more slowly, slowest, like circles made by a spinning top whose end was near. Winding down, wobbling, ready to fall over. Knowing that once it fell it would never spin again.

Is this, Sylvie wondered, what comes just before death?

Time passed but her mind wouldn't click off. Was it morning or was it night? Would they begin their dissection soon?

No matter. In two days' time, autopsy or not, she would be dead. No matter what. Adrien had told her and she knew it was true. For Sylvie there would be no stay of execution.

As a last resort, she turned her mind to God. If she prayed, would He answer? Was there such a Being? She had never been sure. If there was a God, why was He doing this to her? Could there be a worse ending to life than this? Sylvie had not been a perfect human being. There had been indiscretions, petty things she had done that she was not proud of. But did anything she had ever done or not done in her life merit *this*?

And finally, if there is a God, she wondered, could Adrien possibly be his instrument?

Never. In the most vile universe imaginable, no God could ever be so monstrous as to make Adrien Ravel His instrument.

Then there can be no God, she concluded dully. The very existence of Adrien Ravel is proof of that. No God would ever permit Ravel to continue to exist.

Her thoughts went from grey to black. The terror which, like a dark shadow, had trailed her for what seemed an eternity now was dwarfed by a new emotion, one that was far more devastating. A black, numbing despair. Her mind could stand no more. *I have felt the wind of the wing of madness.*

The thing that was her brain finally clicked off. Goodbye. She fell into blessed unconsciousness.

The clock on the wall ticked on.

Galen felt a sick wave of remembrance. Six days ago this was where she had stood when she had come to identify David. Only six days ago.

The autopsy technician opened the door and stepped inside, throwing a curious look in Galen's direction. In fact, everyone in the building was going berserk because of Galen. And because of one good man named Jeremy Calder. While Galen stood guard over Sylvie's body, Jeremy had managed to get her transferred to the Charity Hospital. It had taken him a dozen phone calls and an awful lot of string pulling but he had finally succeeded. Sylvie would be transferred as soon as the people in charge here could get the mess of paperwork cleared up.

The technician cleared his throat. 'Excuse me, are you Dr Wickliffe?'

Galen nodded.

'Dr Calder phoned. Said to tell you he's been called into emergency surgery. Can't be at the hospital when you arrive with . . . with her.' He pointed. 'But he's spoken to Dr Tyron who has agreed to examine her, get her set up. Dr Calder will be there as soon as he can.'

Galen nodded. Thank God for Jeremy.

The technician was still pointing at Sylvie. 'You really think she's still alive?'

Galen didn't answer. 'Would you tell her daughter to come in?'

'Sure.' With a last look of disbelief he left the room.

As soon as Edie came in, Galen moved quickly to the autopsy table and pulled back the sheet. 'Sylvie,' she said, her voice trembling, 'if you can hear me, I want you to know that we're going to try. If you are alive we're going to do everything we can to save you.' She stepped to one side and motioned for Edie to come close.

'Mother.' A broken sob of anguish, and Edie lay her head down on Sylvie's chest, put her arms around her mother's motionless body. 'I can't hear your heart beating, but I know you're alive. I just know it. And somehow we're going to bring you back.'

And she wept.

Sylvie heard a voice and in her mind she knew she had crossed the line between sanity and madness, and now for her the thought of death was welcome. When one is mad what else is there?

Yet the voice seemed so precious, so achingly familiar. The gentle weight of a child's head against her chest, the arms around her, the tears on her cheek, so real. *Was* someone here in the room with her?

And then she heard the voice again. The sweet anguished voice of her own child. *Edie*.

Incredibly, Sylvie heard her whisper. 'They are going to take you to the hospital now, Mother, so I have to go.'

The weight on her chest was lifted, the arms withdrawn, and yet somehow, astonishingly, Sylvie knew that Edie was still there, standing beside her.

Then a second voice, terse, commanding: Galen. 'Lift her carefully, for God's sake.'

Sylvie felt hands on her shoulders, under her legs, lifting. Could this be true, or had she indeed crossed over that line into madness? She didn't know, but she didn't care either. If she *was* insane, this sweet lunacy brought with it an illusion of hope. Whether they were really taking her to a hospital or not didn't matter because in this strange new world of dementia, she *believed*. And she *hoped*.

She felt the gurney move, heard Galen's voice one last time. 'Come on, girls,' Galen said sharply. 'Try not to be seen. We are all going in the ambulance with Sylvie.'

Chapter Twenty-Three

'What do you think?' Katy whispered, unable to keep her voice from quavering. She was in the ambulance, squeezed in between her mother and Edie. 'Is she . . . is she still alive?'

'She is. I just know it,' Edie choked. She had finally stopped crying but her face was still tear-streaked. 'The question is, can anyone save her?'

'Mom?' Katy took her mother's hand. 'Can you?'

'I don't know, Katy. I'm in way over my head. But I'm going to try and so is Dr Calder. I'm just not sure we have enough time.'

The ambulance began to move. It stopped at the corner and waited for the light to turn green. 'How come the siren isn't on?' Katy asked.

'I don't want him to see us.' Galen pointed out the window. Monsieur Ravel's driver was standing on the steps in front of the building, waiting for Edie.

Katy turned to Edie. 'What's going to happen when you don't come out?'

'He'll come in looking for me.' Edie shivered. 'And they'll tell him they don't know where I went, because they don't.'

'Somehow he's going to find out,' Katy said darkly. 'Monsieur Ravel knows everything. I think he's going to search everywhere for you. He's going to look under every rock, behind every bush. He's not going to give up until he succeeds.'

'He isn't going to find anyone,' her mother cut in sharply. 'I'm going to make sure of that. The first thing I'm going to do when we get to the hospital is to put you two in a cab. Send you where you'll be safe. And then I can concentrate on Sylvie.'

Edie stiffened. 'I'm not leaving my mother.'

'You have to, Edie. I can't leave you two alone, and you can't be with me while I'm working.'

'But . . . but where will we go?' Katy stammered.

'Besides Dr Calder, there's only one person in this city who I know will keep you out of harm's way.'

'Who?' Katy whispered but somehow she already knew, and she winced when she heard the name.

'Ti Reine,' Galen said.

Unlike Katy, Edie's face lit up. 'Why didn't I think of her? I am so afraid of Adrien Ravel. If anyone knows what to do it will be Ti Reine.'

'But . . . but why do *I* have to go, Mom?' Katy quavered. 'Can't I stay with you?'

'No, you can't. If you two are going to be safe from Adrien Ravel you cannot stay at the hospital. You were right, Katy. By now he knows that Edie has disappeared. And it isn't going to take him long to find out that Sylvie has been transferred. And then he'll come to New Orleans himself. I want you both safely tucked away before he gets here.' She put her arm around Katy's shoulders. 'Ti Reine is a good woman, Katy. She would never let any harm come to you. And as soon as I can, I'll come for you.'

'This is the best thing, Katydid,' Edie said, and for the first time since they left New York Katy could hear a little bit of hope in her voice. 'Ti Reine will help us. She can do *anything*. She will speak to the *loa* and they will save my mother.'

Katy slumped back against the seat, her heart thumping. She knew her mother was right, that Monsieur Ravel would come looking for Edie. But sending them to Ti Reine? Even *before* this nightmare began Katy had been afraid of her. Now she had to go to the *mamaloi*'s house. The place where she did all her Voudou magic, with no one but Edie to protect her. 'I . . . I wish we were going home,' she whispered.

'We will be soon.' Galen hugged her tight. 'As soon as we know about Sylvie, we'll go home.'

Still unconvinced, Katy nodded. Sure, she thought. If Monsieur Ravel and his zombies don't get us first.

Galen watched while Dr Tyron checked Sylvie's pupils.

'Get the EKG hooked up,' he said to an assistant. 'I need a print-out. And get a tube in her.' He looked over at Galen. 'Any epinephrine administered? Atropine?'

She shook her head. 'Nothing.'

'CPR?'

'Yesterday.'

The doctor looked hard at Galen, then turned to bark a few orders. When he was finished he motioned for Galen to follow him. He went out into the corridor. 'You know, I'm sure, that if it weren't for Jeremy Calder and a lot of pressure from above, I would never allow this farce to continue. That woman in there,' he jerked his head towards the door, 'is dead. Our emergency room is full of patients who are alive, who need our help. So why are you two wasting our time? What are you hoping to accomplish?'

Galen felt a terrible tightness in her chest. This

232

doctor was not overreacting, he had every reason to wonder why they were doing this. Were she in his shoes she would be asking the same questions. 'If I could explain, I would,' Galen said flatly. 'All I ask is that you hook her up, do a complete blood chemistry, then monitor until I get back. Ten, fifteen minutes. Then I'll take over until Dr Calder gets here.'

'Goddamned nonsense,' he said, throwing up his hands. 'Such a crock of goddamned nonsense.' Then he turned and went back into the room.

Galen didn't waste any time. Within minutes she had collected the girls from the waiting room, hustled them outside and put them in a cab. 'You stay with Ti Reine until I come for you.' A kiss on Katy's ashen cheek and they were gone.

Galen half-walked, half-ran back the way she had come, her mind a jumble. She *was* in way over her head. Was there anything she could do?

Forty minutes later, Jeremy still hadn't appeared and Dr Tyron came back into Sylvie's room.

'I can see you have made tremendous progress, Dr Wickliffe,' he said in a sarcastic tone. For a minute he peered at the monitor, then turned to Galen. 'I hate to interrupt you in the midst of such noble effort, but one of the patients here – I want to emphasize that he is one of our *living* patients – would like to see you. His name is Jonas Beauchamp. It seems that one of the nurses told him about the New York cardiologist who was here playing Jesus Christ trying to raise the dead. And it seems that Mr Beauchamp knows you.'

Before Galen could respond his tone changed, softened a bit. 'I don't know why you are here, Dr, I really don't. And I can't imagine what you and Calder hope to gain by all of this.' He waved a hand at the equipment in the room, hooked up to Sylvie's motionless body. 'But from all reports you are a fine cardiologist, not one to go off the deep end gladly. So I'll give you the benefit of the doubt.' He touched her gently on the shoulder. 'Take a break. Go see Jonas Beauchamp. When you get back, the results of the blood tests should be in. While you're gone,' he sighed, 'I will stay with your patient.'

Galen hesitated. 'If Dr Calder arrives, please will you tell him where I am?'

'I will.'

Galen needed no further encouragement. She had come to the end of her resources. Sylvie had not responded in any way. Without Jeremy's input there was nothing left to do but wait. In the meantime she would talk to Jonas. Maybe by some weird chance he might know something. Give them a reason to continue.

Unless we can find one, Galen thought grimly, Sylvie will be sent back to the morgue.

Then, dead or alive, it would be the end for Sylvie Valois.

Galen had never met Jonas, but she wouldn't have been able to recognize him even if she had. His face was swathed in bandages.

'Jonas?' she said quietly.

His eyes opened. 'Galen?'

'Yes.'

'Jesus, what a sorry sight I must be.' He sounded drained. 'But then it was only a week ago that those goddamned dogs tried to devour me.'

She crossed to the bed and took his hand. 'You survived, Jonas. That's the important thing.'

'And David didn't.' Anger.

'No. He didn't. Nor did Camille Carne.'

'I'm so sorry, Galen. I'm so very sorry.'

'I know you are.' She hesitated. 'What were the three of you doing out there, Jonas?'

He lifted his shoulders in a feeble attempt to shrug. 'We were trying to kidnap Sylvie. But the place was deserted and on the way back we had a flat tyre. When we stopped to change it, his dogs got us.' He grew agitated, tried to lift his head up, then fell back. 'But what about Sylvie? Have you seen her?'

'Sylvie is the reason I'm here at the hospital. Everyone thinks she's dead.'

Jonas groaned. 'Oh God, not Sylvie.'

Galen sat down on the edge of the bed and, without mincing words, told him everything that had happened at Shadow Hill from the time she first went there nearly a week ago until the end, yesterday, when Sylvie died.

Jonas listened in horrified silence. When she finished he reached over and grabbed her arm. 'Listen to me, Galen,' he said fiercely, 'forget all about this. Forget Adrien Ravel. Forget you ever heard the word Voudou. You take those girls and you get on the next plane back to New York. Force Ravel into the courts. Let him try to get Edie back if he can. First of all I don't think he's going to want any publicity. He won't take kindly to exposure. And if the worst happens, I have a fabulous home in Monserrat where you can stay until somebody kills the bastard.' He collapsed back on the pillow. 'If I ever get out of here I may just be the one to do it. But in the meantime, do as I say. You get the hell out of here.'

He's right, Galen thought suddenly. I can pick up

the girls and be on the next plane out of New Orleans within the hour. I won't even wait for a flight to New York. We'll just go. Anywhere. Just so we're out of range.

But what about Sylvie?

'But what about Sylvie?' she said aloud. 'I can't leave Jeremy to deal with this alone.'

'You've met Jeremy Calder?' Jonas asked, surprised.

'No, I haven't,' Galen said, and it was her turn to be surprised. She felt as if she had known Jeremy Calder for ever. 'I've only spoken to him on the phone. But I'm expecting him here any minute.'

Through the slits in his bandages Galen saw his eyes narrow. 'As soon as he gets here, Galen, you cut bait. You have more here to think about than Sylvie. Get the girls and go home while you still can.'

Somewhere along the way Katy suddenly thought about Mingo. 'I bet he's dead,' she muttered, slumping down farther into the back seat of the cab.

'Who?'

'Mingo.'

Edie sighed but she didn't answer.

Neither of them spoke again until the taxicab came to a stop in front of a small shabby-looking store. Praline's, the sign said. It hung above a small grimy window.

'We're here,' Edie said, opening the door, sliding out.

An anxious Katy followed and stood close beside Edie while she paid the driver.

'Come on, Katydid,' Edie said. 'Don't be afraid. If we're ever going to feel safe again it will be here with Ti Reine. She won't hurt you. She is the kindest person in the world.'

Katy stuck her hands in her pockets to keep them

from shaking and shuffled along after Edie, down the dark narrow alley and up the rickety wooden stairway. This is an awful place, she thought. Why did my mother have to send us here? But she knew the answer. It was the only thing her mother could do to keep them safe from Monsieur Ravel and his hideous, staring, shuffling, mindless zombies.

At the top of the stairs they stopped. Edie hesitated for a moment, then knocked on the door. 'Ti Reine?' she called. 'It's me. Edie.'

No answer.

She knocked again, this time with more force.

Still no answer.

And then from the foot of the stairs came a voice. 'She ain't here. What you want?'

Katy looked down. A fat woman carrying a baby stared up at them.

'I . . . I came to see Ti Reine,' Edie stammered. 'Will she be back soon?'

The woman shrugged and shifted the baby to her other hip. 'Don't know when she'll be back. Maybe never. She gone home.'

'Home?'

'Back to Haiti.'

Katy saw the tears spring into Edie's eyes and at the same time her own vision blurred. Ti Reine wasn't here, and as much as Katy had dreaded being with her, she suddenly realized that being without her was much, much worse. 'Now what do we do?' she gasped.

Edie sat down hard on the top step and put her hands over her face. 'We have to go back to the hospital. We have to make sure that no one sees us, but we have to go back.'

Chapter Twenty-Four

I am in a hospital. Galen is trying to save me, but she doesn't know how.

Does anyone?

Adrien does.

Adrien.

How many hours left? Forty? Thirty? Twenty? Fewer than that?

Sylvie didn't know. But she did know that strange things were happening to her. Her head had been tilted back and someone had pushed something down her throat. A tube?

And a thousand prickings of needles.

But what for? None of this was doing any good. She didn't need respiration. She didn't need injections of useless drugs. She needed Adrien Ravel and his anti-dote.

At least they aren't cutting you up into pieces.

She drifted in and out of consciousness. She was weaker now than she had been. It was harder for her to stay awake.

From time to time she heard voices. Sometimes Galen's, she knew, because when her eyelids were lifted, sometimes she would see Galen's face.

I am alive. I am alive. Please don't hurt me. Don't let them hurt me.

But she knew they would. In time.

And the black suffocating tide of despair rolled up to smother what had been only a faintest hope. Galen was trying but it wasn't going to be enough.

After a long period of quiet she heard another voice. A vaguely familiar voice. Anxious. 'Hello, Jack. I got here as quick as I could. Any changes?'

'No.'

'Any blood results?'

'Not yet. So what is this all about, Jeremy? What in hell are you doing? Expecting a miracle perhaps?'

Jeremy?

A flash of light, a glimpse of a face, like the voice, vaguely familiar. And then Sylvie remembered. Jeremy Calder. A surge of hope. If anyone knew what Adrien Ravel could do to the human mind, the human body, it was Jeremy.

'Any reaction?'

'No. I haven't time to explain, Jack, but I need some more blood work.' Sylvie felt him pick up her hand. Hold it tight.

'You're kidding.'

'No, I'm not.' A flat answer.

Sylvie's hand was placed back on the bed and she heard footsteps moving away, then the familiar voice again. 'Where is Dr Wickliffe?'

'Up in 305 with Jonas Beauchamp.'

Jonas Beauchamp. The name was an electric shock. What was Jonas doing here?

'Good. I need to talk to him.' A pause. 'Here's the list for the additional blood work. Will you do what you can?'

Sylvie heard Dr Tyron take a deep breath. 'I wish I knew what the hell you were up to.'

'I owe you one, Jack. If anyone needs me in the next

239

few minutes, I'll be in 305.'

'Time is running out, Jeremy, and so is my patience.' Irritation. 'We can't keep this one monitored for ever.'

'I know that. One hour. Not a minute more.'

One hour. Not a minute more.

Not much time. But still enough that they might save her. Jeremy Calder might know what Adrien had done to her. Might. Might. Might.

One hour.

Sixty minutes.

Three thousand six hundred seconds.

And then the end of her life.

She would be butchered.

Unless . . .

Galen knew who he was before he even opened his mouth. He looked like his voice – gentle, concerned, with an air of quiet confidence that made her feel instantly reassured. She had hung on just long enough for help to arrive. She held out her hand. 'Thank you,' she said simply.

He took her hand and held it for a minute. 'Don't thank me yet,' he said gravely. 'I just saw Sylvie. If Ravel has given her one of his Voudou potions, life support isn't going to do her a damn bit of good. I just gave Jack Tyron a list of tests to run, but if I know anything at all about this, I know that we have to move quickly.' He crossed the room to stand beside the bed. 'Can't say I haven't seen you looking better, Jonas. How are you?'

'Lousy. Listen, Jeremy, tell this lady to take her girls and get out of here. Go back to New York where she'll be safe.'

Jeremy turned. 'He's reading my mind, Galen,' he said softly. 'He's right. I'm going to do everything I can to save Sylvie, but I don't think you should stay. Ravel is a madman. I think you should take Edie and Katy and get on the next plane out.'

Galen shook her head. 'I can't leave now. Not yet.'

'Yes, you can,' he said, taking her hand again. 'You *must*. It's not just you in the line of fire. It's your daughter. It's Edie. It's anyone who messes with Adrien Ravel.'

Jonas lifted his head from the pillow. 'Where are the girls anyway?'

Galen was breathing hard. Were these two right? Was she risking more than she dared? 'I sent them to Ti Reine.'

'Ti Reine?' Jeremy said, his eyes lighting up. 'Exactly what I wanted to talk to Jonas about. We need to find Ti Reine.'

Galen was startled. 'What for?'

'We can't help Sylvie by ourselves. We need someone who knows something about the dark side of Voudou. Ever since I've been involved with the Haitians, both here and on the island, I've heard stories about Ti Reine. A very knowledgeable lady. If anyone knows about Voudou toxins it would be the *mamaloi*. Maybe. It's a big maybe, but it's all we've got.'

He stood looking at Galen and for a minute she felt as if she were looking in a mirror. In his face she saw all her own emotions reflected: concern, determination, doubt, sadness. And something more. Something that Galen had lost. Hope.

'I can't promise I'll leave the city,' she said quietly. 'But I'll take you to Ti Reine. And after we talk to her, then we'll decide what to do next.' She paused. 'Okay?'

He nodded, smiling for the first time. 'Okay. First we'll check on Sylvie. Then we'll go to see Ti Reine.'

Still as stone, Ti Reine sat and waited. The flight to the United States had been delayed again and so she waited.

Wedged between her legs was her straw bag and she never took her eyes off it. Tucked inside, under her clothes, was a small red packet wound tight with scarlet thread. And inside the packet was one small part of the magic for which she had come here to Haiti. The only part of her weaponry that had form and substance.

The rest of what she needed could not be carried, could not be seen. It could only come with the *loa*. If the *loa* came at all.

Ti Reine was beset with fear. Fear that she would not be there in time. Fear that when she finally came face to face with the enemy, her *loa* would desert her. Ravel would conquer.

No one looking at the stoic emotionless face of the old woman would ever have imagined that she was afraid of anything. But she was. Deathly afraid.

She was afraid of Adrien Ravel.

Deep in her soul Sylvie wept, but beneath the lids her eyes were dry.

Galen, where are you? Where is Jeremy Calder? How many minutes have I left?

Faint whirring sounds in her ears. Machines humming. But no voices. She was alone in the room.

Where was Dr Tyron?

And suddenly silence. A disconnection. The machines stopped humming. It was as if someone had thrown off a switch.

And then the ripping off of adhesive. The tube pulled from her throat. The wires removed from her flesh. The straps holding her onto the table loosened.

Galen?

Hands behind her neck, under her arms and legs, lifting. She was being carried.

No voices. Only the sound of soft breathing. She was set down. The squeak of wheels on a gurney.

Who? Where were they taking her? Was this the end?

Somebody help me! Somebody please!

Chapter Twenty-Five

Galen felt as if she were walking along the edge of a cliff. *Follow him. Don't look down. Just follow him.* Right now, Jeremy Calder was her lifeline and driven by a renewed sense of urgency, she followed him through the maze of corridors. If he was right, they were racing against time, trying to find answers to a human condition neither of them could begin to understand. *If* such a condition even existed. And if it did and Sylvie was suspended in such a state, was there any hope for her at all? Would a simple old Voudou *mamaloi* be able to save her?

Just outside the door to the examining room she stopped, throwing a last look of quiet desperation in Jeremy's direction. Then together they went inside.

Even before she saw the empty bed she knew something was horribly wrong. There was a total lack of sound. No humming of machinery. No nothing.

Dead silence.

'Jesus,' she whispered.

Jeremy touched her on the arm. 'Where is Sylvie?' And for a split second Galen wondered if in fact they had taken a wrong turn and were in the wrong room.

'What in hell is going on here?' Dr Tyron came in right behind them, face flushed, angry. 'What in hell are you up to, Dr Wickliffe? And you, Jeremy, what have you done with your patient?'

Galen was stunned into silence. Where *was* Sylvie? What had happened to her?

'I have to ask you the same question, Jack,' Jeremy said sharply. 'What *is* going on? Who moved her?'

'Exactly what I'd like to know. I came back from the lab and she was gone. Poof. Vaporized. And I know one thing for sure: that lady didn't move herself.' He threw a sharp look in Galen's direction. 'Or did she?'

Utterly drained, Galen slumped against the wall. 'I don't know,' she whispered, shaking her head. 'I don't know anything any more.' That's it, she thought, closing her eyes. It's all over. We've done all we can. There is nothing left.

'Dr Wickliffe?' A puzzled female voice.

Galen opened her eyes to see a young woman standing in the doorway, but she might just as well have been a rock or a tree. For Galen there was a total lack of comprehension.

'That's Dr Wickliffe,' Jeremy said, pointing.

'This envelope was left for you at the front desk.'

Still not comprehending, Galen took it. 'What is it?' she asked stupidly. She held it out in front of her, a dazed expression on her face.

Jeremy took the envelope, opened it, put the contents back in her hand. A single sheet of paper.

Galen took it.

The handwriting was elegantly scripted. Black ink on ivory parchment.

My dear Dr Wickliffe,

How unfortunate that we have finally come to this sorry impasse, but as Monsieur Defoe so aptly pointed out, even the best of men cannot suspend their fate.

You have led me a merry chase, I must admit. I thought

you had made the wise choice, albeit the less courageous, and had left New Orleans. But alas, it was not to be.

A credit to your keen intelligence that, in spite of what you knew to be true – that Sylvie Valois was dead – you began to doubt. And you were right. Our dear Sylvie is not dead. Even as I pen this note, she lies motionless in her bed beside me here at Shadow Hill, in a state of suspended animation, still alive, but unable to move. Waiting. Wondering. Most assuredly praying.

And I too must wait.

For what, you ask?

For your decision, of course. You must decide whether she is to live or die.

If the antidote is not administered to her within the next twenty-four hours, Sylvie will die. But if Edie is returned to me, and you, dear Dr Wickliffe, return to New York, I will administer it. I will save Sylvie's life.

I needn't remind you that if there is any interference of any kind from any legal authority whatsoever, I shall be forced to let her die.

The decision is yours.

I look forward to Edie's return to Shadow Hill.

In all things I remain your humble servant,

Adrien Ravel

Galen moaned low in her throat. Then fainted.

Galen took a sip of coffee. Scalding. It burned the roof of her mouth but it was a reassuring kind of pain. It meant that she was still able to feel. She looked across the table at Jeremy Calder. 'Well?' she said.

'Do you mind if I smoke?'

'No.'

'I gave it up two years ago,' he said, fumbling in his pockets for some change. 'I feel a strong need of *something* right now.'

Galen took a deep breath and nodded.

He stood up, then sat back down. 'I just remembered. This is a hospital cafeteria. No cigarette machine here.'

'Just as well,' Galen said numbly.

Jeremy leaned forward. 'You want to know what I think?'

She nodded.

'Our worst enemy right now is time. The girls are safe with Ti Reine so we don't have to worry about them for the moment.'

Right. At least the girls were safe.

He continued. 'Like it or not, you and I have to take a trip out to Shadow Hill. We'll tell Ravel that we will send Edie back, but only after we have seen the antidote administered. We have to see with our own eyes that Sylvie is brought back from wherever the hell she is.'

The mere thought of Shadow Hill sent waves of nausea coursing through Galen's body. She blinked. 'You want us to go to Shadow Hill?'

'Yes.'

She closed her eyes tightly for a moment, then opened them. 'Then what?'

'We'll tell Ravel that once we're certain Sylvie has been revived we'll make a phone call. Have Edie brought out to Shadow Hill.' He looked at her over the rims of his glasses. 'But instead of sending Edie, we'll send the police.'

'The police?' Galen echoed.

'Yes,' Jeremy said. 'I know some people downtown

247

in the Police Commissioner's office. Before we head out to Shadow Hill we'll talk to them, tell them what's happened. What we're dealing with. They've handled hostage situations before. Not like this, but they have people who are trained to perform rescue operations.' He let out a long breath. 'I know it sounds risky, but I think it's our only chance.' His voice trailed off.

Galen felt a sudden dryness in her throat and she took another sip of coffee.

There was a long silence, and in spite of the warmth radiating from the mug she was holding, her hands suddenly felt deathly cold. She set the mug down on the table and clasped her hands together. 'I'm scared, Jeremy,' she whispered. 'I am really truly scared.' A single tear trickled down her cheek.

'You and me both,' he said grimly. 'But at least we know that right now Sylvie is still alive. So what other choice do we have? Our first priority is to get Ravel to bring her back before it's too late.' He threw his hands up. 'From there on, it's a crap shoot.'

Galen fixed her eyes on his. 'I sure as hell hope that once we get there the police know how to get us all out. Alive, that is.' She closed her eyes, then snapped them open when she heard her name being paged over the intercom.

'Dr Wickliffe. Dr Galen Wickliffe. Please come to the reception area.'

She looked over at Jeremy.

He shrugged, then stood up. 'Come on, Doctor,' he said, holding out his hand. 'Whatever it is, it can't be any worse than what's already happened.'

When Galen saw the two girls huddled in one corner of the reception room everything else passed out of view, and for a moment she couldn't remember where she was. Where *they* were. Madly the room tipped on its side, then upside down, and if Jeremy hadn't reached out to grab her, she would have fallen onto the ceiling. 'What is it, Galen?' she heard him say. 'What's wrong?'

And then Katy was there, grabbing onto her, holding tight.

Dimly she felt herself being led across the reception room to a chair. She sat down, the dizziness gradually fading, people's faces coming back into focus. Edie, Katy, Jeremy.

'Mom?' Alarmed.

Galen felt like screaming. *Jesus, can't anybody do anything right?* 'What are you doing back here, Katherine Wickliffe?'

'She's gone,' Edie murmured tonelessly. 'Ti Reine has gone back to Haiti.'

Galen looked over at her. There was no spark of hope left in Edie's dark eyes. Nothing but utter desolation.

Galen saw the despair, couldn't help but feel it herself. There was no Ti Reine to help them. But it really didn't matter any more. Adrien Ravel held the ace. He had Sylvie. If there was any chance to save her, they would have to act on their own. And right now. Confront Adrien Ravel, force his hand, do exactly what she and Jeremy had just discussed. Except that now, Jeremy would not be going with her. He would have to take the girls somewhere safe, then get help. Galen would have to go out to Shadow Hill. *Alone.*

'Looks like we have to change the plan,' Jeremy said softly.

Galen nodded. 'Let's get on with it,' she said sharply, getting to her feet. Sylvie wasn't the only one on the

249

edge. Galen's resources were slipping away too. She was exhausted, and she knew if she waited one minute longer she would not have the strength to do anything. If she waited one minute longer, she would run away and never look back.

Chapter Twenty-Six

The curiously familiar scent of almond. The feel of satin against her skin.

Tired. So tired. So hard to think.

Where am I? Am I dead?

But no. If she were dead she would be able to see, wouldn't she?

Of course she would. In heaven there were no blind people.

Unless . . .

Unless this was hell.

And then she heard his voice, and she knew that she had come to a place far worse than hell. She had come back to Shadow Hill.

'Ah, dear Sylvie. Welcome home.'

Galen's head throbbed and she had a bitter metallic taste in her mouth, the taste that comes from a continual overdose of fear. She leaned back in the cab and from sheer exhaustion, she slept. She didn't wake up until the cab driver stopped in Brancheville and asked for directions.

The road to Shadow Hill was hidden in mist, and they went along slowly. Still time to turn around, Galen thought. Still time to get away. She glanced at her watch: ten minutes past three, mid-afternoon, and yet it seemed much later, the roadside already thick with

251

shadow. But then when she thought about it, Shadow Hill was a place that seemed perpetually shrouded in darkness, even at high noon.

How many days ago did I make the first trip to this hellish place, she wondered. Seven? Eight? No matter. The length of time no longer had meaning. Her life now could be measured only in terms of fear. But how does one measure fear? she wondered. How much is too much? How frightened can a person get and still function?

She glanced out at the passing landscape. Would she ever come back along this road alive? It all depended on Jeremy, on how much of what he told the authorities about Adrien Ravel they believed. And then there was Ravel himself. Would he agree to let her see Sylvie restored to life? Would she then be allowed to call Jeremy? Give him the signal to move in?

Deep inside she felt something slip like the gear in a car. Not enough to do serious damage, just a simple reminder that nothing lasts forever. That she was coming to the end of her endurance. She didn't have much left. She prayed it would be enough.

The cab pulled up in front of the house and Galen sat for a moment, staring at the front door.

Here we go, Galen. For better or worse, here we go. She took a deep breath, opened the door and got out.

A warm wind blowing in from the marshes caught the edge of her skirt, rumpled her hair, and with it came a sound. Low, steady, throbbing. The primal sound of native drums, seeming to come from a long way off, at the same time seeming to emanate from somewhere deep inside her head. She was stricken with a sudden paralysis of terror.

The driver leaned out the window. 'Forty-eight dollars, ma'am.'

Somehow she managed to pay him. Somehow she managed to walk up to the front door. By the time she got there it was already open.

Standing just inside was Adrien Ravel.

He didn't speak. For a moment he impaled her with a dark penetrating gaze, then turned, motioning to her to follow.

Keep it together, Galen. If you have any hope of surviving, keep it together.

She followed him down the long hallway and into the library. He gestured for her to sit but she shook her head.

'This won't take long, Monsieur Ravel,' she said, and her voice was so calm, so controlled that she herself was astounded.

His gaze never wavered. Watching her with predatory concentration he waited for her to continue.

'Edie Valois will never be returned to you unless you meet my demands,' Galen said.

'And they are?' Molten metal.

'I want to be there when you administer the antidote. And after you have done so, I want to examine her. Talk to her.' She paused. 'If I am satisfied, I will arrange to have Edie brought here. And I will go back where I came from.'

'Is that it?' A faint hint of a smile.

'It is.'

'No questions?'

'No.'

'That surprises me, Dr Wickliffe,' he said softly. 'I would have thought you would be more curious. From a professional standpoint I would have thought you would want more specific information. Details about how I do what I do so brilliantly.'

'I have no interest whatever in you, Monsieur Ravel, or in your primitive jungle mentality. My only interest here is in Sylvie Valois.'

There was a vague flickering of something in his eye. Disappointment? 'You are a foolish woman, Doctor, to show such open disregard for genius. And you are doubly foolish for having labelled it primitive.'

'I have no disregard for genius, Monsieur Ravel,' she said quietly, 'except when it is coupled with lunacy. Instead of using your knowledge in some worthwhile way, you have defiled it. Your brand of genius is an abomination. It is bestial. It is demonic. I have no interest in it whatsoever.'

A look of amusement came into his eyes and he smiled a genuine smile. 'At least you are intelligent enough to recognize it as genius.' He turned. 'Come then. Sylvie is waiting.'

The warm wind blew through the moss-laden trees on either side of the path, making mysterious whistling sounds as it passed, and beyond the sound of the wind she could still hear the low relentless thunder of the drums.

She had expected Ravel to take her to Sylvie's bedroom but instead he led her out across the lawn and into the misty gloom of the swamp.

Once they stepped outside the house, the calm Galen had exhibited vanished, and now in the quickening darkness the numbing fear had returned with a vengeance. Teeth chattering, she followed Adrien Ravel along the path, in one place missing a

254

step, her left foot slipping off the tussock into the murky stagnant water.

God, I am afraid, she thought. Please God, let Jeremy pull this off. Don't let me die.

From time to time along the way she heard sounds of splashing water somewhere off in the distance. Maybe it's help coming, she thought, breathing hard. Maybe they are moving in. But why would they? Didn't they have to wait until she gave the signal?

The drumbeats grew in volume, closing in around her until she felt suffocated. All at once they were on dry ground, stepping out of the swamp into a small clearing, and Galen realized that they were in a cemetery. In the fading light she could just make out the outlines of tombs. Heart pounding, she pressed her hands to her ears to try to block out the boom boom boom of the drums, but it was impossible.

Suddenly she became aware that she was alone. Adrien Ravel had disappeared.

Quaking with fear, Galen battled for control. Don't lose it, she told herself fiercely. Think of Sylvie. For God's sake, don't lose it. Don't let Ravel paralyse you with this jungle madness. Drums can't hurt you. Only Ravel can do that.

She felt her heart slow down a bit, and she stood where she was, sucking in long deep breaths of air to steady herself. She waited.

How long she stood there she didn't know, but when the last bit of light left the sky, the drums stopped. 'Damn you, Ravel,' Galen shouted. 'Where are you? Where is Sylvie?'

And from behind her his silken voice responded. 'Sylvie is here.'

Galen whirled around to see him standing only a few feet away and the sight of him made her gasp. All evidence of the twentieth century had vanished. Before her stood a barbarian, a pagan high priest. He was wearing flowing red trousers. His chest was bare and around his neck hung a huge golden disc.

'Come with me, Dr Wickliffe,' he said.

Her heart in her mouth, she followed him past the rows of whitewashed tombs and along the side of what looked like a mausoleum. Ahead, she could see a circle of white-smocked worshippers, each one holding a flickering candle. In the centre of the circle, two open coffins.

He is going to put me in there! she thought wildly. One for Sylvie, one for me!

But she was wrong. As she drew closer she could see that both coffins were already occupied. She could see bodies. Closer still and she could see the faces.

One was the masklike visage of Sylvie Valois.

The other was Jeremy Calder!

Her mind pulverized, Galen reeled back and dropped to her knees, but before her mind could shut down entirely, she saw Ravel's giant henchman step forward into the circle.

In one huge hand he held Edie in a vicelike grip. In the other – horror upon horror upon horror – he held a sobbing, terror-stricken Katy Wickliffe.

Incoherent with fear, Katy wrenched free and ran for her mother. The giant made no move to stop her, and she threw herself into Galen's arms. 'Save me, Mommy!' she shrieked. 'Save me!'

Her mother grabbed her by the shoulders and spun

her around. 'Run, Katy!' she gasped. 'Run! Get away from here! Run!' And she pushed Katy hard.

With a look of sheer bewilderment on her face Katy took two stumbling steps backward, then turned and threw herself once again into her mother's arms. 'I can't, Mommy,' she choked. 'I don't know where to run.'

This time her mother pulled her close, held her, rocking back and forth. 'I know, Katy,' she whispered. 'I know. I don't know where to run either.'

Holding her child tight, Galen turned her head. The circle had opened and Adrien Ravel had stepped inside. In candles' glow she could see him clearly, his features twisted into a feral snarl of triumph.

'You came very close to victory, Dr Wickliffe,' he said in a tone of pure malevolence. 'Had the superstitious old *mamaloi* not fled the country, had Edie not been forced to return to the hospital, I might never have found her. You might have won. But I was watching you. Edie came out of hiding, and without even knowing, you delivered me the prize.'

Hearing the terrible truth, seeing the unremitting savagery in his eyes, Galen buried her face in the curve of her child's shoulder so she wouldn't have to see any more.

I am asleep but I want to wake up, Edie thought, sucking in great gulps of air. I want to wake up. Mama, I love you. Please wake me up. Please tell me it's okay. That it's all a nightmare. Nothing more. Only a nightmare. She tried to throw her arms around her mother's neck to hug her. Oh, Mama, wait until I tell you about it. It was the most horrible nightmare, the most horrible nightmare.

But her arms wouldn't move. For some reason they were pinned to her sides.

She opened her eyes.

Mama?

But she didn't see her mother. Or anything else to reassure her that she was really safe at home. She was here, in the cemetery at Shadow Hill, held captive by a demon, unable to do anything but wait for the end to come.

Paralysed with fear and horror, Edie watched as somehow Katy managed to wriggle free from the giant's clawlike hand and hurl herself into her mother's arms. The giant made no move to bring her back, but he tightened his grip across Edie's chest.

Edie's range of vision was clouded by tears but she could still see the two open coffins, the circle of silent white-garbed onlookers and, just beyond, Adrien Ravel. Drained of all strength, she sagged, wanting nothing more now than to curl up into a tight ball and die, but the giant held her up. She let out a low strangled sound, the cry of a helpless, hopeless, terrified child.

The sound echoed through the cemetery, and when Adrien Ravel heard it, he turned.

Edie's eyes widened. Around his neck she could see a great golden disc marked with the twisted serpent symbols of Damballah. But it wasn't the sight of Damballah's disc that filled her with renewed terror. It was the gleaming curved machete that Ravel carried in his left hand, the terrible instrument of Voudou sacrifice.

He is going to kill us! Edie thought wildly, her

breath coming in sharp jagged gasps. We are all going to die!

As if she had spoken out loud, Ravel stopped in the centre of the circle and turned to stare at her. 'The spirits are hungry, young Edie,' he said softly. 'They must be appeased. But you are not one of those who will die. You do not belong to the spirits. You are mine.' He raised one arm and the drumbeats sounded again, low at first, then growing in intensity, harsh and merciless. And with the drums came the chant.

Edie knew what it was: the ritual chant of blood sacrifice. Unable to bear the sound she tried to clamp her hands over her ears but her arms were pinioned to her sides.

And all at once the drums stopped. The chanting stopped. A thick silence fell over the crowd, and underneath the silence Edie could feel a sudden strange undercurrent of uncertainty.

Adrien Ravel must have felt it too because slowly he turned to stare in the direction of the swamp.

'*Mystere p'vini*,' someone whispered. A mystery approaches.

But what? Who?

And then Edie heard the giant rumble low in his throat. 'It is Ogou who comes!' His grip across her chest loosened.

Incredulous, Edie peered into the darkness. She knew all about Ogou. He was the great Voudou spirit of war, the one Ti Reine always turned to when she needed strength. Ogou holds the key to the storm-clouds, the *mamaloi* once told Edie. But Ogou would never come here, not to aid a *bocor*. Not to help Adrien Ravel.

Edie turned her head, searching the crowd for an

answer. She saw nothing. But the others did. Their faces strained, fearful, the men in the outer circle drew back and, one by one, trembling, they bowed low. 'We feel your presence, great Ogou. Do not devour us. We are your people.'

'You are *my* people!' Adrien Ravel screamed. In a fit of savage fury he took one step forward, the machete held high above his head. 'Silence!'

But the pitiful entreaty continued.

'Silence!' he screamed again. 'What imbecilic absurdity is this?'

In response, a voice, deep and dreadful, came out of the darkness. 'Don't you know?'

'Come forward, fool,' Ravel commanded.

Out of the gloom, draped in the blood-red cloak of Ogou, moving as if in a trance, came Ti Reine. She glided forward to stand before a seething Adrien Ravel.

Edie stared, her terror mixing now with disbelief. The face she saw was not Ti Reine's. It was the rigid mask of someone else, the eyes wide open, unfocused, like those of a blind person. Clenched in one gloved hand Edie could see the great ritual sword of Ogou. But even as she gaped, incredulous, she could see the others dropping to their knees, hear their terrified whispers. 'Great Ogou, spare us. We tremble in your sight.'

Edie was thunderstruck. Was this what Ti Reine had meant when she talked about the *loa* descending, when she prayed for spirit possession? Had Ti Reine called the Voudou warrior down, given her body over to him so that somehow he could save them?

An eerie stillness fell.

Then Ravel spoke in a tone filled with unmasked

contempt. 'We meet at last, old woman,' he said scornfully. 'Am I to assume that you have come for my head?'

'*You are!*' Two words. Deeply masculine. Terrifying in their simplicity. In the next instant the blade of the great sword went up, slicing the air in a wide arc.

A look of stunned surprise came across Ravel's face but before he could take a breath or raise his machete in self-defence, the sword of Ogou came around with lightning speed, and with a swishing whistling sound it separated Adrien Ravel's head from his body.

For a moment the only movement was Ravel's. A slow sagging, a fountain of blood gushing from his neck, a final folding over at the waist, his headless body dropping to the ground.

Behind her Edie heard the giant groan. He released his grip and fell to his knees. The rest of the group surged forward, falling prostrate at the feet of Ti Reine. 'Forgive us, O Lord Ogou. Forgive us.'

But Lord Ogou was gone.

In his place stood a dazed trembling old woman, the bloody sword dangling at her side.

Weeping, gasping, Edie rushed forward, arms outstretched, but before she could reach her *mamaloi*, Ti Reine collapsed to lie motionless in the spreading pool of Adrien Ravel's blood.

Edie fell to her knees beside the old woman. 'Don't leave us, Ti Reine!' she cried. 'Help us! Ravel is dead but you must save my mother!' And dimly she became conscious of someone kneeling beside her. Galen.

Ti Reine's eyes fluttered open to stare at the doctor. Without speaking she reached inside her robe and took out a small pouch. Motioning for Galen to come close, she began to whisper. Edie couldn't hear the words. She could only pray that somehow those words would save her mother.

Tired. So tired.

   This is the end. So sad. But everyone has to die sometime.
   But not like this. So sad. Not to say goodbye. Never to say goodbye.
   Please God, take care of Edie. Don't let Adrien have her.
   Tired. So tired.

Even sound had ceased to have meaning. Only distant indiscernible echoes. Voices coming and going like ghosts.

   Tired. So tired.

Sylvie had been drifting in and out of consciousness for a long time, with great periods of nothingness in between.

But suddenly something broke through the nothingness.

Suddenly she became aware that her arms were being lifted. Something was happening? But what?

All at once there was pain. Exquisite, razor-sharp pain. A thin ribbon, slicing down along the underside of her arm.

   Have they begun? Dear God, am I being dissected?

'It's all right, Sylvie. Hang on.' An anxious voice. Galen?

Fingers pressing along the edges of the open wound. Coating the raw flesh with something powdery. Mixing it with Sylvie's blood.

And then the right arm. A blade, cutting.

Again the searing pain. Again the voice. Gentle, reassuring. 'We're almost there, Sylvie. Hang on.' And the fingers moved again along the line of the incision, mixing something with her blood.

The pain in her arms spread like electric current running along wire. Excruciating electric pain.

Sylvie blacked out.

It was the tingling that brought her back. A weird, waking-from-sleep, coming-back-to-life tingling that began in her toes, spread to her feet, to her legs, then up across her chest to her neck, across her face to her eyes. And in the next instant her eyes opened! No one had opened them for her. She had done it all by herself. And she saw the tearful eyes of her child staring down at her.

Impossible. Could it be?

Sylvie felt her mouth open, heard her own voice rasping the three words she had tried for so long to utter. 'I am alive.'

Epilogue

New York City, 29 January.

It wasn't that late in the afternoon. Not yet six, but outside on the avenue the streetlights had come on. That's the trouble with winter, Katy thought, reaching across her bed to flick on the light. It gets dark too early.

Curled up beside her, Mingo lifted his head, blinked, then went back to sleep. Katy rolled over on her back to reread what she had just written in her new diary. The diary had been a Christmas present from Gram but Katy never had a chance to make a single entry. So this morning when Edie and Galen went off to the hospital to see Sylvie, Katy had opted to stay home with Helen so she could work on getting everything down in writing before she forgot it.

She frowned. The trouble was that when she got to 25 January she couldn't write *anything* about that hideous day. Not one word. But now, staring at the blank page she decided it really didn't matter. What had happened on 25 January didn't have to be written. *Couldn't* be written. But none of them would ever forget.

Katy shivered and turned the page: 26 January. She propped herself up on her pillows and began to write.

After it was all over, Edie and I shared the same room at the hospital. The doctors wanted to observe us, see if we were okay. And I guess we were because, like all the experts say children are very resilient. But we didn't talk about it. Maybe we won't ever talk about it.

Anyway, after the doctors were satisfied that we hadn't lost our minds, Edie went off to be with her mother and I spent most of my day with mine. First we visited Dr Calder and Mom told him about the powder Ti Reine had given her. Something about how she had to cut under their arms to get it into their blood. And she told him that she had sent what was left of the powder to the lab for analysis.

I didn't pay much attention to the rest of their conversation because Oprah was on Dr Calder's TV set talking about animal abuse. I sure am glad we found Mingo.

After lunch we went to see Edie's mom. Edie was with her. Sylvie looked awful but she seemed very happy. Not that I'm surprised she's happy OR that she looks awful. After what she went through, who wouldn't? Yikes.

Monsieur Ravel's zombies are somewhere here in the hospital, too, and Mom says that the doctors aren't sure what their chances are for recovery. Only time will tell, I guess. I wish them good luck but I sure don't want to ever see them again.

I stayed with Sylvie while Mom and Edie went to visit Ti Reine. I didn't want to go and they didn't make me. They know that in spite of everything, Ti Reine still scares me. Especially after what she did to Monsieur Ravel.

Not that I'm sorry he's dead. Good riddance to bad rubbish is all I have to say.

Anyway, tomorrow we're all flying back to New York. Sylvie is going to be admitted to the Medical Center so

Mom can keep an eye on her. Edie is going to stay with us until her mother gets back on her feet. And Dr Calder is coming to see us as soon as he can make arrangements. I'm happy about that because I really like him.

Enough for this page. I've just about covered everything for 26 January.

Katy closed the diary. She was tired of remembering. She rolled off the bed. 'I think I'll see if Helen will let me make cookies,' she said to Mingo. With a last pat on his head, she left the room.

☐	CRACKDOWN Val McDermid	0 00 649008 5	£4.99
☐	THE RED SCREAM Mary Willis Walker	0 00 647861 1	£4.99
☐	NOBODY BELIEVES ME Molly Katz	0 00 647602 3	£4.99
☐	BAD CHEMISTRY Nora Kelly	0 00 647853 0	£4.99
☐	DOLL'S EYES Bari Wood	0 586 21862 9	£4.99

All these books are available from your local bookseller or can be ordered direct from the publishers.

To order direct just tick the titles you want and fill in the form below:

Name: _____

Address: _____

_____

Postcode: _____

Send to: HarperCollins Mail Order, Dept 8, HarperCollins *Publishers*, Westerhill Road, Bishopbriggs, Glasgow G64 2QT.

Please enclose a cheque or postal order or your authority to debit your Visa/Access account –

Credit card no: _____

Expiry date: _____

Signature: _____

– to the value of the cover price plus:

UK & BFPO: Add £1.00 for the first and 25p for each additional book ordered.

Overseas orders including Eire, please add £2.95 service charge.

Books will be sent by surface mail but quotes for airmail despatches will be given on request.

24 HOUR TELEPHONE ORDERING SERVICE FOR
ACCESS/VISA CARDHOLDERS –
TEL: GLASGOW 041-772 2281 or LONDON 081-307 4052